Midnight Dance
A Corsair Novel
Douglas Pratt

MANTA
PRESS

MANTA PRESS

For Ashlee

Cartagena de Indias
Historic Walled City

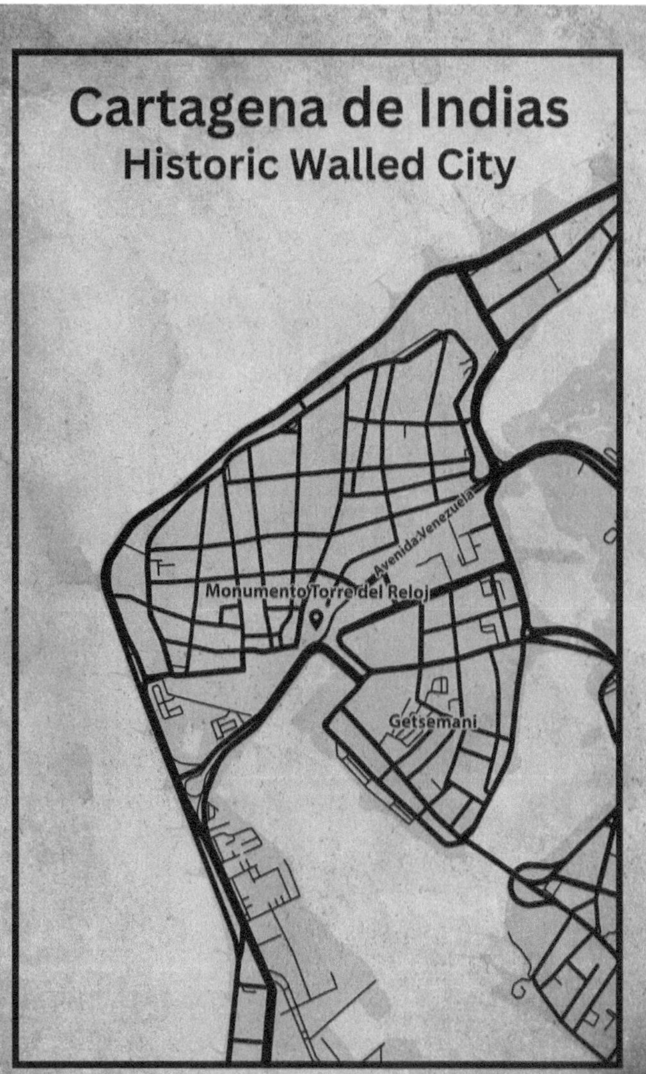

2012

Marseilles, France

The open pane brought in a hint of salt in the air. Camille's apartment didn't have air conditioning. Instead, she found an old, metal, oscillating fan that made Caleb think of something from a black-and-white Humphrey Bogart movie. Despite the thin electric cord, it created a draft in the flat. Her window faced the sea, and the Mediterranean breeze blew through the blades of the old fan.

He rolled over on the feather mattress to see the naked and sleeping form of Camille Dubois. Caleb assumed she was awake, even though the rhythmic breathing suggested otherwise. The American agent lay on his stomach and studied the flawless skin of his lover. Her naked back faced him, allowing his eyes to trace along the nubile curves.

At only twenty-six—that was the age she claimed—she proved to be a deadly asset. Caleb didn't like the particulars of this assignment, in part, because of how close he'd gotten to Camille, the agent code-named Minuit. It was closer than he'd been with anyone—ever.

But it was a mission, and Corsair continued to remind himself of that fact. She was a means to an end. Albeit a fabulous means.

His fingers reached out and trailed along the fair skin. The Mediterranean sun had bronzed the woman in the last few months she'd been in Marseille. Her assignment from the DGSE, France's equivalent to the CIA, had been to establish her presence in the coastal French city. The Riviera attracted the elite from around the world, and Marseille's cosmopolitan atmosphere ensured that the upper crust would pass through. Camille Dubois developed enough of a back story so that her target, Khalid Al-Zayyat, would take her to his bed in an instant. Any man would, but Camille applied that truth to Al-Zayyat. The Libyan businessman carried suspected ties to the Libyan Guardian Front, which has spread some cells into Paris and other parts of France. Reports indicated he had been funneling money to the group for the past few years.

The Office of Compliance sent Corsair into Marseille to connect with Minuit. Their mission involved Minuit's infiltration of Al-Zayyat's private yacht to gain access to his private network. Once she'd gleaned the information needed to isolate the many cells set up across France, Corsair's task was to assassinate Al-Zayyat.

Once he made contact with Minuit, his superiors expected him to remain on her until he could kill his primary target. For the last month, he'd done just that. Caleb and Camille bonded, and although he'd never loved another person in his life, he couldn't help feeling like he did now. So much so that as he lay on his side staring at the naked figure lying next to him, he wanted to abort the mission. That was an option he'd never done except in extreme circumstances.

Unfortunately, feelings didn't constitute an extreme circumstance. Duty was something he hadn't ignored yet, and he was aware that today would not be the first time he did.

But he didn't like the stirring it left in his gut.

If he explained it to Minuit, would she understand? After all, she was a professional. Death for her, at twenty-six, was all too commonplace. Just as betrayal and repercussion were.

No, he knew the answer. Minuit—Camille—was driven by the same sense of duty to her country as Caleb was.

There's no way around it, Corsair told his sentimental self.

He rolled his feet off the bed, letting his bare soles touch the cold tile floor.

"*Où vas-tu?*" her voice asked. *Where are you going?*

"Nowhere *ma puce*," the man answered in French.

Her fingers curled around his biceps as she pulled him back down onto the bed. He flopped back, sinking into the feathers as she threw her leg over him. Her lips moved along his neck, and Caleb's hands trailed along the curves of her hips. The logical portion of his brain warned him that this was the last time he'd be with her. His baser emotional side, which never showed itself, begged him to stay in this flat with her.

They kissed with fevered passion. Camille's fingers held his face to hers as she rocked on his pelvis. As she reached a climax, her back arched in a moan. Despite the struggle to keep up with her, Caleb lost control. His eyes struggled to remain focused on the lithe form astride him.

A moment later, Camille collapsed across his chest. He breathed her in as she kissed his pecs and neck while running her fingers through his hair.

"Do we need to go?" she wondered at him.

No, he thought to himself. *You don't have to go.*

Corsair responded, "I'm afraid so."

"At the least, can we repeat this later?" she asked, pushing up so that she could stare him in the eyes.

"There is nothing I want more," he told her.

Camille kissed him again. This time it was intimate and loving, a divergence from the passioned, breathless ones they'd shared earlier.

She threw her leg over, dismounting Caleb like he was a horse. "I must shower or I'll smell like you all day."

Caleb gave her a half smile and watched her naked ass as she strode into the bathroom. He wondered, not for the first time, if this was a test. Perhaps his orders were wrong.

But he'd never questioned them before, and it would do no good to question them now. Laden with duty, Corsair followed his tasks to the letter. He wasn't making the command decisions. All he did was perform as instructed. Corsair was a scalpel. He wasn't the surgeon.

The shower started running, and Caleb sat up. He scanned the room for anything that might trace back to him. The day before, he'd done a thorough inspection, but Corsair didn't want to leave anything undone.

He slipped his pants on and walked to the door to the bathroom.

"I'm going to run to get some coffee and croissants," he told her. "Maybe grab some clean clothes."

Camille's head appeared around the shower curtain. Curls of steam billowed from behind her. "Don't forget the marmalade," she reminded him.

"Of course," Caleb agreed, grabbing his shirt off the floor.

Five minutes later, he was back at his own flat, which was little more than a closet with a shower and toilet in the corner. Unlike Camille's apartment, his water was tepid and only for a short time. He stepped into the tub before the water hit the drain to make use of as much of the warmth as he could. Two minutes after getting into the streaming water, he was dripping dry.

Once dressed, he swept the room again for anything that would identify him. His habits involved removing anything daily, so he expected to find nothing. Still, he performed the search with the same diligence. It was far from the first time he'd come to the end of a mission, but it was the first time he did so with regret.

Once he satisfied himself that his temporary domicile wouldn't offer any clues to his identity, he exited the flat, locking the door behind him. Corsair paid his rent up for three months, and while he didn't expect the landlord to wait that long to discover Caleb no longer lived there, he expected a few weeks—perhaps a month or more—before he came looking around. Caleb only met the man once, and he'd come across to the OOC agent as somewhat trustworthy. That was a high praise from Corsair, who viewed the nuns and other people of the cloth on the same scale.

On the street, Caleb found a *pâtisserie* on the corner. He picked up two croissants and two *cafés au lait*. As he headed for the door, the man asked for a handful of small marmalade packets. When the girl offered him a selection, he requested extra raspberry, knowing Camille's preference for them.

When he got back to Camille's flat, she stared out the open window in a zebra-striped silk shirt that hung just over the curves of the tight jeans.

"Coffee?" he offered her a cup. She leaned over and kissed him, taking the proffered cup as she eyed the bag in his hand.

"Did you remember the marmalade?"

His smile twinkled as he handed the bag of pastries to her. He wasn't hungry. On the day of any job, his appetite vanished. Sometimes he would go for days after completion before he ate. It wasn't nerves or anxiety that stifled his appetite, but it came down to a sort of Zen-like mindset. This was the clutch moment, not unlike a championship football game when the time clock was almost to zero and the team was at the fifteen-yard line.

Long ago, he learned nothing was set in stone. The adage of best laid plans held true. If anything was going to go wrong, it happened between the time he woke up and the kill moment. Every second that carried him closer to the end seemed more precarious to Corsair.

Today, it was more than just that mental acuity he sought. He didn't enjoy the knowledge of where the morning would go while Camille ate her croissant with raspberry marmalade. It struck him as unfair—an unfamiliar feeling.

Caleb considered reaching out to Carl to bring up the idea of recruiting Camille. He never did, knowing that any undue attention to her might incite an order that Caleb didn't want to follow.

He smiled as he watched her tear off flakes of buttery bread and dip it into the raspberries. In this moment, he sensed something about himself that he liked. If he could live in any moment, it would be this instance.

"We have to go," Camille stated. "You didn't eat your croissant."

He leaned over and kissed her. "I think I'll save it for later. The last thing I want is for you to find me getting pudgy."

"Not something I'm concerned about, but if you don't eat it later, I can't promise I won't."

He smiled at her, and the French DGSE agent grabbed his hand, squeezing it. "Come, let's go."

"Do you know what your boss wants to see me for?"

She shook her head. "Only that he asked for me to arrange to meet you. Somewhere out of prying eyes."

It hadn't been part of Caleb's plan, but when Camille's boss, Marc Lefevre, told her he wanted to speak with the American, everything fell into place. Camille hadn't told him about Lefevre's desire until last night, but he'd known about it two days earlier, having hidden a listening device in her flat. She made a habit of sweeping the room daily for bugs, but Caleb soon figured out her routine. Camille enjoyed kombucha, which she made in a thermos every day. Caleb placed the device in her thermos, knowing she'd sweep the apartment, determine it was clean, and then go about her work. Since she swept it after coming back to the flat, it would be after she determined no one planted a mic that she'd retrieve her drink from the refrigerator where the insulated walls shielded the device from her scanner.

Corsair had two full days to know not only that Lefevre wanted to meet but even where he intended to hold the rendezvous. Twelve hours would have been enough, and it concerned him that Camille and Lefevre's conversation was so far in advance.

The pair were soon on the street, strolling along the roads hand in hand. Any passerby would judge them to be a couple enjoying a sightseeing day. Camille led him along toward Fort Saint-Jean, a structure dating back to 1660 when Louis XIV constructed it to protect the Old Port. Now it has become one of the iconic sites of the old city. Thousands of tourists daily traipse along the parapets and visit the museums.

"The fort?" Corsair asked, feigning surprise.

Camille offered him a smile. "Marc's going to meet us here."

"I'm still surprised your boss even came out, much less to see me," Caleb commented. It was true. Marc Lefevre never left Paris, and even in the city, he maintained a well-armed escort at all times.

That was part of Corsair's paranoia. It was like Lefevre delivered himself on a platter to the agent. Corsair didn't mind things working out, but he suspected it always. Coincidences were never predictable, but sometimes, they worked to his benefit, as long as he was prepared for them.

This time he was, and that left him uneasy. He had the discretion to call off the job if the need arose. He'd considered it for several reasons. In the end, Corsair recognized the selfish motives behind that idea. Or, at the minimum, he couldn't distinguish the legitimate reasons.

Still, his instincts remained flared up, searching for the slightest reason to pull the plug.

They entered the fort, and Camille led them through the arched tunnels and walkways toward the tower. At the southern edge of the fort was the Tower of King René rising almost a hundred feet over the entrance of the Old Port.

It was still early, and the fort and museum had just opened. In the middle of the week, the tourists hadn't started filing in yet. There was only one cruise ship in the harbor, and those passengers hadn't disembarked yet. It would be at least an hour before the crowds flowed into the fort.

"He said for you to go up," Camille told Caleb when they reached a stone staircase angling around the square structure.

"What about you?" Caleb asked, staring at her green eyes for a few seconds longer than he should have.

"I'll be here when you get back," she promised. Again, he felt trepidation. It was too easy. Until now, he'd wondered how he could handle Camille, not knowing that if he were in the position where he needed to kill her, he could do it.

Caleb took the stairs with caution, resisting the urge to glance down at the Frenchwoman. The stonework on the castle gave off a dusty aroma. Under different circumstances, Caleb might enjoy absorbing the architectural marvel. Today he didn't have it in him.

Don't look back! Corsair scolded himself.

He didn't, but as he came out on the roof of the tower, he shielded his eyes from the Mediterranean sun. As he squinted, Camille's face flashed before him. What would she think of him?

A thin man in his late forties stood on the far side of the tower next to the parapet overlooking the blue waters. As Corsair approached him, the man seemed to sense the agent's presence. He turned to face Corsair. Silky brown hair danced in the sea breeze. Marc Lefevre matched the file photos Caleb studied. His pointed, stony jawline and brown eyes gave the man a stern countenance.

"You must be the famed Corsair," the DGSE agent proclaimed. "You have quite a reputation."

Corsair didn't respond.

Lefevre held a pair of aviator sunglasses in his hand, twirling them around like a whirligig. Corsair thought they were an odd choice for the man who was wearing a tailored suit.

"I wanted to speak to you about your employer."

Caleb waited.

When Lefevre realized he wasn't responding, he continued, "I don't blame you. There is no need to verbalize—just yet. However, Minuit assures me you are honorable. She even said trustworthy. I'm bowing to her assessment to bring this information to you."

"Go on," Corsair urged. He wasn't sure what game Lefevre was playing, but he knew the longer the pair stood on this parapet, the larger his chance of failure became. Still, he listened.

"The Office of Compliance is no good. Rotten."

Corsair observed the man.

"You know it, don't you?" Lefevre remarked. "Minuit says there's no way you would be involved."

"I'm not sure what you're talking about." Corsair shifted on his feet, catching the man's eyes flit off to the corner as if he was checking something over Corsair's shoulder.

Damn, I knew he was too smart to come alone.

A sniper, Corsair guessed. He didn't want to turn to look. Corsair didn't have to. If he'd set up a sniper nest, it would be in the church across the road.

With a step toward the DGSE agent, Corsair remarked, "Who is it? Who's dirty?"

Lefevre furrowed his brow. "That bastard Winston."

Corsair took a step forward, whipping up his arm as a thin blade came out of his sleeve. Lefevre saw it, swinging his left arm up to block it. The OOC agent anticipated that, grabbing the Frenchman's wrist to jerk him toward the American.

The blade pierced Lefevre's chest, slicing between the rips to puncture the man's heart. Corsair spun the DGSE man around as a shield. He didn't hear the shot, only the *thunk* of bullet hitting stone. Corsair dragged the dying spy back with him against the parapet before dropping to the ground.

From where he crouched, there was no line of sight to the church. He'd have less than a minute before the sniper reported Lefevre's assassination. Less than sixty seconds before Camille Dubois charged up the steps to see him over her superior's corpse.

Lefevre wheezed as the last of his life escaped. Corsair ripped his shirt off, removing a packet from the seams. Then he fished a lighter from his pocket, ignited the pouch, and tossed it away. The canvas bag flared up for a second before green smoke billowed out.

As the cloud filled the air, Corsair rose to his feet, stripping off his pants. Underneath, he wore a full bodysuit made of Lycra. With the breeze coming off the sea, the smokescreen wouldn't last more than a few seconds. Caleb climbed up onto the edge. Looking down, he saw the rocks that sloped down into the water. Fifty feet from shore, an older sailing sloop floated at anchor. He took a deep breath, jumping and spreading his arms and legs at the same time.

Today was the perfect day for this. The strong wind from the south filled the wingsuit in the split second before he launched himself off the tower. Still, he felt like he was falling.

Because he was.

BASE jumping, parachuting from fixed heights like bridges, antennae, spans, and earth or mountains, required more than a hundred feet for the suit to do its job. The suit had a 2.5-to-1 glide ratio, meaning that for every 250 feet he fell, he could go forward a hundred feet. None of that helped him here as the water rushed up at him.

There was no sensation of flying. It felt more like he was falling forward. In the second or two it took to drop, he saw the rocks roll past him. He hit the water headfirst, pulling his arms and legs together to dive deeper.

The impact into the water wasn't bad, and the wingsuit had done its job, carrying him past the rocks to where the depth dropped from eight feet to eighty in a step.

Once he pushed past the stunned effect crashing into the sea had on him, he ripped at the suit, tearing it open. Strapped to his back was a small air cylinder with a mouthpiece. The six-cubic-foot tank had a head strap that wrapped around his head, securing the rubber mouthpiece. He inhaled a quick breath as he stroked forward.

Corsair glanced up to see the surface of the water, and he estimated he was ten feet deep. With the sunlight reflecting above, it would be difficult to see him. He didn't dare go much deeper with only the pony bottle of air to sustain him.

He could make out the shadow ahead, and the agent kicked his feet toward it. When he saw the anchor chain stretched into the depth, relief passed over him. It had been a challenge to put everything in place, but it had worked.

Corsair took the chain and used it to descend into the depth, careful not to shake the chain. It would be a give-away to any DGSE on the surface. Thirty feet below the surface, he found his stash.

A battery-operated underwater scooter floated there, attached to the chain by a carabiner and some paracord. There was a full-sized scuba cylinder on a backplate with a mask. As he sucked on the last bits of the pony bottle, Caleb stripped the rest of the wingsuit off him and donned the back plate. He exchanged the near-empty tank for the second-state regulator attached to the cylinder and took a deep breath now that conserving air wasn't the priority. With the mask adjusted on his face and cleared of water, Corsair unhooked the scooter. He checked the compass on his gauges before heading east.

The scooter could carry him up to three miles, and if he didn't exert too much energy, he could stay on this tank for at least an hour. Enough time to get away from the Old Port and Camille. As the motor pushed him away, he cleared his mind, only thinking about his next move.

1

Rio de Janeiro

Six Months Ago

To say the smell assaulted her olfactory senses was an understatement. The combination of rotting flesh, soured water, and fresh grilled meat almost turned her stomach with the confusion. She stepped to the right when someone behind her shouted. A flurry of air whipped past her as a teenage boy zoomed between Minuit and the wall. He didn't seem to mind that he was going downhill so fast, with nothing to stop him until he hit a wall farther down the favela.

Minuit hoisted the bags she was carrying up on her hips. With enough dirt smeared across her face, she could pass for any mother struggling through the steps toward whatever shitty hovel she called home. The assassin was a chameleon in the truest fashion. Her skin tone was such that with a little extra sun, she could quickly pass for Brazilian, like she did today. Or let the color fade over time, and Minuit would fit into any European city with ease. Her long, dark hair often assisted in obscuring her features. A few strands across the face masked the striking green gaze she always had. If she left it draped over the front of her shoulders, it detracted from the high-boned features that distinguished her.

This weary woman continued through the steps and alleys of Rocinha. The slums of Rio de Janeiro climbed up the side of the mountain surrounding the coastal city. Despite attempts by the government to curb the growth of buildings on top of buildings, the lack of affordable housing in the area perpetuated the favela's spread. While parts of it have become tour-worthy for tourists searching for a sliver of culture during their seven-day all-inclusive resort, most of Rocinha struggled with prevalent crime.

The drug trade in Brazil funneled from countries like Bolivia and Peru, where cartels processed coca leaves into cocaine. With thousands of buildings crammed onto the hillside, the labyrinth of tunnels and paths through the structures offered ample avenues to move cocaine through the city.

Like any population where the criminal enterprise sustained it, the rivalries grew. Wars began, and in tight quarters like Rocinha, those battles often wrought more damage to the innocents than to either side.

Minuit passed the damage. She'd seen it over the last week as she worked her way through the hillside slums, searching for her target. It took her three days of strategic meandering and asking the right questions, under the guise of a woman seeking her brother or son or husband, depending on the audience.

Ricardo Silva didn't live anywhere. That much she knew coming into the job. A man didn't work his way up into the most—no, second most dangerous gang in Brazil without a fair amount of caution. As a chief of Amigos dos Amigos, Silva was vilified by some and revered by others. He earned the villain status by brandishing an iron fist in the favela while the veneration seemed like idolatry.

Minuit knew enough to vilify him, but she recognized him as weak, using force and threats to enforce his edicts. However, despite his rank in Amigos dos Amigos, Silva offered the organization next to nothing. He wasn't smart enough to develop new trade routes or come up with better methods of smuggling the cocaine out of the favela. But he could run the organization like it was.

Basically, Minuit thought, he's a typical middle manager. But that didn't prevent him from becoming the target for the Red Command. Silva's attempts to elevate his importance fooled not only the leaders of Amigos dos Amigos, but their enemies at Red Command. Minuit's employer believed that Silva's removal from the Amigos dos Amigos network would cripple them. Had she pointed that out to Cairoca, the leader of Red Command, it would have saved them two hundred thousand reals. However, it would have painted Cairoca as an idiot on the same level as Silva. Weakness like that was as deadly as strength in the favela.

Minuit didn't care either. It was a task, and while it was less than most of her payouts, it had been quiet the last few months. Most of the drug cartels quieted down during the political circus, and right now, the United States, the supreme ringleader in political chaos, was amid a presidential election. The drug manufacturers and runners kept their heads down so as not to draw the ire or attention of an incoming policymaker. Nothing was more damaging to business than a political face passing off an executive order to interfere in the drug trade as a political promise. It was an easy ploy, too. Short of the rising marijuana popularity across the United States, most people didn't speak out for the cartels, especially if the news showed them murdering people on international television.

She turned down a narrow tunnel that ran beneath the apartment above. Much of Rocinha grew up on top of the rest. Similar to stacking building blocks, houses rose like a LEGO village against the mountain. It created caverns that were unlighted.

The warren curved into darkness, and Minuit ventured inside. Her senses flared up as the tunnel went to pitch black. Many residents carried lighters or battery-operated flashlights to maneuver these paths. The bag in her right hand slipped off her hip, and she lowered it to the ground. From the other pack, she pulled out a jacket, stripping off the oversized shirt she'd been wearing. As soon as she slipped into the sleeves of the threadbare jacket, she pulled her hair up into a bun.

The man's musk reached her before he did. In the black of the tunnel, a shadow grunted toward her. He stopped in the middle of the path. Minuit heard the *click-click-click* before an orange flame popped up from the man's lighter. She saw the grizzled face shrouded by an unkempt beard. He reeked of sweat and grime.

The stranger's head cocked to the side as he studied her. His raspy voice called, "Hello, miss."

Minuit didn't answer, only nodding.

"You don't have something to say?" he growled.

"No, I don't," Minuit retorted, pushing past the odorous man.

A thick, calloused hand caught her forearm. "Don't be rude."

"I have to be somewhere." Minuit tried to pull away.

"Oh, you can go," he assured her. "Just take a few minutes to tell me hello."

With more force, she yanked free of his grip. "No!"

In the flickering yellow light, the man's eyes raged. He shoved her against the stone wall, pressing his face close to hers. She smelled the cachaça on his breath. When his rough tongue scraped across her neck, she drove her forehead into his nose, cracking the cartilage.

"*Puta!*" he howled, stepping back to raise a fist.

Minuit moved faster than he did, driving her fingers like a knife into the soft tissue under his skin. The fiend gasped, jerking his head back. In the dark, the French assassin swiped a stiletto across the man's throat. The air in the tunnel filled with the warm, coppery aroma of blood as her attacker fell back to the ground.

Damn, I'll be covered in blood. She could move back down the path where she left the shirt she'd stripped off, but it would put her behind.

No backtracking.

She wiped the razor-sharp edge on the pants leg of her dead attacker. The blade slipped back into the sheath on the inside of her forearm. She walked through the dark, distancing herself from the body in the dark corridor.

When she emerged from the dark, Minuit examined her clothes. Blood splattered across her front, but the killing slice was clean, leaving only speckles of brown on her clothes. It would go unnoticed in the favela, and as long as no one attempted to do any forensics on the jacket, the lifeless scum she left in the dark would be marked down as random violence. That assumed that anyone would even investigate. A man like that oozed violence, and he would have plenty of enemies. Besides, the police did little as far as investigating or even policing Rocinha. Outside of the bits that the tourists visited, the favela was a forbidden zone.

She hiked up two flights of stairs before heading through a small tunnel that led to a quasi-courtyard constructed between four block buildings. A green building constructed from concrete blocks backed up into the mountain.

Minuit ripped the front of her shirt, exposing her cleavage beneath the splattered jacket. Without exposing her breasts, she assured herself that anyone looking at her would find their eyes drawn to the visible curves of dark skin rather than the speckles of blood.

The Frenchwoman straightened her back and approached the green structure. Before she got to the door, it swung open, revealing a gaunt figure. Like the slaves of vampires, this guy let the mixture of cocaine and amphetamines drain him of life. Minuit gauged the man, knowing he'd die on this doorstep, eventually. He'd sworn fealty to Amigos dos Amigos in return for a constant stream of chemical feelings.

"What do you want?" he demanded.

"Rafa sent me to talk to Ricardo."

"Wait here." The wasting figure faded back inside, closing the door. She noticed no click of a lock. He'd developed a sense of security. A false sense. It was complacency like that which killed powerful men. She considered entering now, but there'd be a chance Silva's slave overreacted. It wouldn't do to have to kill him here and end her subterfuge.

She waited. Five minutes. The door reopened and the sad figure of a man reappeared with a snaggletoothed grin.

"Ricardo said to come up."

It was a given. The lieutenants in Amigos dos Amigos communicated across the city through couriers who were often girls. It was like a gift with the message because the recipient would almost always rape the girl—if she put up any resistance. Although they kept most of the women high enough that they were nothing but pliable; there was little resistance.

Ricardo Silva would have stolen a peek out the window at the woman at the door. The exposed cleavage and tight skirt marked Minuit as a trophy to be conquered. That the message she brought was from the head of Amigos dos Amigos fed on Silva's ego.

Minuit followed the doorman through a small apartment that stank of mold and rotting food. Two rats shared a scrap of molding bread on a mound of what Minuit guessed were clothes.

Holes in the walls between the buildings created a larger space that spread along several buildings. Doorways between the structures were nothing but jagged openings created when sledgehammers and sweat broke through the concrete walls. Minuit wondered how structurally sound the building was now that so many walls had wide openings.

"Who are you?" Silva questioned as she entered the room where he sat. The glorified drug runner slumped on a worn sofa that had once been hunter green. Someone cut a hole in the roof and installed clear polycarbonate roofing to allow the sunlight to illuminate an otherwise cavernous room. Two bare bulbs dangled from thin electrical wire on either side of the makeshift skylight. At night, this room would still be gloomy, like so much of Rocinha.

"Rafa sent me to bring you to meet him," Minuit explained in Portuguese. All traces of her French accent vanished when she spoke. Not that Silva would notice or care. His attention remained on her loosely buttoned shirt.

"We can do that soon enough," Silva told her. "Why don't you sit with me first?" His tone had been congenial and suggestive when, in fact, he wouldn't take any refusal.

Minuit offered a diminutive smile as she turned to stare at the doorman who'd brought her up.

"Are you sharing?" she asked with a trace of disgust in her voice.

Silva snapped his fingers at the doorman. "Marcos, get back out front."

Marcos didn't hide his disappointment when he nodded. As he left the room, Minuit took a step toward the door, closing it behind Marcos and leaving her alone with Silva.

"Is that better?" Silva asked, moving his hands to his belt to unfasten the buckle. His eyes danced up her body as Minuit ambled toward him. Her fingers fumbled with the plastic button at the front of her shirt. As the button released, her shirt fell open, allowing Silva an eyeful of her breasts. His face widened into a smile, and he remained fixated on her nipples as he jerked his pants down.

Minuit swung her left leg over the man's lap and settled onto his thighs. Silva grabbed her around the waist, pulling her toward him and burying his face in her bosom.

The stiletto stabbed through his ear into his brain. The man arched his back as what remained of his brain sent shock waves through his central nervous system. Minuit leaned back to see the man's last few seconds of life, which turned into convulsions.

When the seizure ceased, Ricardo Silva's head flopped forward. Minuit pushed the forehead back. The thin blade came out of Silva's skull, and she wiped it clean on the man's shirt. Standing up, she noticed the man's erection remained, causing her to sneer as she fastened the buttons on her shirt.

From her pocket, she removed a large-tipped marker. On the wall above Ricardo, she scrawled the words "Red Command" in bold cursive lettering. Her employer wanted the Amigos dos Amigos to know who dealt the blow. To Minuit, it seemed dramatic, but these were men who believed in their own mythologies.

The skylight offered her an exit from the building without passing Marcos or any of the other Amigos who might be in the house with her. She dragged the table under the clear plastic roofing and climbed up it. Nails secured the polycarbonate material, and Minuit pressed against the corner to pop it up. The edge gave way instead, breaking off a chunk at the corner with a loud crack.

Minuit paused, holding her breath for a second. When no one came charging through the door, she moved to the opposite corner. Years of direct sunlight turned the plastic brittle, allowing her to break the other corner before the nail holding it down gave way.

She heard the footsteps outside a few seconds before the door opened. The former DGSE agent turned with a jagged piece of plastic in her hand as the door swung open.

Marcos appeared in the opening. His initial reaction was confusion. The doorman stared at the lifeless figure on the couch, and on instinct, his eyes shifted away from the man's death erection to the woman on the table staring down at him.

As his brain pieced the puzzle together, Minuit launched herself off the tabletop, swiping down with the plastic in her hand. The pointed edge of the polycarbonate roofing drove into Marcos's neck as she slammed into him.

The bigger man shoved her off him and rose to his feet. Rage filled his eyes as he lunged for her. Minuit jumped back, knocking the table over.

"You whore!" Marcos growled as he jerked the plastic shard from his neck.

Blood erupted from the artery, and Marcos's eyes widened as he realized his fatal mistake. He dropped the plastic and grabbed at the spurting wound. It took a second before his legs collapsed and he landed on his knees. His mouth opened and closed like a fish in an aquarium just before his eyes rolled back in his head and he fell face-first to the floor.

So much for leaving quietly.

Minuit turned to look at the table in the middle of the floor. The already-dilapidated table had a broken leg from her overturning it.

She let out a scream and ran from the room. "He killed Ricardo!" she shouted as she scurried through the house toward the front entrance.

Two Amigos stepped out of a room as she ran past.

"He killed Ricardo!" she repeated, waving her arms about.

The two men dashed back toward the room with the two corpses, and Minuit pushed through the front door, stepping out into the sunlight. Her hand shielded her eyes as they attempted to readjust to the bright outdoors.

"Get her!" someone inside shouted, and Minuit ran for the tunnel across the small courtyard.

Three Amigos, including the two she'd passed in the corridor, came out of the building. Minuit didn't turn back. There was no time for that, and any slowdown, even for a second, gave them time to catch up.

She'd chosen a different route than the one that she used coming up to the house. If a passerby discovered the guy she'd killed in the other tunnel—by now, someone must have walked that path—she wanted to avoid the scene. When she came out of the first labyrinth, a boy on a bicycle almost ran her down. He weaved as she appeared, slamming the front wheel into a cinder block step and flipping over the handlebars.

Without checking on the boy, Minuit righted the bike and threw her leg over the saddle. A second later, she was careening down the slope toward a flight of stairs.

The three men came out only a few seconds behind her. All of them leaped over the downed bicyclist who was struggling to get to his feet. Minuit chanced a glance over her shoulder to see the Amigos still in pursuit.

She gripped the handles as the wheel came off the top step. The woman pulled up on the front wheel and leaned back. The front tire came up as the rear one bounced off the next several stairs. Minuit maintained control despite the bumpy descent. When she hit the concrete at the bottom of the stairs, Minuit braked the bike into a skid before pedaling downhill again.

Her rapid drop down the stairs added vital seconds to her lead, and with a straight downhill path, she gained even more of a lead. When she whizzed through an opening into a darkened tunnel, she pumped the pedals harder and shouted ahead for anyone in her path to take cover.

Ten seconds later, she came out of the dark and turned on the first path she found that took her down the hill. When she reached the next junction, Minuit threw her legs off the bicycle, rolling it over to a corner beside a shack that doubled as a convenient store. She started walking down a flight of steps to the next level. Her pace dropped back to a casual walk, but she maintained vigilance. In a place like the *favela*, word spread like wildfire. People would hear soon about Ricardo's murder and the woman who fled the Amigos dos Amigos house.

When she passed a woman peddling t-shirts, she bought one with an LA Lakers logo on it. Slipping it over her top, she tied the extra-large shirt at the bottom in the attempt to disguise its size.

She'd lost the Amigos, and now she was almost to the bottom of the *favela*. Ten minutes after that, she was on the bus heading east on Estrada da Gávea. In the back of the bus, she stripped off the Lakers shirt, ripping a strip at the bottom. With the extra fabric, Minuit tied her hair up in a ponytail.

When she stepped off the bus in Jardim Botânico, Camille Dubois, without changing clothes, looked like any expat living in Brazil. She thanked the bus driver in broken Portuguese and with a British accent.

Her route home took her on a circuitous walk through the neighborhood, where she stopped for a bottle of wine, fresh chicken, and a handful of vegetables from the market. No one was following her, and she hiked the last kilometer to the blue and white cinderblock house on the hill.

Camille set her groceries on the counter, and she pulled a cold bottle of water from the fridge as she dialed a number.

"It's done," she told her contact when he answered.

"Any problems?"

"Nothing out of the ordinary." Camille swallowed some water.

"Word will be out by now."

"I assumed as much," Minuit acknowledged. "I'm clean."

She didn't point out that the only two people who got a good look at her face were dead.

"Money is in your account," the voice on the other end of the line reported.

Without a word, Camille carried the phone and her water to the balcony that looked down the mountainside.

"There's another job," he told her.

"I just finished this one," she pointed out. Camille preferred to space the work out. Too many jobs drew unwanted attention from people she preferred forgot about her.

"I know, but this one you might find interesting. There's a contract out for the Corsair."

Minuit straightened her back. "Corsair? He's dead."

"Apparently not. He's back, or at least he was."

"Where?"

"He surfaced a few days ago in Puerto Vallarta. He's gone back under, but there's a very large bounty on him."

She didn't have to tell him that she'd kill her former lover for free.

"Give me everything."

2

Belize City, Belize

Present Day

He'd been sitting in the front seat of the 2005 Toyota Corolla for three hours. Caleb cracked the windows to get a breeze, but despite that, sweat dripped down his face. Without the car running, the air conditioner wasn't cooling the interior, and the sun at the 17th parallel baked the car, raising the temperature to close to 130° Fahrenheit.

Caleb wasn't about to approach the house yet, though. He'd been too careful over the last few months since he'd left Puerto Vallarta with Khloe Evans and his daughter Amanda. They'd stayed under the radar, and this would be the first contact he'd had with either of his former lives since then.

Caleb Saunders had been a dead man. In fact, he'd remained dead for just over a decade when he'd faked his demise during a mission that he'd thought was for the Office of Compliance. The OOC was an offshoot and off-book intelligence branch that fell somewhere under Homeland Security where 9/11 shrouded its creation in the wake of patriotic fear. Recruited straight out of Parris Island, Caleb Saunders, codenamed Corsair, became one of the OOC's best assassins, working across the globe in what he thought were missions for the good of the United States.

Things changed in Turkey when Caleb learned he'd been operating often as a personal assassin for Carl Winston, the head of the Office of Compliance. Caleb scrubbed the last mission, faking his death in an explosion.

For the last ten years, Caleb found some contentment and joy, living under the alias Thomas Harrod. Until his path crossed with two carjackers that kidnapped his daughter after killing his wife and son. In order to get Amanda back, Corsair resurfaced. Now his former employer knew he was alive and branded him a traitor with a kill-on-sight order.

As if the OOC wasn't enough of a problem, his sudden resurrection caught the attention of several of his former enemies as well. He compounded the problem in Puerto Vallarta, where he faced off with the Cincinnati mafia and the Cortez cartel to save Khloe's life.

Caleb had years of preparation and planning to drop off the grid. Even while he and Audrey were married, a persisting fear weighed on him that one day someone would uncover his identity, forcing his family to run. He'd confided in his wife all about his past, and she understood the risks and the potential need to vanish. Caleb spent years crafting a few identities for them. While he lacked unlimited funds, he'd established enough to survive for a few months.

Unfortunately, none of his plans involved a woman who wasn't Audrey Harrod. Khloe Evans had no alias or fake passports. To get a solid identity takes time. He'd back-stopped several of his aliases in case he needed them. That meant creating paper trails. With the ease of data retrieval online, a false identity needed more than a new name on a passport. It needed a credit history, rental history, even an Amazon purchase history.

Khloe had none of that. There was no way to know that the mob or the cartel weren't still after her. That meant Caleb had to reach into his past to find someone who could craft a new life for the woman.

All of that led the former assassin to sit in a Toyota Corolla about ten miles west of Belize City on a scorching afternoon. Corsair planned to meet with Driver later, and being a man who liked control, Corsair opted not to make a scheduled rendezvous in the city later. Instead, he tracked down Driver to his home in the Los Lagos Community, a neighborhood populated with American and Canadi-an expats who moved to Belize for the laid-back, tropical lifestyle.

Corsair connected with Driver fifteen years earlier, and he'd done some business with the forger until his apparent demise. Caleb did not know what Driver's real name was, having only known him as Driver during their previous interactions. He guessed the man was a former agent of some alphabet agency, perhaps even the OOC. Although he didn't think that was the case. As far as he could tell, Driver never knew Corsair by anything but that code-name.

After three hours, Caleb believed the man was alone in the house. He hadn't left all day, and he'd confirmed Driver was home. He counted six cameras hidden around the property, and Caleb suspected there were more that he couldn't see. It would be impossible to make the approach without being spotted. However, he wanted to eliminate as much notice as possible. Although he didn't want to surprise Driver to the point of his taking a full-defensive position.

He'd watched long enough. Caleb exited the car, leaving it down the road. Even leaving it out of sight meant he would need to get rid of it. Driver had been paranoid a decade earlier, and Caleb expected that paranoia multiplied over the years. If he wasn't tracking who came and went in this neighborhood, Caleb would be surprised. It didn't matter since Caleb stole the car. Once he left here, he'd dump it before heading back to the house where he was staying with Khloe and Amanda.

Caleb approached, scanning the street as he walked. As he came through the front gate, Caleb saw movement in the curtains at the far end of the square cinderblock structure. It was a typical Caribbean construction built from blocks with a concrete finish and painted a turquoise and white that matched the tropical theme.

Ten feet from the front door, Corsair stopped and folded his arms. He was far enough from the door that a shotgun blast wouldn't take him out. It wasn't enough distance to stop anything else, but if Caleb wanted a new passport for Khloe, there was no choice but to risk it. Driver might be kooky, but he liked money. Caleb fanned out a stack of one-hundred-dollar bills, making certain the denomination was visible and could be estimated. It was five thousand dollars, and Caleb knew it might not be enough for the job. He expected Driver to ask for at least that much more. Ten thousand seemed high. He could buy a perfect passport in Europe for three. But, of course, they weren't in Europe.

Still, Caleb hoped five thousand would get the job done. The last few months cost more than he'd planned. In order to get to Belize, they had to get Khloe across the border from Mexico. It took some bribes to ensure they made it without incident. If he could get her ID for what he had on him, then he could book passage on a freighter to skip across to Portugal. If one wanted to remain under the radar, it cost more. A decent cabin on a freighter was about two grand each. But if one didn't want to be on a manifest, it cost a little more.

There was a loud click as the deadbolt snapped. Two more clicks sounded as more locks disengaged from the inside. Caleb watched as the door swung open and a man in his fifties—late fifties, Caleb noted—stepped into the opening. The man cocked his head, studying the person on his front walk.

"I thought you were dead," Driver said after he'd traced the former agent with his eyes.

"It wasn't as permanent as I would have preferred."

"Is it ever?" Driver motioned for him to come inside. "You could have called."

"That never occurred to me." Caleb followed him inside.

Driver's home reminded Caleb of the bridge of an aircraft carrier. He assumed there was a more livable section, but what Driver led him through was a room filled with monitors showing at least two dozen angles of his house. There were an additional ten monitors showing the street, including the section where Corsair parked his Corolla.

"Where have you been?" Driver dropped into an ergonomic chair with an array of controls on the right armrest. It seemed like the chair where Blofeld might sit and stroke a cat.

"That doesn't matter," Caleb reminded him. "I need a passport."

"For you?" Driver leaned back in the chair as his index finger keyed a switch. A low hum sounded from the chair.

"Massage chair," Driver explained. "Bad back."

"Old age is nothing to sneer at."

"Who are you calling old?" Driver leaned forward.

"Cool it, man. I was kidding." Caleb forgot how strange the guy had been. "I have a picture, name, and birth date."

Caleb slid an envelope with Khloe's face picture and the name they'd chosen. Driver removed the photo and studied it.

"Cute," he remarked. "Daughter?"

Caleb didn't remark, and Driver nodded. "Do you want it backstopped?"

"No." If Driver set up the backstory, he'd know all the information. Corsair preferred to get the ID only. His plan was to get Khloe to Europe, where he could build her a permanent background. That would take months to develop, but it would be foolproof.

Driver shrugged. "Easy."

"Great," Corsair sighed.

"Well, kinda easy," Driver amended, letting a hint of a Midwestern accent bleed through.

"What do you mean?"

"I can do this for you, and I'll do it at cost."

Caleb narrowed his eyes. "At cost?"

"I need a favor."

"Driver, I don't have time to do any favors." If Driver knew enough to assume Corsair died ten years earlier, he would know what it was the agent did. That meant any favor Driver might want in exchange for the passport would involve Caleb killing someone.

"It's nothing like that." Driver waved his hands at Caleb as if whatever ran through Caleb's mind was absurd. "Just a pickup."

"A pickup?"

Driver shrugged again. "Last year, I was in Colombia doing some work. After a bit of a misunderstanding, I had to leave rather quickly. Ended up leaving some of my tools."

"What kind of tools?"

"I have about ten perfect US passports. They only need the photo and details. These include the watermarks and everything. Cost me a fortune to get them."

"Why don't you go get them now?"

Driver leaned forward. "There's a good chance every immigration booth in the country has my picture posted. I made some enemies."

"You can't make yourself a new identity to slip past?"

"I haven't been so inclined," he commented.

"What does that mean?"

Driver put his hands at his lower back and stretched. "The risk for me is too great."

"What's the cost?" Corsair inquired.

"Tell you what, I'll give you one of the US passports—those would be about 10K—and I'll throw in a couple of grand for your time."

Driver's suggestion sounded too good to be true. Caleb didn't care for it. Nothing was that easy. He suspected there was an ulterior motive underneath it.

"What if I just pay you for the passport?"

"I'd have to tell you I can't do it. Best I can do right now is a shoddy Nicaraguan passport. And your girl here would have a hell of a time getting anywhere with it."

"Bullshit."

"Not at all. Times are tough."

Corsair glanced around the room at the thousands of dollars' worth of equipment.

"Come on, you know this is just business. It's an easy two days, tops. You can grab an arepa, maybe dip your dick in a little *colombiana*, then be right back."

"Ten passports?"

"And some cash—but not enough for you to get flagged. In fact, you can take the two grand from that."

Caleb shook his head. "Here's the deal. I'll get your passports and bring you two. While you make two for her—I enjoy having options. When you finish them, I'll deliver all the cash and the rest of the passports."

Driver curled his lip. "Two?"

Caleb shrugged. "Take it or leave it. I can get a passport anywhere for less trouble."

Driver made a gesture as if he was giving up. "Fine. Deal." He extended his hand to Caleb, who ignored it.

"Give me the details. I'll leave tomorrow."

3

Qatar

Mahmoud Abbas sat in the chair looking out his penthouse window at the moonlight reflecting off Doha Bay. The book in his lap hadn't held his interest, but Abbas was a principled man of habit. He found he needed to slow his thoughts down, and while some meditated or prayed to do that, Abbas struggled to find any peace in those rituals. As a devout Muslim, he performed those rote prayers, but he found even while chanting praises to Allah, his mind twirled around whatever he'd been working on.

He only slept about four hours a night. Often, the businessman would toil till two or three in the morning. Those hours were sometimes a necessity when conducting business with people on the other side of the globe.

But that schedule caught up with him, and last year, his doctor advised him to rest more. After all, at his age, his expectation that he could keep up the same amount of work he did in his twenties and thirties was unreasonable.

The same amount of work indeed. I work ten times more now than when I was younger.

Still, he felt the wear on his frame. Now, Abbas attempted to sleep by midnight or one. He'd developed a transition to shift from the constant churning of thought during the day to a somewhat peaceful slumber by reading poetry. The book in his lap was *The Conference of the Birds* written by Farid ud-Din Attar, and while he enjoyed the imagery of the poems, tonight his mind wouldn't focus.

His cellphone beside his chair lighted up. He kept the phone on silent most nights to avoid disturbing his wife. Tonight she was sleeping in the other room, but as Abbas was a man of habits, he still turned the phone's ringer off.

The number on the screen belonged to Salar Tolazar.

"Salar, my friend, it is late."

"I hope I didn't disturb you," his chief of security apologized.

"No, I'm still awake."

"Reading?"

Abbas smiled. Salar was more than just his employee—he was Abbas's most trusted friend. Only he and Abbas's wife knew the billionaire immersed himself in poems before retiring. It seemed to Abbas to be a sign of weakness that the man either wasn't focusing his complete attention on work or that the fact he couldn't sleep.

"I have news that I wanted to share with you."

"Please, don't leave me waiting." Abbas closed the book.

"Corsair surfaced."

Mahmoud Abbas straightened in his chair as his mind ignited.

"Where?" He tossed the volume onto the table beside him. There would be no more reading tonight, and Abbas suspected that sleep would not happen either.

"After Mexico, I reached out to contacts around that part of the world. I assumed that at some point, Corsair would reach out for something. Today, he called upon a forger in Belize."

"Belize? How soon can we task someone there?"

"There is no need for that," Tolazar explained. "Our contact has offered to tell us exactly where Corsair will be. Provided, of course, that we pay him."

Abbas frowned. He'd miscalculated last year when Corsair first reappeared after a decade. His haste and rage caused Abbas to offer a hefty bounty on Corsair's head. While the agent escaped, the word of the bounty meant that any information about Corsair would cost him. It also led to countless false leads from people hoping to get a small percentage of that money.

Salar cautioned Abbas then, but not even the sensible, tempered friend could assuage the rage Abbas still carried toward the American who killed his only son over ten years ago. He'd swore at the time to hunt the assassin down, but fate intervened when reports surfaced saying Corsair died in Turkey.

A decade later, Abbas learned his son's murderer rose from the dead. The man had enjoyed years of life with his own family. Years that his son, Farid, would never have.

"How much does he want?"

"Two hundred thousand in American dollars," Tolazar answered. "He will give us the location to find Corsair."

"For just the location?" Abbas clarified.

"Yes."

"If he fucks us, I want him dead."

Tolazar cleared his throat. "That goes without saying."

"Tell your contact that I want the information now, though. We can wire the money."

"Of course."

"Call me back, Salar. I'll be awake."

The phone disconnected, and Abbas rose to his feet. He walked to the massive window. The glow of the lights from the Burj Doha Tower would have illuminated the penthouse even if Abbas turned off the lights in his home. He had a remote that tinted the glass as dark as Abbas liked it. If he adjusted it to blackout mode, the room would be pitch black in the middle of the day. He never darkened the glass until he was ready to sleep. The view from his bedroom was one of the most expensive ones in Qatar, and he enjoyed seeing the lights of the city. Somehow, it gave him a sense that he was one of the few who oversaw the city.

Mahmoud Abbas built a name for himself over the last twenty years. His legitimate business spread from real estate to shipping and included an aspect of almost any industry. His company-owned restaurants around the globe, airlines, and even a citrus grove in southern Florida. *Forbes Magazine* featured him three times in the last eight years, and the magazine listed him in the top twenty billionaires in the world.

Despite that success, Abbas made almost as much in arms sales. With manufacturers in North Korea, Abbas supplied everything from ground-to-air missiles to Glock knock-off nine-millimeters. His weapons found their way to terrorist organizations around the world, but the lion's share ended up in the hands of the Libyan Islamic Fighting Group.

He folded his arms, thinking about Corsair. The man had killed his only son, Farid, twelve years ago. Since then, Abbas longed to kill the man. He came close last year when the agent resurfaced, but somehow the men he'd sent after the American died—likely at Corsair's hand.

A coppery taste filled his mouth. It was what Abbas assumed was the flavor of rage. His stomach tightened. It frustrated him because he wanted to bring Corsair here. Abbas wanted to execute the man himself.

The information he'd received over the last year told him Corsair found a wife over the last decade. He'd developed roots, having children. It thrilled Abbas to learn someone murdered Corsair's wife and son. Almost in front of him, if the reports were accurate. But that was a pleasure he'd desired for himself. To watch the man who'd killed his only son beg for the lives of his family would have offered Abbas satisfaction.

There was still a daughter. Though no one had seen her since Florida, Abbas assumed she was still alive. If he could find her, then Corsair would come to him. That would be the only way. Corsair had been the deadliest man in the world, and capturing him was a near impossibility.

No, he decided. Abbas would find contentment in knowing he'd arranged the American's death. That would be enough. Once accomplished, he might have Salar hunt down the daughter and eliminate Corsair's line, just like he'd done to Abbas.

The phone flashed again, and Abbas answered it.

"The man agreed. Corsair will be in Cartagena, Colombia, in two days. He's given us the location and time for the meet."

Abbas did something he rarely did—he smiled. "How soon can you get there, Salar?"

"I'll be pushing it to make it there in two days," he admitted. "If I could leave first thing tomorrow, there'd still be some delays getting into the country."

"What about the Frenchwoman?"

"Minuit? She's already in South America. I can call her now and get her to Colombia."

"I want him dead this time, Salar."

"Of course, sir. I'll go to ensure it happens."

"Call this woman. I want him to know it was me that killed him, too."

"Yes, I'll handle it all."

"For Farid."

"For Farid," Tolazar repeated.

4

Mexico City, Mexico

She'd watched this footage at least a dozen times. The camera covered the sidewalk where six tables sat in a small cordoned-off section of outdoor seating. Almost out of the camera's view, half a table hung on the edge of the screen.

Lee Hubbard leaned toward the monitor as if that allowed her to see clearer. Only half of Caleb Saunders's face appeared. The other side fell off the display. He'd been careful to stay on the outside of the zone covered by the coffee shop's security camera, but he'd miscalculated. The angle screwed up the facial recognition software the guys in the Basement at the Office of Compliance used.

Just finding the video had taken months. The OOC team on the ground in Puerto Vallarta worked for months to find any footage of Corsair. By the time they did, though, the forensic team concluded the former agent fled the city. Lee Hubbard knew they'd located his apartment—again, too late to find him or any clues to where he might go.

She'd lived in Mexico now for months as she followed up leads on the former OOC assassin. The trips home on the weekends flew by too fast, and Lee didn't like that she remained out of the office, unable to monitor her boss, Carl Winston. The evidence she'd been gathering on her superior seemed razor-thin, but if she could locate Caleb Saunders before the OOC team, she felt confident he'd hold the coffin nail on Winston. Her boss, though, displayed dogged determination in trying to kill Saunders. He'd declared Corsair a traitor, and given Winston's unmitigated power, he didn't need approval from anyone to assassinate his own people if they turned. Based on Winston's allegations, Corsair did just that.

Lee didn't believe the story to be as cut-and-dried. Corsair's sudden departure, including his faked death, didn't strike her as a betrayal. An escape, perhaps. He wanted out, and Lee suspected he chose the path he did because he knew too much about Carl Winston and the Office of Compliance to retire in peace.

She'd also miscalculated when she chased after a Corsair sighting without notifying her boss. Her hope had been to catch up to him first, but she'd failed. Corsair not only escaped, but he left a bloody scene with her at the center. By the time she alerted Winston, her actions enraged him. He responded with an entire OOC forensic team to scour Puerto Vallarta for Corsair.

They'd come up empty-handed, except for a few clips of video which took months to find. Saunders must have mapped where almost every camera pointed, and the team's best efforts only narrowed it down to a small section of the city. Then a concerted, door-to-door search found someone who pointed them to his apartment.

She knew he'd left the city. It seemed pointless to continue to dig for him there. The man knew enough to cover his trail, and Lee suspected he'd been prepared to run all along. Her instinct suggested getting ahead of him. He only had so many ways he could get out of the country. With the help of the Mexican Federal Police, the OOC cut off access to airports. Unless he made it to Mexico City, the other airports in the country were smaller. It would be easier to search the security footage there. Of course, that was what her OOC team did. They struck out in Puerto Vallarta and Guadalajara, the closest city.

Lee assumed that would be the case, and she diverted a couple of her team to search Mexico City. The capital offered a large enough population for Corsair to blend in.

It was futile, or almost futile. It was a lucky hit on a camera outside a bank that led Lee to the coffee shop.

She restarted the loop again. The half a face stared at a computer screen as if he were working on something.

An escape plan.

The timestamp on the video was two days after her encounter with the man. He'd taken some injuries in the fight, but other than what looked like a bandage on his right hand, he didn't show signs of massive injury.

He'd been shot, though. She knew that. It was bad enough that Corsair would have needed medical treatment soon after leaving her. The fact he wasn't prone somewhere so short a time later was a testament to the man's strength. It further confirmed the difficulty she faced capturing him.

Corsair could have killed her. That also rattled around her brain. It was further confirmation to her that the man wasn't quite the traitor that Winston made him out to be.

At the twelve-minute-and-thirty-six-second mark, the woman and girl show up. The angle of the camera didn't show the little girl, but the bank across the street offered a grainy image.

Why was the Khloe Evans girl still with him? To Lee, it seemed like a dangerous calculation. He'd almost died protecting Khloe. Perhaps he didn't believe her life was out of danger.

The man was a conundrum. He was a merciless killer. She'd witnessed that firsthand. Even his history with the OOC showed a ruthless agent.

He was a rule follower. She'd examined the details of the last job he was to do before he supposedly died. The files had been redacted despite her clearance, leaving murky evidence at best. He'd been in Turkey, but one of the blacked-out lines was the identity of the target. That wasn't unusual. Allegiances change over time, and the US government doesn't want evidence of a hit from a decade ago to sour the relationship with a new ally. However, some higher-up power redacted that information in order to prevent a publicity nightmare if discovered. Lee had learned not to trust the reasons behind censorship. She just assumed the worst.

In this instance, her gut considered that something triggered Corsair on that mission. Whatever happened caused him to walk away from the agency, fake his death, and vanish. She wanted to ask him what it was. Why had he given it all up?

She stared at the screen. The frozen image of Khloe Evans was mid-step. A tiny figure, obscured by Khloe, walked along the other side. Amanda Harrod.

Caleb Saunders was a ghost, but the two females in his life weren't. Hell, the girl was only three or four. If she stayed on the run with Corsair, she'd have a fucked-up childhood.

Khloe, though, was the key. Lee was certain. The woman was an unpracticed civilian. She'd been lucky to hide from the criminal element in Cincinnati, but they didn't have the same resources as Lee. They'd found her without those avenues. It was just a matter of time before Lee found her again.

Corsair had a weak link. Two. Khloe and Amanda. If she shifted her attention from tracking Corsair to finding the two girls, Lee was certain she'd succeed.

As she leaned back in the chair, she watched the paused video. What mistake was Khloe going to make? If she could anticipate that, she'd have them.

5

Cartagena de Indias, Colombia

Anonymous travel was rarely comfortable. It wasn't impossible, and frankly, much easier than most people thought. Caleb read the news articles and editorials about how porous the US-Mexico border was, and he almost chuckled. The truth would appall the typical Fox News and CNN viewer. While Border Patrol guarded all along that imaginary boundary, there was no way to close off the gaps. Even if they did, what stopped the more industrious from traveling to Canada or hopping on a boat and sailing across the Gulf of Mexico to the Florida panhandle?

However, any effort to skirt the border control of any country came at a cost—usually equal parts comfort and money. This trip had been just that. Most of the flights from Belize to Colombia routed Caleb through Miami. There was too great a chance of the OOC locating him on airport footage. Instead, he found a cheaper flight that took him to Barranquilla, where he used a fresh passport under the name Damon Alexander from just outside of Berlin. His accent shifted flawlessly into the *Hochdeutsch* dialect that most recognized. He slipped through immigration with ease, explaining he was here on holiday.

Once out of the airport, Caleb found a bus that traversed along the coast the 120 kilometers between Barranquilla and Cartagena. Corsair found a seat in the back of the bus where he'd used the five-hour ride to sleep, waking long enough at each stop to ensure no threats boarded the bus.

Unable to shake the uneasy feeling about this trip from the instant Driver mentioned it, Caleb repeated to himself that it was the fact that he'd been nonoperational for a decade. This had the earmarks of several missions he'd embarked on for the Office of Compliance.

But it bothered Corsair that Driver needed someone to make the pickup for him. In this line of business, it wasn't uncommon to make enemies and become *persona non grata* in other countries. During the last few years that he worked for the OOC, he'd done just that in a few places. After so long, he wondered if he still needed to worry about it. After all, he'd been "dead" for a decade.

But you aren't anymore.

It was a reminder that he'd risen from the dead. The woman he'd crossed paths with in Puerto Vallarta and Florida was an agent for the OOC. He wondered, not for the first time, if leaving her alive had been a mistake. When he was operational, that wouldn't have been an option. He would have put a bullet in her head and left her on the floor of that living room with Sonny Departi and his men.

Caleb Saunders wasn't the same man. Corsair was still deadly. Although Caleb wondered if the past ten years were more sedentary than he believed. His gut scolded him, knowing that he'd grown complacent. The Corsair, who once took out a small unit in Germany, would never have allowed two gangbangers to kill his wife and son.

He let his head touch the window of the bus as he stared out at the countryside. Moments like this plagued him. Quiet seconds when Audrey and Jackson invaded his thoughts. He'd allowed them to get killed. In the past, Corsair would have spotted the two kids and registered the danger before pulling into the gas station. Hell, he'd have never allowed the gas to get that close to empty.

Complacency killed Audrey and Jackson. It didn't matter to him that most people would have been in the same situation. None of those hypothetical people had the training and experience that Corsair did. Since then, he'd seen his daughter kidnapped and placed in danger twice. Was he good enough still to protect her now? How did that even look?

When these morose moments hit, Caleb struggled to find balance. The two parts of him struggled. The grieving husband only wanted a few moments to reflect on and remember the face of his wife or the laugh of his son. But the operative fought to keep him on target. His life no longer had room for any lack of vigilance. Not if he wanted to protect Amanda.

That goal drove him forward. It was what led him to Colombia. Amanda liked Khloe, and having the woman with them completed the familial image. If all they did was get to Europe, then Khloe could choose her own path. For now, she offered a perfect disguise.

Are you replacing Audrey, though?

He argued that over and over. Logic explained to him that no, Audrey was never replaceable. Guilt, though, screamed louder, calling him the worst of things. All of it sat in the pit of his stomach.

The bus jarred as it traveled along the rough highway. As it passed through small villages between Barranquilla and Cartagena, Caleb watched the small glimpses of daily life zipping past at only about thirty miles per hour.

He checked the time. According to the ticket, his arrival in Cartagena de Indias would be around six. The last sign he'd seen was about fifteen minutes ago, and it indicated thirty-five kilometers. Despite the rugged terrain, the driver was on time.

His timetable remained solid. The rendezvous with Driver's man wasn't until tomorrow evening. That left him plenty of time to secure a room somewhere. Corsair already scoped out several options within the touristy section of the city. There would be less chance of standing out if he resembled every other Euro-American visiting the historic locations. Again, anonymity sometimes costed more. Any hovel in the shittiest part of Cartagena would draw attention. White Americans avoided those places like the plague. The denizens of those *barrios* might not report him to the authorities, but there was more than just the OOC on the hunt for him. Corsair had a solid share of enemies who would love to see him dead.

With a mental snap, he brought himself back to attention. He'd reach the city and map it out, locating where he wanted to stay in relation to the meeting point. Corsair wanted to know every avenue of escape from any point in the city.

It was an impossible task for the entire metropolitan area, which was another reason for Corsair to remain within a smaller section. During the flight, Caleb memorized the streets off a map. It was a technique he'd developed during operational training with the OOC. Preparation resolved most of the situations that came up during a job.

He wanted to be prepared. He didn't trust Driver or the reason he'd asked Caleb to retrieve the forger's documents. After leaving the man's house, he returned, aware now of the various cameras the paranoid man used to surveil his property. Armed with that knowledge, he found cover and stared at the man's house for several hours. There'd been only a small gap from the time he left Driver until he set up surveillance for the forger to contact anyone. Unfortunately, there was no way to gauge or monitor the man's virtual communication. Corsair assumed it was a setup.

Driver never left his house, and well after midnight, Caleb resigned to the fact he wouldn't get any more information about Driver's intentions until he went to Colombia.

But he'd remain wary. Caleb had Khloe arrange the rental house, a bungalow off Seashore Drive, just north of Belize City. It wasn't a waterfront property but one whose owners hoped to break into the vacation rental market with a lower tier property. Corsair found it perfect for their needs—just off the beaten path enough to go unnoticed while being close enough to the water to have foreign tourists about.

He'd assured Khloe there was nothing to worry about despite his own anxiety about this trip. However, the woman would be with his daughter, and he wanted to know she remained vigilant but calm. They'd gone over every contingency plan, something Khloe recognized as a necessity for Caleb. He found she was adept at it, too. Not a surprise, given how well she'd vanished from the Cincinnati mob last year. With some training, Khloe could develop excellent countersurveillance skills.

"Don't go anywhere you don't need to," he urged her before leaving for the airport.

"It's only a few days," she assured him. "We have plenty of food in the house."

"I won't be in contact until I'm out of Colombia," he explained. His overly cautious behavior grew normal for Khloe, who displayed remarkable patience for Corsair's instructions. He wondered if it was a level of trust they'd developed or the realization after Puerto Vallarta that her life hung precariously over a den of lions. Caleb thought that in truth, it was a mixture of the two. She thought she'd been careful when she took refuge in Puerto Vallarta, only to be discovered by pure chance. That made her almost as wary as Corsair.

The bus pulled onto a four-lane highway, and Caleb sighed with relief. The last road rattled the bus like a cocktail shaker with its numerous potholes and spots where Caleb wondered if there'd ever been asphalt. It was a road best traversed in a truck or off-road vehicle, not a thirty-two-foot bus with three axles.

From his window, Caleb saw the rise of buildings in the distance. Cartagena de Indias. He sat up a little straighter in his seat as he observed the outskirts of the city develop with each passing mile.

6

Cartagena de Indias, Colombia

Music echoed off the walls along the street. A taxi blared its horn at a car blocking the one-lane road as its passengers spilled out of the back seat. Nightlife was in full swing in Getsemani, a neighborhood inside the walled city of Cartagena. As dusk arrived, artists pulled their works along the street. Vagabond vendors stretched blankets out on the narrow sidewalk to display the jewelry, trinkets, and art they wanted to sell. At the same time, fruit carts appeared out of nowhere with an array of fresh items. Sliced pineapple, papaya, and mango filled cups lined along the cart with an assortment of tropical fruits.

Camille Dubois stepped out of the large wrought-iron door of the Hotel Monaguillo. The heavy metal door scraped the concrete step as she pushed it open.

"Pizza! Delicious, hot pizza! You know you are hungry!" a male voice called through a handheld speaker. His mechanized voice ricocheted off the walls. It was out of sync with the beats of music already drifting down from the Café Havana and Trinidad Plaza.

Minuit thought it odd. She'd been in the city for several hours now, and that was the first English she'd heard. No doubt the pizza place hoped to bring in the American tourists in the area. She hadn't encountered any yet, but she'd been resting in her room since two this afternoon.

When the call came through yesterday, she sprang into action. It had been months since her contact reached out to her about Corsair. At first, her blood boiled with anticipation. Like a hunting dog pulling at its owner's leash, she expected to be released on her former lover in a matter of days. Yet, days turned into weeks. Weeks into months. All with no word on Corsair.

All her contact told her was that Corsair emerged in Mexico. Would she be interested in the eliminating the agent? Of course she would.

However, Minuit remained professional. Her past relationship with Corsair became the source of her demise. When Corsair killed Marc Lefevre, the DGSE disavowed Camille Dubois, attempting to arrest her for conspiracy and treason. Lefevre's tactical team confirmed that Minuit escorted the American agent to the Tower of King René, where Corsair murdered Lefevre before escaping.

The fallout sent Minuit into the shadows. She barely escaped France. Angered and broken, she retreated to the streets of Kiev, hiding in a flat for several weeks. On the run, she began the hunt for Corsair, only to find he died in a botched assignment in Turkey. Devastated that the only hope she had to clear her name with the DGSE died, Minuit built a name for herself as a skilled assassin.

She began in Ukraine, working for a crime boss, rebuilding her life, albeit one on the run. Her services weren't cheap, but she developed a reputation as a chameleon.

Camille inhaled a breath, smelling the fried arepas being sold from a house window three doors down. She'd grown to love South America. It was far enough from Europe that her fear of discovery lessened. The drug cartels offered a constant supply of high-paying jobs that sustained her for a while.

But she hadn't had a kill in three months. Not since the Amigos dos Amigos man in Rocinha. Minuit wanted to be ready to go when the call came about Corsair. She'd almost been to the point of accepting a new job when the phone rang yesterday.

Now she was back in Cartagena. The last time she'd been in the city was three years ago. Tasked with acquiring a file from an American businessman. It had been a different job for her. The American couldn't die, and he couldn't know that the file had been compromised. An easy job, too. Men were always easy targets. She'd mastered the art of manipulation. Most couldn't think if their dicks were activated. Others required stroking their egos. If somehow, neither libido nor pride worked, she moved to greed. Her ability to read a mark so accurately allowed her to change gears in the middle of an operation.

Except for Corsair. Or could it be that because of Corsair, she learned that? He'd fooled her thoroughly.

"Pizza! You want fresh pizza!" The hawker with the loudspeaker ambled down the road toward her. A dark-skinned, lanky man in his fifties held the microphone against his lips. The repeated phrase had a rhythm to the cadence leading Minuit to guess he'd memorized the English. The Frenchwoman studied his face as he passed her. When he spoke into the loudspeaker, his eyes glazed over, and he trundled forward through the sea of people.

The echoing voice receded down the road as she moved toward the church at the end of the street. A few Colombian men eyed her as she walked. Minuit, aware of the attention a single female might draw, acknowledged each stare with enough eye contact to intimidate the men without drawing them in. Colombia in recent years developed a reputation for sexual tourism. Prostitution was legal in the country, leading men from around the globe to travel there strictly for the women.

Minuit appraised each man with a passing glance. Most were only curious—there were not many single foreign women walking the streets after dark. Some, she thought, might be interested in hiring her for sex, and at least one she pinpointed as a predator—perhaps he thought himself a pimp. Her terse expression seemed enough to prevent any initiation of contact.

As she reached the end of the street, an intersection forked around a three-story yellow building. The Church of the Trinidad stood as the center of Getsemani. Crowds were forming around the front of the plain church. The locals filled into the plaza. Groups of teenagers clustered near the steps of the church as a man stood next to a small, round platform with blaring speakers and flashing lights.

Sizzling meat caught her attention, and Minuit turned to see a man grilling chicken and steak kabobs over an open flame.

"Cerveza!" A man with a Styrofoam cooler hanging from a makeshift strap stepped in front of her. He opened the lid to reveal bottles of water and cans of Aguila beer nestled into ice.

If she weren't working, Camille would settle onto one of the concrete benches and watch the crowd gather. While beer wasn't her drink of choice, she counted three portable bars set up around the square with signs offering mojitos, margaritas, and other mixed cocktails.

Instead, she wanted to find a coffee and a small bite to eat. Tomorrow would be important, and she wanted to keep her mind on target. A satisfied smirk filled her face as she thought about the coming evening. As she crossed the plaza, her attention turned to the faces around her. Groups of young men in their twenties laughed and joked. Camille noticed two that she'd enjoy taking back to her room. Minuit averted her gaze.

Perhaps tomorrow night.

For the moment, she needed to keep her focus. Twelve years of hatred culminated, and in the next couple of days, she would dip into that well.

Minuit considered it had been twelve years. She didn't remember the exact date she had gone with Corsair to Fort Saint-Jean, but she recollected every detail of that day in Marseille. The most distinctive memory struck her with certain aromas. Often the hint of oily salt water on the breeze triggered her, however the one that used to bring tears to her eyes had been that of exhaust and baked bread. The combination, usually heavier on the yeast, flour, and butter scent, had been a constant in the flat where she spent so many nights with Corsair. The *pâtisserie* two doors down and the bus stop beneath her window fueled the smells.

She shook the thoughts away. If she let her mind dwell on the happy memories, she worried that she would forget the pain. Despite that fear, no such loss would come. Minuit was certain of that. The lingering, almost burning, agony flared up at the thought of her mentor, Lefevre.

Marc recruited her into the DGSE. He'd become the father figure she never had. Her father abandoned her mother and Camille when she was nine. Camille never saw the man again—not until she was twenty-four and ran into him in Paris. Minuit, already working with the DGSE, broke the man's nose when he attempted to reconcile.

Reconcile, indeed. He approached her, telling her who he was. The man stank of cheap wine. When he blamed her mother for his leaving, Minuit punched him in the face. The blow rocked him back into the grass with blood dripping from both nostrils.

His face flashed with anger. Camille recognized it from her childhood, and in that instant, she felt grateful the bastard left. With a warning that if he ever approached her again that she would kill him, Minuit turned her back on the man.

She wanted to do the same to Corsair. He deserved worse.

Not only did he kill her mentor, but he stole some part of her in the process. Camille thought they were in love. Corsair tricked her. He lured her in—just like she'd been taught to do. Her defenses dropped, and Minuit pointed the assassin at her boss. Too many nights after that morning were spent in fitful sleep as she saw her hand holding the blade that killed Marc Lefevre.

Like salt in a wound, though, her situation became worse. Her country branded her a traitor, slapped a target on her back, and hunted her. Corsair took far more away from her than her father ever did. She lost her mentor and friend, her career, her country, and her lover.

Minuit gritted her teeth as she moved through the crowd. A small café in the corner shared a wall with the cathedral. Six round bistro tables, each with two chairs, sat on the stoop overlooking the street. Camille climbed the steps to the raised level and found a seat.

A girl no more than thirteen appeared at her side.

"Would you like something to drink?" she asked Camille in Spanish.

"Coffee. Black." Minuit took the menu, scanning it. "Shrimp and rice, please."

The young Colombian girl smiled at the Frenchwoman and nodded before scurrying into the restaurant. Minuit stared back down the street the way she'd come. It seemed that with each passing minute, the crowd increased as the people of Getsemani poured out of their homes and hotels.

Camille Dubois leaned back in the chair. By tomorrow, she might be free of a burden she'd previously been unable to release. She sighed. The disavowed agent knew better. Minuit would accomplish nothing more than revenge. Simple as that.

Nothing would assuage the guilt she'd carried.

But the satisfaction of revenge would make an adequate substitute.

It would do just fine.

7

Cartagena de Indias, Colombia

Six buses barreled down Avenida Venezuela, swirling exhaust and dust in the air. Caleb stepped back from the curb. Once the vehicles rumbled past, the street, dedicated to bus traffic, was empty. Crowds of people crossed from the base of the clock tower that served as the main entrance to the older part of the walled city.

Caleb took advantage of the passing traffic to move away from the people and seemingly meander up the road a few hundred yards. He performed some countersurveillance as he walked. The action was habitual, and he'd paused at least six times since leaving the hostel where he found a small cubby that doubled as a room. He didn't need comfort, but privacy.

His choice of accommodation remained predicated on his desire for anonymity. Since leaving Florida, Corsair operated as if someone actively hunted him. In Mexico, he proved that was accurate when the woman from the OOC appeared. Since his unease about this mission hadn't settled down, he intended to maintain vigilance.

Nothing caught his eyes as he turned to gaze at the architecture. A few girls stood under the clock tower, but he'd made them as prostitutes setting up for the evening. A handful of policemen patrolled aimlessly around, almost as if they were watching the working girls more than the crowd. It didn't surprise Caleb. He spent his time waiting at the airport by scanning recent news reports coming out of Colombia. There'd been an uptick in crimes against foreign travelers. The implication Caleb gathered was that most of these victims were men looking to partake in the country's legal prostitution. Most of the reports were robberies where the men found themselves drugged and their bank accounts cleaned out. A few incidents involved murder—probably an overdose of scopolamine administered by the girls the men took to their rooms.

Caleb crossed Avenida Venezuela. His motions were casual as he strolled down the side street between the towering buildings. Children sat in plastic lawn chairs where they sold corn on the cob. A roiling pot of water bubbled on a propane burner in front of them. The girl holding a cob up toward Caleb wasn't more than six years old. The boy, obviously her brother, had a few more years on his sister. He offered a wide grin and asked Caleb, "Corn?" in Spanish.

Caleb gave the boy a polite shake of the head and continued past. An older woman who might have been the kids' mothers stood next to a blue cart advertising ceviche.

Her smile was as wide as the boy's but lacked the majority of her teeth. She motioned toward the cart where a pot of premixed ceviche sat in a tub of ice. The metal exterior displayed a thin covering of frost.

At least it's cold.

On the opposite side of the street, a couple of old men in their sixties squatted on milk crates. An array of used tools, from greasy screwdrivers to worn hammers, spread out over the three crates they used as a makeshift table. Neither of them gave Caleb more than a passing glance.

However, Caleb slowed. He'd come into the country unarmed. It wasn't a condition he wanted to remain, either. Kneeling down, he touched a six-inch Phillips-head screwdriver.

"How much?" he asked the old man in Spanish.

The vendor pulled a tattered blue baseball cap off his head as he surveyed the potential customer. "Four thousand pesos," the answer came.

Caleb peeled eight five-hundred-peso notes from a wad in his pocket. It equated to about a dollar. Caleb grabbed the red-handled screwdriver with a quick *"Gracias."*

By the time Caleb straightened up and started walking, the screwdriver disappeared into a pocket. The old man slipped the hat back on his head as he folded the bills in half and slid them into his shirt.

The fellow next to the old vendor watched Caleb trail down the alley with a curious stare.

"Why does a *gringo* need a screwdriver?" he asked his friend.

"Who cares?" the old man replied as he went back to his table, rearranging the tools to fill in the gap where the red screwdriver had been.

Caleb passed a guy selling cookies that he'd taken out of a package and placed in plastic bags. Each bag held four plain cookies that looked like simple shortbread. A hand-painted sign said they were four thousand pesos each.

A minute later, Caleb reached the end of the alley, where he turned right toward the park. Centennial Park was the green oasis in the middle of the walled city. Trees covered the walkways and shrouded the park from the glow of the city lights. With only a few lamps lighting up the center path, most of the park offered shadows, something Caleb appreciated as he weaved through the trees. Beneath a banyan tree, he leaned against the trunk, allowing the silhouette of his form to disappear against the massive tree. It gave him a view of the park and a perfect spot to watch for anything unusual.

As was his custom, he had plenty of time to make the rendezvous. It wouldn't matter though, because he also intended to be late. The man that Driver arranged for Corsair to meet would likely get into position early, assuming he was a professional at all. Caleb didn't like being predictable, and while he'd been out of the game for a long time, anyone he'd crossed paths with in his years working for the OCC would expect him to be early. If he was going to be unpredictable, he'd need to arrive late. But that wasn't an option. It would be too difficult to watch the area all day. He'd need to find the perfect place for that.

All of that preparation would be for naught if he picked up a tail on the way to the meet. He'd prefer arriving clean and dealing with whatever awaited him there.

Motionless, Caleb remained against the huge trunk, watching. A dirty figure pushed a cart full of garbage bags that rattled as he drew closer. The man's stench wafted across the park on the breeze, and Caleb doubted anyone would face that aroma on purpose. Even in his days of deep disguise, he could never master that smell.

Still, he watched the man roll the two-wheeled cart along the path. A strange murmur echoed off the trees, and Caleb listened. Was the man talking to someone? Perhaps he'd been wrong, and this wasn't just a vagrant.

"You don't know what I am!" the man argued. "I told you that already."

Corsair studied him as he drew closer. His head turned to address an invisible companion, and Caleb breathed with relief.

Once the man's odor faded and he had left the park, Caleb straightened up and crossed the path, intersecting with the lights for only a second before the darkness of the other side of Centennial Park absorbed him.

His rendezvous was in the courtyard of Terraza Municipal, a park overlooking the bay. Six food trucks created a semicircle around a permanent bar constructed in the open. Each truck had two-foot letters across the top with lightbulbs illuminating each letter. They spelled out in English: Pasta, Sushi, Burgers, Tacos, Ice Cream, and Hot Dogs.

Very American, Caleb thought as he paused off to the side, remaining out of the perimeter of hanging Edison-style lights draped between poles and trees to light up the terrace.

Caleb meandered around the edge of the food court. Past the bar, he saw tables arranged along the waterfront. It was a popular spot, perfect for catching the sunset, and it drooped below the boatyard on the opposite side of the bay. Not quite as picturesque as Caleb got on the Mexican Riviera, but still a nice place to order a margarita and watch dusk descend on the city.

He'd long missed that magical moment, and now the city lights outshined the stars. Across the water, Caleb saw the lighted dome of the San Pedro Claver Church rising up in the walled city. Spotlights splayed up the side of the yellow and white church.

Three tables back from the water's edge sat a slightly overweight man with glasses. He donned a white Panama-style hat that would have pinned him as a non-native if it weren't for the pasty white skin he flashed when he removed the hat to wipe sweat from his bald head. Caleb stood behind the sushi truck watching the guy that had Driver's documents.

After six minutes, the man's phone lit up his face as he glanced at the screen—checking the time. Caleb should be making contact any second now. Or, at least, the man expected that. However, Corsair had no intention of meeting that expectation. In this business, one never fully expected on-time service. In fact, the longer the man sat there patiently waiting, the more Caleb suspected him for a professional.

Driver never intimated who the man was, and Caleb only guessed that a paranoid like Driver would take care to work with someone as equally careful. But someone completely oblivious to the ins-and-outs of tradecraft might prove even safer. After all, if they were completely expendable and ignorant, they could cause no trouble if they were caught and interrogated.

However, Caleb had no plans to interrogate anyone. If this plan went according to Driver's information, he'd sit down next to the mark, take the briefcase at his feet, and leave. Just to be safe, Caleb would take a bus south to Bogotá, where he could catch a flight to Mexico City and connect to the Belize City airport. It added three days of hard travel south, but the safety of staying off the grid gave him a sense of security.

He looped through the shadows of the Terraza Municipal again, keeping his eyes out for anyone else, maintaining surveillance on the fat bald guy. Nothing set off any alarms, and after the third circuit, he checked on baldy. He fidgeted in his chair until the young cocktail server appeared. He ordered another drink that Caleb thought was a frozen Piña Colada. The white hat rotated 180 degrees as he looked around.

Not a professional.

It wouldn't be long before the man decided Caleb was a no-show. He'd leave with the passports. Caleb considered waiting until he did that, but once he was on the move, the situation became less controllable. While Corsair handled his share of tales and surveillance, it was usually on a known target. This man was still an unknown, and the former agent didn't want to reach out to Driver to arrange another meeting. The sooner he was back on his way to Amanda and Khloe, the better he'd feel about it.

Caleb stepped under the drooping string of bulbs and onto the concrete terrace. He moved to the bar in the center of the half circle of food trucks.

"Mojito," he ordered when the bartender, a Colombian man in his twenties, approached.

Caleb watched the man as he crushed the fresh mint leaves. His gaze drifted just over the man's shoulder to watch the bald man across the terrace. As the bartender shook the cocktail, mint filled Caleb's nostrils. The liquid poured out of the metal shaker into a tall Collins glass that the young Colombian garnished with a wedge of lime and a sprig of mint. With pesos in hand, Caleb passed a handful across to the bartender before he could give him the price. He'd estimated the amount and added enough to appease the man.

Caleb sipped the mojito from the paper straw, something he hadn't expected but was pleased to see. With an approving nod to the man behind the bar, Caleb carried his drink toward the empty seat next to the bald man. The mojito assured Corsair that the young cocktail server wouldn't disturb him as soon as he sat down. His mouth sucked another drink through the straw.

That's a damned good mojito, Caleb considered.

Corsair dropped into the colorfully striped chair. As he sat next to the bald man, his eyes flicked to the messenger bag on the ground at the man's feet.

"Is that mine?" Caleb asked in Spanish.

"You're late," the other man growled in English.

"You were just too early," Corsair replied in Spanish.

"Fucking asshole."

Caleb didn't respond. He took another drink from his glass as his eyes scanned the tables around the edges.

"Is that my bag?" Caleb asked again, leaving his tone as flat as possible. He already didn't like the guy, and Caleb reminded himself that there was no prerequisite to enjoy the man's company. Just get the stuff and leave.

"You were followed?" the man asked.

"No," Caleb confirmed.

"No, asshole. You were followed." There was no question in his tone.

Corsair shifted in his seat to see two men moving along the water's edge toward them.

8

Cartagena de Indias, Colombia

The concierge at the Casa del Arzobispado eyed Valentina as she slipped through the marbled lobby. It wasn't the most elegant hotel she'd been to since arriving in Cartagena, but it was much nicer than most she visited.

The American—he said his name was Dale like the race car driver, whatever that meant—had been one of the most unpleasant she'd experienced. Unpleasant seemed a little harsh. He was rude, hateful, and smelled like old laundry, but he didn't hurt her. This Dale wasn't even the oldest or the fattest American she'd fucked this week, but for someone staying at the Casa del Arzobispado, he was grosser than she expected.

That's all it was. When he approached her earlier, she expected exactly what she saw—a dirty, obese asshole that was unable to get laid in his own country. But then he took her to the Casa, and she got her hopes up.

Hopes? What fucking hopes? There was nothing to hope for. Except that the Captain didn't find out she was freelancing on the side.

No, the American was tolerable. She reminded herself that she now had another two hundred thousand pesos that the Captain would never see. If he stayed in the dark, she'd put together enough to get on a bus back anywhere. Hell, even back to Venezuela was better than here. Her home country was crumbling so that families like hers fled across the border into Colombia or Brazil. The chaos at the border had been too much, and Valentina somehow found herself separated from her mother and father and two brothers.

Stupid. She should have known better. He promised to take care of her and help her find her family. After all, he was a police officer.

Her brothers warned her about the police. They were never trying to help. Javier, her oldest brother, had the most trouble with the cops in Venezuela. That was the impetus for her family to leave the little village in the south of Venezuela. Another visit by the *policía* would likely end with Javier beaten to death or in jail.

But now she was held prisoner by the *policía*. She didn't even know what happened. They'd come across the border, and her father said they were meeting some people. He'd left them with a Colombian family that he knew while he arranged to get a ride for all of them. While her father was gone, the police raided the house, and her brother told her to flee.

Valentina did. She'd run for what felt like days through the woods until she had no idea where she was. When she found the road, it felt like salvation. Three days of sleeping in the woods wore her down, and the truck driver heading toward Cartagena offered her a ride—for a price, of course.

She eased out of Casa del Arzobispado and onto the street. She'd held her breath as she stepped through the iron doors, praying to God that there were no police on the street. If Captain Torres discovered she'd been working on the side, he'd take what she earned and rape her for the trouble.

The street was busy, but there were no cops out. Torres commanded a unit of police in the walled city, and each of them made sure that Valentina and the other girls did what Torres said. If they spotted her in the wrong spot, they'd report it to Torres—if they didn't confront her themselves.

Valentina had been lucky to run across Dale on her way to the clock tower this afternoon. Torres didn't expect her out there until dark, and she'd gotten an early start in the hopes of finding a man like Dale. She'd decided last week after Torres and one of his men, who Torres called Carlos, took turns raping her because she told Torres she wanted to leave.

They thought they'd forced her into submission, but all their brutal tactics accomplished was to teach the young girl that her plans to escape had to remain secret.

Valentina had no clue how much a bus to Bogotá or Medellín would cost. She was certain that wherever she went wasn't far enough. She assumed that the police anywhere were just as corrupt as him. He might even have people watching the bus stations once he realized she'd disappeared.

Some of the girls she lived with told her stories of whores that ran away. Torres always found them. Either they ended up back in Cartagena or they were dead.

"Are you sure they're dead?" she asked.

"Torres said so."

"He's lying," she pointed out. Even at thirteen, it seemed obvious to her that Torres benefited from the other girls thinking that escape was only a death sentence. He had to find her to kill her, and if she got far enough away, she thought she'd disappear.

But Torres controlled everything. In Colombia, prostitution was legal, if you were an adult. Valentina wasn't, and when she got arrested by Torres for giving a guy a hand job, he explained it to her, offering her protection and a place to stay.

Once he got her into the one-bedroom apartment that she shared with ten other girls, it became obvious that he was the one she needed protection from. He did keep the girls supplied with coke and grass, usually used to counteract the other. Within a day, she'd become nothing more than a compliant body for him to sell.

"Be under the clock tower by sunset," he ordered. "I'll tell you when you can go home."

Those were her marching orders. Occasionally, he'd give her some drugs for whatever john took her back to his hotel. If he appeared naïve or he flashed too much money, Torres would send one of the girls to him. Most of them were dumb Americans. They seemed the most oblivious to the dangers. Some were convinced they were invincible. But dose them, and they let her lead them to an ATM and clean out their account.

As soon as they woke up the next morning, those idiots would call the police. "I've been robbed," they'd cry to the man who ended up with all their money. Valentina turned over 25,000 US dollars one night to Torres. He thought she was holding out on him and forced her to strip in an alley.

Now she was late, and if Torres caught her before she got to the clock tower, he'd want her to tell him where she'd been. But she hoped she would miss him and find her first john. At least, the first as far as Torres was concerned. Then she would have something to hand over to him without him causing a scene.

Valentina felt the wad of bills stuffed into her panties. The edges of the bills rubbed against her skin, making her uncomfortable. She needed to find a place to hide the money. In the little apartment, it would be impossible. One of the girls might find it. They'd either steal it or give it to Torres.

A bank seemed logical, but she didn't think there were any banks that would open an account for a thirteen-year-old girl with no identification. Most likely, the bank teller would just call the police. Then Torres would hear about it and wonder what she needed a bank account for.

She needed a better plan. It frustrated the girl. This wasn't what life was supposed to be like. In moments like this, she wondered where her mother was. When they crossed, her parents never explained where they planned to go. Her mother had family in Bogotá—an aunt, Valentina thought. No one Valentina ever met. But if she got to Bogotá, perhaps she could look up this family member. What if that's where her parents escaped?

What if they were still looking for her, though, near Cúcuta, where they crossed the border? She could go down there, but Torres knew where she came from. He might think she'd done just that. Hell, he might know exactly where her family was.

The thought infuriated her. It suddenly dawned on her that her parents might have gone to the police when Valentina went missing. If they had, then it would make sense Torres knew who she was.

What if that's how he found you?

The girl clenched her fist. She wanted to hit him again. Valentina did that the other day when she demanded he let her go back to her family. She pulled back and punched him. It was hard too, just like Javier taught her.

"Don't swing your arm. Let it shoot out," he told her one afternoon. "Keep your fist in a ball or you'll break a finger."

Valentina recalled those words a split second before she threw the punch. She fired her fist out and Torres stepped to the side, letting it hit his chest. The Kevlar vest took the brunt of the punch, and he simply struck her with the back of his hand while Carlos cackled to the side. If she hadn't punched him, the pair of them might have let it go. Just put her back to work.

But they wanted to teach her a lesson.

It wouldn't happen again. Valentina reminded herself of that. Her fingers loosened from the fist she'd been making. She couldn't fight Torres. He'd just make her pay for anything she did.

I just have to get away. It developed into a mantra for her. She decided if she would get a million pesos, that would be enough. Maybe she'd take the bus part of the way to Bogotá. If Torres started looking for her, he might look in the bigger cities. With a million pesos, she could find some place to wait a week until he got tired of looking for her.

Valentina figured some girls had to have gotten away. Unless they were all just stupid and didn't leave Cartagena. Torres had the police on his side, but he wasn't that smart. Plus, he didn't have the time to go hunting all over the country for a runaway girl. If she disappeared for long enough, he might not search that hard.

Plus, he'd expect her to act like a kid and not think it through. The other girls were mindless dolts. All they wanted was the next hit of coke he'd bring them. Valentina realized that. She'd started cutting back what she took. If she didn't snort any, the girls or Torres might notice. But she'd figured out how to dump it and make it look like she'd done a line. The weed was different, though. It was tough to fake that, but then the high only lasted until morning.

Valentina intended to stay clear-headed. She needed to hide the money somewhere. That was her first goal. After that, she needed to get out when Torres wasn't in the plaza. She'd made 200,000 pesos with Dale. If she could do one

American like Dale a day, she could have enough in less than a week.

After that, she could make her getaway. *I just have to get away.* Valentina knew she had to be smart, though. This wasn't something to rush. Strangely, that thought reminded her of learning to sew with her *abuela*.

"Take it slow, *hija*. Every stitch is important or the seams will tear. It's about the details."

She'd get it right. Valentina knew that. It was the only thing that mattered now. Don't let Torres find out. Don't mess up.

Ahead, the crowds filled the plaza behind the clock tower. The city erected a movie screen to one side where a cartoon played that Valentina had never seen. She stared across the crowd. There was no sign of Torres, and she felt some relief. Her eyes began focusing on the faces of the men, and she wondered how many of these fat Americans she'd have crawled all over her tonight.

9

Cartagena de Indias, Colombia

Corsair reached for the messenger bag.

"What the hell, man? You going to leave me here?"

Corsair cut his eyes up to the fat, bald man. "You're lucky I don't kill you for setting me up," he snarled.

"I didn't fucking set you up," the man whined, but Corsair was already on his feet, pulling the messenger back up onto his shoulder. He took long strides toward the water's edge, glancing over his shoulder.

The fat man was out of his seat, scurrying like a scared squirrel away from the two—no, three men now. The third appeared near the food truck that read "Tacos" in bright lighted letters. The other two looked to be Latino, but the new guy was a tall, broad-shouldered white man. Caleb decided he was military or, rather, ex-military. The neatly trimmed hair and edges of a skull tattoo peaked out from under the bottom of his right shirt sleeve. The fabric of which stretched around pronounced biceps crafted from years of weight training.

The two Latinos weren't quite as big as the Caucasian, but that didn't make them less formidable. Caleb sensed the danger from them. These were men that, like him, had killed before. All three of them focused their eyes on him and continued pacing forward.

An ordinary individual, knowing that three killers stalked after him, would sprint in fear. Corsair wasn't normal. Certainly, not in the same way that the people enjoying their handcrafted cocktails under the half-moon were. He didn't scare.

Well, that wasn't true, was it? He'd been scared before. But that had been when Amanda was in danger. Even after finding the bloody bodies of his wife Audrey and their son Jackson, he didn't feel fear. Anger—yes. Rage drove him after the men who killed his family and took his daughter.

It wasn't until he had been wounded and unable to rescue Amanda that he felt scared.

Right now, he had nothing to worry about. He knew Amanda was safe with Khloe. If something happened to him here, she'd take care of the girl. It would actually be better if he met his demise somewhere far from the females in his life. In his line of work, he expected to die. It was a matter of odds. One can't play against the house and never lose. As long as he protected his daughter, there was nothing to concern him.

That didn't mean he intended to roll over and let these men catch up to him. Corsair might not fear death, but he also didn't welcome it. At least not his own.

Caleb took a step to the right, changing his heading back toward the food trucks. He drew an imaginary line toward the burger truck. His head swiveled to scan toward the three men who had now added a fourth, another Caucasian who appeared near the bar.

They're funneling me. It was subtle, but the four men cut off three direct routes. If he wanted to draw attention to himself, he could sprint past the two Latinos and escape behind them. However, that would draw every eye in the crowd to him, which in today's world meant they would attract phone cameras. The last thing he wanted was the OOC to catch a sighting of Corsair.

He'd only get past those two if he ran, so he vetoed that option.

The men were pushing him toward the burger stand, likely expecting him to cut between the burger and sushi truck. Past the vendors, the park was dark. It would be ideal to set up a net of people to catch him as he escaped the lighted terrace.

It was a fish trap, called that because it referred to a netted trap placed in a body of water. Usually, there was bait in the trap to entice the fish to swim into the opening. But often it was placed in shallow streams between rocks along the path the fish swam. A fish could get into the opening because it acted like a funnel. However, it was impossible to swim back through the small opening.

The fourth man moved forward, pressing him toward the gap between the trucks. That wasn't an option for Caleb. He let the man move a few steps closer before he feinted toward the funnel. Instead, he broke into a sprint toward the fourth man.

Caleb's sudden charge surprised the man who pulled a Walther P22 from the small of his back. Corsair let the messenger bag slip off his shoulder, catching it in his grip and swinging it at the man. The canvas tote caught the man in the chest, stunning him for a split second. It was long enough for Corsair to plant a stomp kick into the man's knee. His heel drove into the patella with a snap, buckling the man forward with a grunt.

As he fell, the P22 bounced out his hand. Caleb took a microsecond to consider grabbing the gun. Instead, he sprinted past the fallen man who made a weak attempt to reach for the American's ankles.

Caleb vaulted over the man, hoisting the strap over his head and letting the messenger bag flop against his back as he ran.

"Get him!" a thick accent shouted. Corsair didn't look back to see who called out, assuming it was the other Caucasian.

As he dashed under a sign set up across the path that read in lighted lettering, "Municipal. Kitchen-Bar-Terrace." His eyes flicked up at the words for a split second as a shape moved out of the shadows.

Corsair dropped and swept his right leg forward as a Latino man swooped from the dark. His shin collided with the man's legs with an agonizing thud, but Caleb pushed that discomfort away as he bound to his feet. The other man toppled to the ground, and Corsair spun back toward him with an ax kick to the man's left shoulder. His foot drove the man face-first into the concrete, and a second after the attacker appeared, Caleb was walking quickly out of the park.

10

Cartagena de Indias, Colombia

Minuit furrowed her brow as she watched from the front seat of the Nissan Kick. Corsair shifted away from the trap, dropping one of her men as he ran past the fallen mercenary. The move was swift, and even from this distance, she knew the knee Corsair just shattered would never be the same. A few seconds later, he dropped to the ground, sweeping a second man off his feet just as he came after the American.

Such a turn of events didn't surprise her. The man she'd shared a bed with so many years ago had always been reactive. While Tolazar assured her that Corsair had been out of the business for a decade, she doubted he was soft. The man who killed her mentor and left her in the wake of that destruction never went domestic. It was foolish of Tolazar to think that.

But the man insisted, and like most men, he needed to see the failure himself. Seven men weren't going to be enough to capture Corsair.

"You don't need to capture him," Tolazar scolded. "My employer only wants confirmation that he's dead."

What kind of confirmation did he want? Corsair had been a ghost for the last decade, and while she recognized his features at a distance, most people never got that close to the assassin. Or they never lived long enough to describe him. If she killed Corsair without some evidence that he was who she promised, Tolazar's employer might not be inclined to pay for her trouble.

Those were only excuses, though. Minuit longed for the last thing Corsair saw before he died to be her face. She relished that thought, wondering if he would express surprise or anger. It wouldn't be fear. He was formed of the same mettle as she was. Neither of them had courage because that was an idea that overcame fear. Corsair and Minuit didn't sense that emotion. They'd been built from the ground up to charge into the face of danger without a regret.

No, Corsair would be shocked. Or would he even remember her? Of course he would. The man might not care, though. After all, she had been only a means to reach Lefevre.

She watched the man cross the street, disappearing into an alley. Three of her men followed several seconds later.

"Idiots," she cursed under her breath. They'd lost any advantage they had now. She'd warned them to make sure

Corsair didn't escape Terraza Municipal. Once he got into the labyrinth of streets, Corsair could evade them.

She opened the door of the Kick and stepped out of the Nissan. Her brown ankle boots clicked against the stone sidewalk as she approached the park. The breeze off Cartagena Bay flicked at the stray hairs that came loose from the bun. The strands tickled the nape of her neck, but she swiped them back with her fingers.

T'mon, one of the Colombian thugs she'd hired, was helping Caruso to his feet. The Australian had been in the 2nd Commando Regiment before an incident with a young Iraqi girl got him booted from the military. Minuit didn't consider him smart, but he'd been a capable fighter. Although, judging from the angle of his knee, Corsair didn't bother fighting the man. He'd dropped him with a single, well-placed blow that Minuit thought had shattered the former commando's patella and taken him out of play.

Minuit pursed her lips. No matter what anyone thought of Corsair, he hadn't lost much of an edge. A little, perhaps. Minuit conceded that he hadn't seen the men before he made his meet. She didn't think the man she'd known in the past would have missed them. But likewise, her people didn't spot him until he made contact with the mark.

Another of her men, a German whose name she forgot, now struggled to his feet. She'd seen that attack from her car. It was the moment she knew this operation was beyond salvaging. Corsair seemed almost surprised by the German's sudden appearance. Had the man been more competent, he might have stood a chance.

"Leave him," she ordered T'mon in Spanish. "I want the target cornered."

"I can't walk," Caruso howled.

Minuit stared into T'mon's face. "Go!" she growled. The Colombian ran down the path past the German, who was now on his feet.

"Lady, I need some help," the Aussie commando called.

Minuit turned, dropping down on her haunches. The fingers on her right hand shoved a lock of hair behind her ear.

"You let one man get past you," she reminded him.

"He was quick." His strained voice warbled as he swallowed back the pain.

Minuit let her eyes drift down to the bent knee. "I'm thinking that now he'll always be quicker than you."

She stood up and turned. "I'm sure the locals will call an ambulance for you."

"Foockin' bitch!" he screamed.

The clip-clop of the boots on the pavement stopped. Without turning around to face the hobbled Aussie, Minuit announced, "I'll remember that, Caruso."

On the ground, the man watched her walk away.

She crossed the street. It hadn't been enough men. But the former DGSE agent knew that going into the evening. With only a day to gather a small force, she had to use what she could. A few contacts put her in touch with Caruso, who brought in the German and a Brit who Minuit assumed was among the ones in pursuit of Corsair. Tolazar connected her with a leader in the National Liberation Army, a guerrilla group operating in Colombia. The organization dabbled in several criminal activities, including drug production and export, illegal emerald mining, and human trafficking. They were organized enough to train their foot soldiers, and according to some of the reports, they'd grown to develop their own intelligence gathering network.

So far, the Liberation soldiers hadn't fallen victim to Corsair. Although, Minuit didn't expect them to go unscathed. However, she did appreciate the value of the National Liberation Army's reach.

Minuit barely glanced down the street before walking across it, following in the footsteps of her former lover. Ahead of her, she saw T'mon pause in the middle of the street. The pedestrian traffic through this section was steady but not nearly as heavy as other parts of the neighborhood.

Still, witnesses could be an issue. Minuit wasn't worried about being identified or even described. She knew what people's perception was when they saw her. Most witnesses would describe a beautiful woman who may have been Latino, but then again, perhaps she was European. They'd get the color of her hair close, but that wouldn't matter. In South America, brown-haired women were abundant. Since it was pulled up in a bun, they'd never guess the length.

Even her height would be inaccurate. The ankle boots she wore added two inches to her. But most importantly, neither men nor women would notice much more than her beauty. It triggered a response in the primal portion of the brain, especially in men. They'd know what she looked like but couldn't describe her past whatever they found most attractive on her.

Minuit could walk away from a crowd of witnesses, change her shoes and drop her hair to vanish. It made her a chameleon, and most of her employers didn't believe she'd go unnoticed like she did. It was a rare quality, and one that the assassin used to her benefit.

T'mon glanced back at her as she approached. He had a look of trepidation, and when she reached him, she found the source. Two of her men lay on the sidewalk, half a block down the alley.

"Fuck!" she moaned.

"Come on," she ordered T'mon as she stalked down the narrow street.

Both of the Liberation Army soldiers were still alive, but she counted two broken arms and another smashed kneecap. Past them, Minuit spied a pair of feet jutting out of a doorway. Corsair left the third man crumpled up on the stoop under an arched doorway. This one hadn't fared as well as the rest. His neck bent to the left farther than should have been physically possible. Corsair drove the man's head into the steps. When she saw the broken fingers on the man's left hand, she guessed Corsair caught the man's hand during a fight before twisting him around and hammering him into the stone stairs.

Minuit turned back to T'mon. "Do they have their guns?"

"No, they're over there." The man pointed to a bag of garbage where two Beretta 92 FS handguns sat on top of the rotting trash. Minuit walked over and hoisted both guns. The magazines were missing from both, and she checked the chamber, finding a single nine-millimeter round in each one.

She turned to look at the corpse in the doorway. There was no need to check on him. Her initial evaluation was wrong. The broken fingers happened when Corsair disarmed the Colombian. He'd taken the man's gun along with extra magazines.

"Get those two out of here," she ordered T'mon. Without another word, Minuit turned and marched out of the alley. Corsair slipped away, and now he was armed. It almost made her smile. At least he didn't make it easy.

11

Cartagena de Indias, Colombia

Corsair stretched out on the balcony. His right hand cradled the Beretta 92FS with the index finger of his right hand pressed gently against the trigger. With deep, slow breaths, he controlled the oxygen intake, allowing his blood vessels to replenish his body.

The free climb up the side of the building exerted more energy than he'd expected. While he was in excellent shape and maintained his training, scaling a wall with little or no hand or footholds hadn't been part of his regular regime. Mostly, his training comprised heavy cardio with some running and calisthenics.

After dropping the first two men, he'd had to contend with the third. He'd made a fatal error—rather, whoever sent the men made an error. It was obvious they wanted him alive, and the last man standing thought that the Beretta was incentive enough for Caleb to comply.

His mistake. It cost the gunman, too.

Caleb assumed more were coming, but a firefight on the streets of Cartagena would draw more attention than he wanted.

He didn't sit up when he heard the voice echo off the building across from him. Caleb remained motionless despite the urge to steal a peek at the female barking orders in Spanish. His refuge was six flights above the street. High enough that the din of city noise from the busier roads drowned out the voices below.

Caleb cursed himself. No one followed him to the rendezvous. That meant that the men who came after him were already at the Terraza Municipal. Yet, he'd made two complete circuits of the park without spotting them.

They couldn't have been in the park waiting for him. It didn't matter how rusty he thought he was, those men were all soldiers or some sort. They weren't the covert type. Otherwise, they'd have gotten closer to him before he spotted them.

Or rather Driver's man spotted them. How did he do that? The fat, bald guy wasn't that observant. The man put Caleb on defense. If he'd have waited another fifteen seconds, the men in the park would have closed their circle around him, and Caleb might not have found the opening to escape.

He sat up slowly. There'd be little chance of anyone below seeing him as long as he stayed back from the edge. To ensure he did that, Caleb scooted up against the glass French doors. With deliberate and slow movements, he opened the messenger bag.

Caleb's shoulders slumped. It held stacks of newspaper cut into strips and bound together. Caleb removed a packet, finding the newsprint wrapped with a rubber band. He removed it and leafed through the pages. It was somewhat new, but he couldn't find a date on it.

Dammit.

Driver set him up from the beginning. That opened up a lot of questions for Corsair, starting with "Why?"

These guys in the street weren't government issue. Well, they weren't currently employed by the government—certainly not the United States. The ones he put down in the alley were Colombian. Of that, Caleb was certain. The other two could have been any number of Euro-white soldiers, but neither dressed like an American. That didn't mean anything, neither did Caleb.

Whoever they were, Caleb felt confident they weren't with the Office of Compliance. Driver didn't strike him as the type to work with the American government at all. Too much paranoia.

He would, though, work for cash. That made the most sense to Caleb. Driver took a payout to hand Corsair to someone on a platter.

Word spread fast in the last year since Corsair reemerged in South Florida. Within hours, Caleb had to contend with a pair of hitmen and OOC agents out to kill him. With months behind him now, his enemies across the globe would hear the whisper that Corsair wasn't dead.

That list of enemies was too long for Caleb to contemplate. He'd crossed many people in the OOC's employ. Many of those had more money and power than they ever needed. It would be as easy as a few keystrokes to send a squad of men after him.

Caleb stuffed the loose newspaper cuttings back in the messenger bag. He riffled through the bag, hoping to find anything of use. Even a scrap of identification for the fat, bald man would be enough.

No luck. Nothing to lead him to find out who wanted him dead.

Doesn't matter.

Something bothered him more than having a target on his back. He'd given Driver pictures of Khloe for her new passport. It wasn't a lot of information, but a man with the technical knowledge that Driver had could easily use it to find Khloe's real name. Even Caleb could do that. A reverse image search would find news articles dating to last year when Sonny Departi, a gangster in Cincinnati, had Khloe's boyfriend killed.

The first step to finding someone was to discover who they were. He'd harped on Khloe about keeping away from her old life, but it was too much to expect her to do it a hundred percent. Caleb sensed Khloe had been missing her family, and he'd warned her about reaching out without discussing it with him.

The big worry to him was that Carl Winston and the computer gurus at the Office of Compliance might be able to track Driver down if he started searching into Khloe's past. If they pinpointed Driver's location to Belize, it narrowed down their search. It would start them searching border crossings, which wouldn't be a problem for Caleb, who avoided the border controls. So far, he found it easier to avoid the cameras in Belize City than it had been in Mexico City. Most of the tourism in the area was limited to the ports and resorts. Only a few intrepid souls walked past the shops to see the real city.

More shouting below piqued his interest. The female voice called out, asking about the men's guns. A second later, she spoke again. The words were in Spanish, but through the din of street noise, Caleb thought he detected an accent. Something not Colombian at all. Not even really one from Latin America, but it was hard to distinguish.

"*Fils de putain.*"

Caleb understood that. It was French.

12

Cartagena de Indias, Colombia

Captain Alejandro Torres snatched the wad of pesos out of Teresa's grip. The police captain towered over the young girl. His dark uniform imposed a frightening image. "*Policía*" in yellow lettering on his left breast marked the officer, but even without the label, the tall Colombian officer dominated the street. His muscular build and height were enough to strike fear in most people. The dour countenance frozen on his face declared that Torres trifled with no one.

"It better not be short!" he growled as he stuffed the colored bills into his shirt pocket. He couldn't count it here in public, and the officer's anger bubbled up when the young girl approached him with the cash.

"Discretion!" he reminded her in a raspy voice. However, it didn't stop the man from yanking the money out of the prostitute's grip. He believed that the less time the girls carried their payments around, the less time they had to contemplate stealing it.

"Get back out there!" he snapped. "Next time, flag me down. I'll meet you somewhere more secluded."

"I'm sorry." Teresa nodded as she turned.

Torres thought the girl was about fifteen, but he'd had her on the streets for over a year now. Her once smooth features sagged, leaving bags under her eyes—an effect from the coke that kept her going all night. She'd started showing track marks on her arm in the last month, and more showed up daily as she tried to find fresh veins to take the needles. So far, she was still bringing in top dollar, but before long, he figured he'd need to replace her. Drugged-out whores didn't earn much around the clock tower, and American men wouldn't pay much for a worn-out *puta* when the cleaner ones were so readily available. Perhaps he could trade her to some local pimp in Barrio Nelson Mandela, an area where thousands of societal castoffs migrated, for drugs to supply the other girls.

It meant he would need to replace her. His enterprise had grown since last year, when he only had three girls working for him. Those three were all dead now. Overdosed. Well, two overdosed, and the third vanished. At least that's what the other girls thought. She'd gotten the virus and almost gave it to Torres on purpose. The bitch thought she could kill him slowly. It scared him at first, and he carried her south into the jungle, where he took his time dismembering her.

Once he confirmed he hadn't contracted HIV, he took steps to ensure he wasn't with any girls that might carry it. The ones that did he stayed clear of.

He turned back to the crowd. A head above most of the people in the plaza, Torres could scan over the tops of them. He counted his men stationed around the area. The mayor recently decreed this area a high-traffic tourist zone, and as such, he wanted a heavy police presence to discourage the prostitutes and drug dealers from approaching the foreigners in town for some wholesome family fun by the beach.

For most of Colombia and South America, Cartagena de Indias was a beach destination, with people coming all the way from Brazil and Argentina for a few days of sand and surf. However, Torres found that the real money came from the United States, England, and a few other European countries whose men came to this tropical paradise to sample the local women. Like most Colombians, Torres understood the reasoning. Colombian women were renowned for their beauty. Since prostitution was legal in the country, it enticed men to make it a sexual destination.

Torres assumed that like so much of the American culture he saw on television and movies, the women in the States were more difficult. They wanted to have control. The culture was bleeding into South America, and more and more of the local girls began acting differently.

Carlos gave him a nod across the sea of people. His lieutenant gestured with his head toward a group of three girls lingering together. Torres recognized two of them as his girls. Malia and Valeria. The other was an older one that the captain had seen around. She was barely in her twenties, but that was old enough that he didn't want her filling his girls with ideas. Torres motioned for Carlos to break up the group.

As his lieutenant moved over to harass the older prostitute and split off the teen girls, Torres scanned for the rest of his hookers. It was difficult to track all of them and maintain his duties as a police officer, but several of the men in his unit were privy to his business. Carlos was his number two, and he'd already picked up two girls he was running on the street. His lieutenant wasn't making enough yet to pay for a decent room for the girls, but he'd stuck them in one of Torres's flats with a few girls. It allowed Torres to use Carlos to help keep his own girls in line. The other three guys in his unit only benefited from a weekly visit to the girls' apartment and a few thousand pesos a night.

Where was Valentina? He hadn't seen her all night.

Torres checked his watch. It was almost midnight, and there was no sign of the little bitch. She'd been nothing but a headache since he found her. But she still had the freshest face, which meant she could earn the most for a few months. Torres found most of the girls began to lose that virginal look after six months. Then the perverts coming down from America didn't want them.

This little bitch couldn't earn if she wasn't out on the street. He'd told her more than once that unless the mark was worth a lot more, she had an hour to finish him off before he expected her back in the plaza. Torres figured that on a normal night, she could turn eight to ten men in the evening. At close to a hundred US dollars per trick, it was a solid income, especially when the average monthly salary in Colombia was around a thousand US dollars.

Torres walked around the perimeter of the crowd, keeping the wall on his left side. He scanned the faces, searching for Valentina's. She was smaller, and it would be easy for the crowd to engulf her. However, he knew better. She stayed on the outskirts of the groups, and it took one of his men actually prodding her to approach a mark. She was too soft. The few times she'd drugged the guy to rip him off, she'd moaned and whined about it.

"What if he died?"

"Why do I have to do that?"

It was always fucking questions with her. He had the same problem with his own daughter. She was twelve and not out here working, but she complained about everything. He'd be damned if he let little Valentina act the same way.

There she was. Across the mass of heads, Torres watched Valentina crossing from the Hotel Casa Cartagena. That was one of the nicer hotels right here. Most of the guys coming from America stayed in the hostels or a few boutique hotels. Hotel Casa Cartagena, though, usually hosted guests with more expendable income. Those were never the ones Torres targeted to rob. Too much clout. If someone with some money and influence were drugged and robbed, they'd complain all the way up the police chain of command. The people like that want to keep the illusion of power, and they'll stir the pot until it seems they are still in control.

Torres preferred the younger, naïve men who allowed the shame of being taken advantage of to keep them quiet.

Valentina took up a position on the opposite side of the plaza. She was doing what she always did—just standing and waiting. It infuriated Torres. Most of the men here were used to the rules of law in the States, and they were too nervous to approach a girl. It was up to her to make initial contact and lure them away from the crowd.

Torres pushed through the crowd that was thickening as the night carried on. The movie screen rolled credits as the movie ended. The families in the crowd watching whatever inane drivel the city showed on the inflatable screen would be leaving the plaza soon. After that, the police presence was supposed to deter the sketchier denizens of the city. To some extent, they did. Torres and his team worked to chase off any of the drug dealers or whores that weren't working for them.

If they couldn't chase them off, they'd arrest them, take their money and drugs, and shuttle them off for the night. Almost all the ones they arrested were illegal aliens that crossed over from Venezuela, and those didn't have the means or desire to fight the charges. Certainly, they weren't going to point out that the cops that arrested them stole their drugs.

Torres stepped out of the crowd and crossed the expanse toward Valentina. Her eyes widened, and she visibly flinched just before he caught her upper arm in his grip. Torres tightened his hand around the girl's bare flesh. He didn't care if he bruised her. It wouldn't stop the men from going after her. Nothing seemed to matter to those people.

"Where the fuck have you been?" Torres growled as he dragged her off the plaza.

"I'm sorry," Valentina stammered. "I overslept, and then I wanted something to eat."

"There's food at the flat."

She shook her head warily. "The other girls don't let me eat." It was a blatant lie, but it had been a problem among some of the girls. A hierarchy developed, and the more popular girls—usually the youngest—were bullied.

"What were you doing at the Hotel Casa?" he demanded.

"I thought I could pick up a guy in the bar who might buy me dinner."

Torres narrowed his eyes to slits. "You're too young to be at the bar, and I've told you about hustling in the hotels. The managers will get angry and cause trouble."

She nodded. "Yeah, the asshole threw me out."

"Which one?" Torres asked.

"What?"

"Which manager?"

Valentina paused for a second too long.

"You are a fucking liar," Torres snapped, pulling her down the alley. "You are holding out on me?"

"No, I'm not," she insisted.

Torres shoved her back onto a step. Valentina stumbled up the two steps into the doorway.

"Fucking bitch!" Torres growled, throwing his arm up and striking her across the face with the back of his hand.

Valentina let out a squeal of pain.

"Shut up!" Torres shouted at her as he stepped closer. "What do you have?"

13

Cartagena de Indias, Colombia

Caleb remained prostrate on his back, watching the sky. Most of the stars were washed out from the light pollution of the city, but a few twinkled into view. It had been two hours since he heard the voices of the people below. During that time, he hadn't chanced looking over the railing. Through the city's noise, he made out the men talking as they picked up their injured comrades. Caleb wondered if they grabbed the corpse he left behind.

During the past couple of hours, he heard more voices—mostly jovial—pass below him. No one called out in alarm at a dead body.

Caleb pulled himself into a seated position, stretching his back from the inactivity. Two hours was a drop in the bucket compared to a few jobs that required him to remain motionless for days as he surveyed a potential target.

Now, he shifted to peer through the railings at the street below. Two young girls in their late teens, or possibly their early twenties, were coming down the street. The clicking of their heels against the concrete echoed between the buildings. He watched them as they progressed down the alley. They talked in hushed tones, and Caleb couldn't understand them.

When they were gone, he waited another ten minutes, searching for anyone out of the ordinary. A few stragglers came down the street, and a pair of young Colombian men carrying guitars on their backs stumbled along the way.

As he waited, he considered the men who came after him. They weren't all local. Corsair dispatched two white guys, and while neither had much of a chance to exchange words, they struck Caleb as foreigners. They could have been agents, and Caleb thought that both had an air of military to them. Still, his gut told him they weren't part of the OOC. He had heard a woman's voice. Could it have been the woman in Mexico and Florida? He barely allowed her a sentence before he rendered her unconscious in Mexico. She was certainly American, and the voice he'd heard on the street below had a thick accent.

No, he was sure it wasn't the same woman. That might not exclude the Office of Compliance. Carl Winston had plenty of agents to dispatch after Caleb. Not facing off against the same one didn't mean much.

Now, he had a problem. Driver set him up. There was never a pickup, and the fat, bald man at Terraza Municipal was a ruse. He was probably long gone, too. Not so long gone that Caleb couldn't trace him if he wanted. The only satisfaction Corsair would get was confirmation that Driver was involved. If the fat, bald guy had been connected to the woman, then the trap would have been better. The guy tipped Caleb off to the men. Perhaps he didn't know they were coming, but he had to know the meet was some sort of set up. Otherwise, he wouldn't have stuffed the messenger bag with newspaper.

Caleb swung his legs over the railing, letting them dangle sixty feet above the pavement. It hadn't been an effort to free climb up the building, but getting back down was going to prove a little more difficult. Now it was dark, and in any climbing scenario, it was easier to scale up a cliff or wall when one could see the hand and footholds. When he descended, it would be by feel. One wrong move and he'd hit the concrete with a thud.

Caleb glanced up. He could just go up and find a way off the roof. It was only two more stories to the peak of the building. That seemed easier and safer than going down. Plus, if anyone was still waiting for him to come out of the alley, he might be able to skirt around them—or over them, as the case might be.

It took him five minutes to ascend the wall, using a terracotta drainage pipe bolted into the stonework. He hoped the anchors securing the pipe to the wall would hold his weight, and when he was almost to the top, he wondered for a brief moment how long ago the pipe had been installed.

On the roof, he rose to his feet and surveyed the city. Music thumped and lights pulsed from between the buildings. He stood over most of the other structures in the neighborhood of Getsemani, and it allowed him to absorb the sounds of Cartagena's nightlife from a surreal vantage point.

After what might have been a few minutes, Caleb crept along the roof toward an access door at the east end of the building. The metal door was locked, but a firm kick just beside the knob thrust the latch inward, ripping through the ancient wood frame.

At least it wasn't a steel frame.

He came out onto the street, where he stepped in time with a group of younger men in their twenties. They chattered back and forth in German, mixing in some laughter.

"Where are the girls?" Caleb asked jovially to one of the men in German. His accent matched the High German dialect they were using.

"We are going over to Café Havana," he responded. "Devon picked up a sexy local girl there last night."

"Oh, I'll have to check it out," Caleb replied with a grin as he turned to check the street behind him. He didn't see anyone following, but he'd missed the guys at the Terraza earlier.

Perhaps I'm losing my touch.

As the German men turned on the next street, Caleb crossed the street as another group wandered down the sidewalk. Caleb drifted along with that crowd, keeping pace to stay close enough to seem like he might belong. At the next corner, Caleb turned right, walking back toward Centennial Park. He stayed along the east side of the park, passing the shuttered vendor stands.

One older man, who still had his booth filled with paperback books, gave him a nod. Caleb paused for a second, picking up a Spanish edition of *The Da Vinci Code* and checking behind him. The park was quiet, and the only people around were him and the bookseller.

Caleb replaced the book and walked on through the park. He didn't want to stop again until he had a crowd around him. It might be easy for someone on his tail to hide in the shadows, but despite all the eyes in a crowd, it was easier for him to spot someone giving him too much attention. Most people in populated areas keep to themselves. There are a few curious ones who look from face to face, but even they don't tend to remain focused on any one person. If that person notices them, they'll look away, ashamed to be caught.

But if someone is trying to follow a target through a crowd, it becomes vital to keep them in their sight. A person can vanish in a crowd in the time it takes to glance away and back. Caleb had been on both ends of that disappearing act. If someone followed him under the clock tower, they'd need to keep their eyes on him, and Caleb counted on finding them in that mess.

Back on the curb of Avenida Venezuela, Caleb stepped into the street. The buses weren't around, and he wondered if they stopped running at some point in the night.

"*¡Déjame mostrarte algo!*" a voice cried to him over the din of the street. Caleb turned to see a gaunt man approach quickly with a handful of jewelry. Most appeared to be homemade trinkets.

"*No, gracias,*" Caleb responded, waving off the man that didn't look like he'd slept indoors in quite a while. His face carried scars and open sores that he'd scratched. Now the reddened skin past irritation.

"Where're you from?" he asked in slow, heavy English.

"Europe," Caleb lied.

The man cackled. "I think America. Right? Don't let me scare you. Look." He jutted his gnarled hand forward to show the junk jewelry. A couple of crosses molded from plastic and a dove all hung on thin leather strands.

"You want some emeralds?" he asked under his breath. Caleb assumed they were fake or illegal. "Very cheap," the guy promised, almost confirming Caleb's suspicion.

He shook his head and continued walking. The gaunt man raced after him.

"Coke, maybe? Weed?" He dragged the last word out to a point.

"No, thank you," Caleb assured him.

"Ah," the man announced, as if some obvious realization finally hit him. "Single man like you out. You looking for pussy, no?"

"No," the American confirmed.

As if he didn't hear his negative, the frail man pointed toward the clock tower. "Come, I'll show you the best ones. Some are dirty—have the virus. Some will steal from you."

Caleb couldn't help but smile. "But you won't?"

"Me?" the man questioned, slapping the palm of his hand against his chest. The feigned shock and embarrassment of such an accusation was too much for him to take. "Vidalgo's my name. I'm your friend." He tried to shake Caleb's hand.

Corsair cut his eyes down at the grimy, outstretched palm without moving toward it. Most tourists instinctively reach for the grip, afraid they'd come across as elitist or unfriendly for not wanting to touch a street person.

But Caleb had seen people die thirty seconds after contact. It was an easy transfer that used a thin silicone patch on the palm of the hand. Even during the contact, the victim didn't register the difference between the skin and the patch. But the patch delivered a deadly neurotoxin that quickly absorbed into the skin. Within seconds, the blood vessels in the hand deliver the toxin through the heart and toward the brain. Death was as near to instantaneous as it could be. Without a detailed tox screen, it resembled natural causes.

Of course, there were plenty of incidents where the meshing of the two palms transferred a microdose to the killer. That resulted in a similar collapse, usually a few seconds after the target dies. The method was as covert as could be, but Corsair didn't like the risk associated with it. If he planned to kill someone, he intended to get away as cleanly as possible.

Caleb turned his back on Vidalgo.

"You don't want to talk? Eh, fuck you!" Vidalgo shouted after Caleb as he strolled casually away. If the man caused much more of a scene, Caleb would need to take steps to vanish from the streets. While Vidalgo's voice raised a few octaves, the more distance Caleb put between himself and the man seemed enough for Vidalgo to lose interest. After all, he hoped to sidle up to other tourists in the area, and if he created a scene, it might discourage others from talking to him.

Caleb sidestepped behind a group, and the scratchy voice of the street man faded into the crowd. As he moved across the plaza, Caleb focused on the corner near the Hard Rock Café. He passed in front of the windows, pausing to admire the guitars in the window. The reflection on the glass offered him a decent view behind him, and Caleb sighed in relief that there seemed to be no one following him.

He continued away from the crowd and turned down a smaller street. Just a block from the plaza, Caleb found an empty street. All the shops along this block closed hours ago, and with no destination, most pedestrians stayed on the plaza or in the crowds moving up and down the sidewalks. They probably thought the crowds offered more protection. It just depended on what you wanted protection from. Just like the trick with the silicone patch in the palm, there were plenty of ways to kill someone in a crowd and get away scot-free. Caleb preferred the empty streets. If trouble approached, he knew he could handle it. No one can slip up close on an empty sidewalk. Caleb preferred it that way. If he had to fight someone, this would be the better location.

A sharp, high-pitched squeal followed by the sound of someone being slapped. Caleb took two steps forward and turned to see a brawny man in a uniform swiping his arm down in a fast motion. It took a microsecond for Caleb to register the uniform as a police-issued one. The officer's back was to him, and when the cop raised a balled fist,

Caleb saw the intended target—a young girl barely into puberty who cowered in the corner of the stoop.

14

Cartagena de Indias, Colombia

Caleb cocked his head to the side. "What are you doing?" he demanded in Spanish.

The officer turned slowly toward Caleb. Inside the brown iris of his eyes, the pupils shrank to a pinpoint, causing Caleb to wonder what form of amphetamine the cop was using.

"You need to move on," the policeman demanded.

Caleb focused on the man's rugged face. He had a few marks and scars, but most reminded Caleb of deep scratches or cuts. A pair of white marks on his neck popped out on the man's dark complexion. They were the type of scar one might get if someone with long fingernails fought them. In fact, Caleb wondered if the wounds were delivered while this girl struggled against her attacker. They were weeks, if not months, old.

His attention moved off the cop, who still glowered at Caleb, to the girl on the ground. She was young. Very young, he decided. But she dressed as if she were going to one of the nightclubs in town. Caleb passed several women as he crossed back into the walled city. Almost all the Colombian women dressed for the night, but this one felt more like it was artificial. The skirt she wore hiked up on her thigh. Caleb noted the small scarring that looked an awful lot like they were the diameter of a cigarette. He'd seen scars like that before.

"Are you okay?" he asked the girl.

"I said she's fine," the cop stated. His voice deepened and grew louder as he spoke. "If you don't want to find yourself in jail, you need to move on."

"Tell you what, Officer," Caleb said. "Why don't we go back to the square and address this in a less private place?"

"Why don't you listen to me?" growled the cop who Caleb noted had a badge that read "Torres."

"Miss, do you need anything?" Caleb asked the girl again.

The girl turned between Torres, who towered over her and the American standing in the street. Slowly, she shook her head.

"I think we should take this out of this back alley," Caleb suggested, eying Torres. "You know, we want to make sure everything is on the up-and-up."

Torres pulled a handheld radio off his belt. "Gutiérrez, I need backup."

"Don't! They'll kill you," the girl squealed.

Corsair spun back, bringing his right foot around. The heel soared up and caught Torres in the chin. Actually, it struck the hand holding the walkie-talkie. The radio smashed into his chin, and the foot followed with a resounding snap. Torres's head popped back, slamming into the stone facing.

The officer's eyes rolled back as the impact stunned him. Caleb reached for the girl when he saw the cop reach for the Jericho 941 in his holster. Corsair threw himself at the man. His left hand caught Torres's right wrist. All of Corsair's weight slammed against Torres, driving him into the wall.

Caleb wrenched the gun-wielding arm back, twisting the flexor carpi radialis muscles. He felt the hand release its tenuous hold on the Jericho, and Corsair swept his right hand down to take the weapon by the barrel and pluck it free from Torres's grip.

"Motherfucker!" Torres howled. He threw his head forward in rage, smashing his forehead into the side of Caleb's face. The blow glanced off Caleb's cheek, and while it didn't do any major damage, it felt like taking a fist to the face.

Caleb, still holding the Jericho 941 by the barrel, brought his right hand up and used the gun like a hammer, driving the bottom of the grip down on Torres's nose. He swung the pistol three times, smashing into the cop's face. A stream of blood spewed from his nostrils, and the policeman slid to the ground as if all his bones had vanished.

"Are you okay?" Caleb asked the girl.

She nodded. "He's going to kill you. Me too."

"Do you want to come with me?"

The girl pushed herself back into the far corner of the doorway. Her eyes drilled into the face of the unconscious Torres.

"He's going to kill me."

"I won't let him," Caleb promised, realizing as he said the words, it was a mistake.

Just walk away, Caleb.

It was the voice of his training and experience. The advice was a reminder of what happened when he got involved in other people's problems.

But this wasn't just a random person. This was a girl. A child.

"Mister, he's going to kill you," she repeated. "Kill you."

"I'm not an easy target."

As he said this, Caleb turned his head slowly to the cop. It was true—Corsair wasn't an easy target. But in that instant, he realized he might have poked a bigger bear than he intended. Even if this Torres was dirty—from what he'd seen in those few seconds indicated he was—he was still a police officer. In fact, judging from the insignia on his uniform, he wasn't a rookie, either. An officer would have some backup somewhere close.

"Come on," he urged the girl. "Let's get you out of here before he comes around."

"Where?" she wondered.

"We can go to my hotel so I can figure out what to do with you."

She shook her head slowly. "He'll find you," she warned in a flat, emotionless voice.

For a moment, he stared at the girl. What would happen if he left her here? Perhaps that was best for her. He shouldn't have gotten in between a pimp and his hooker.

That's what it had to be. She had those soulless eyes of someone who'd been lost to society.

No, she's not lost. Yet.

There was anger in there. He could feel it underneath the heavy layer of makeup and skimpy clothes. He almost grinned at the realization. In his mind, he classified her as potentially dangerous. In her present state, she was nothing more than a downtrodden teenage girl under the heel of an oppressive pimp. But Corsair recognized the spark of rebellion. This wasn't the first time Torres beat her. She wasn't going to be the compliant girl, and it wouldn't take Torres long to see that it was too much trouble to manage her.

Caleb supposed that there wasn't much of a retirement program for a street whore. If he left her here, she'd die. At that very moment, Caleb knew that for a fact. It wouldn't happen today or tomorrow, but soon. She'd mouth off to Torres or even attack him.

Yes, she'd charge at the cop. It would seem like an act of desperation for her, but it would come. Then Torres would kill her.

"No time to worry about this," he urged. "Come with me."

The girl studied Caleb's face. How many men had she encountered on the streets of Cartagena? How many false promises had she heard? Caleb didn't want to know, but he suspected. She had to decide if it was better to go with Caleb or try to rectify the situation with Torres. Her eyes flitted between the two men for two seconds before she pushed up off the ground.

Caleb offered his hand to her, and she glanced at the Jericho 941 still in his hand. He checked the safety on the gun before slipping it into his waistband.

"I'd rather he didn't wake up with it, don't you think?" Caleb remarked. Although, his thoughts went back to the ambush he walked into. If he ran into any more trouble, he'd be in a better position to handle it now.

The girl nodded to him. Caleb let her start down the street, and he stepped along with her.

"What's your name?" Caleb asked.

"Valentina?" a voice interrupted them, and Caleb stopped in the middle of the road. Twenty feet ahead, at the intersection, stood another cop.

"You know him?" Corsair asked under his breath. His fingers touched the grip of the nine-millimeter under his shirttail.

She gave a curt nod.

"What are you doing?" the officer demanded.

"Working," the girl answered in a demure voice. She made a gesture toward Caleb.

"Officer, I'm sorry," Caleb muttered in English. "I don't want any trouble. I just met this young lady. Valentina?"

Valentina smiled a half smile. "We are going to his hotel."

The new officer bobbed his chin. "Sorry, go ahead," he replied in English for Caleb's benefit.

"Carlos, stop them!" Torres shouted from the doorway.

Corsair shifted his head back to see Torres stumbling out of the doorway. Carlos stared past Caleb and Valentina in stunned silence. By the time that his brain registered that Torres was calling to him, Officer Carlos found himself staring down the barrel of Torres's Jericho.

"Give me your gun," Caleb ordered the cop.

Carlos pulled his own Jericho from his side holster.

"By the barrel," Caleb told him.

The cop rotated the barrel of the gun towards himself and offered the weapon to Caleb, who looked at the police motorcycle parked at the corner. The Suzuki V-Strom 650 had the custom paint job that marked it as a police vehicle. The word "*Policía*" stenciled on either side of the gas tank helped to distinguish it as well.

"That your bike?" Corsair inquired.

Carlos looked back. "Yes."

"Sorry, we'll be taking it," Caleb explained. "Give me your radio, too."

Carlos pulled the radio off his belt. He stared into Caleb's eyes before making a move to bring the radio up to his lips. He clicked the call button as the Jericho hit him, knocking the radio to the ground. The barrel of the nine millimeter swung down. Corsair squeezed the trigger. The gunshot echoed between the buildings as the walkie-talkie exploded.

Caleb struck the officer in the temple with the side of the Jericho. The impact jarred the cop's brain, disrupting the signals keeping him on his feet. Both eyes rolled back in his head as he collapsed.

"Valentina, you whore!" Torres shouted. "I'll kill you."

Caleb threw a leg over the saddle of the Suzuki, raised the barrel of Torres's sidearm, and shook his head. Torres stopped suddenly, stumbling forward. Valentina grabbed around Caleb's midriff as he cranked the bike.

Torres narrowed his eyes as he glared at the two. Caleb shifted into gear and roared off down the road.

15

Cartagena de Indias, Colombia

The metal door creaked and scraped across the marble floor. Its hinges were somehow off-kilter enough that the corner of the decorative black, wrought-iron security door dragged over the tile. A scratch was forming in a six-inch arc. Whatever caused the problem was a relatively new issue, but the Hotel Monaguillo de Getsemani's staff had let it go on too long. Now they'd have to replace that marble tile.

Minuit gave a short nod to the young man sitting behind the regular wooden office desk that took up most of the small lobby. A woman wearing a shirt monogrammed with the hotel's lettering sat opposite him. Minuit felt the young female employee's eyes drill into her. It was a common occurrence. Even women without the training that Minuit endured were often far more emotionally aware—able to detect and distinguish other's personalities and traits. For Minuit, it was a life-saving skill that allowed her to be vigilant in new encounters. In this instance, the girl seated in the alcove was no threat to Minuit, but the French assassin suspected the other woman had a sixth sense warning her about Minuit.

She's right to do that.

The Hotel Monaguillo de Getsemani didn't have an elevator—not that Minuit would choose the confines of a lift. She preferred to take the stairs in case she needed an escape or even just room to fight. The steps leading up to her room on the third floor traveled up the concrete wall at a steeper angle than normally expected. Each step was deeper than whatever standard builders used. It didn't affect her ascent, but she'd noticed on the way down that it created a faux vertigo feeling.

As she neared the third level where her room was, she froze, sensing someone was there. Minuit proceeded slower until she peered over the top of the landing. The hotel had two sun lounges on the third-floor veranda next to the small bathing pool. Salar Tolazar stretched out on the second cushion. At first glance, the man appeared to be sleeping, but Minuit knew differently. The rise and fall of his chest didn't match that of a man in slumber.

"What are you doing here?" she asked.

"Why don't we go for a walk?" he suggested.

"Tolazar, I just got back. Honestly, I'd prefer we just spoke here."

The man glanced past her at the other room on this level. Light streamed through the crack in the door.

"I would prefer we went someplace with fewer prying ears."

Minuit sighed with resignation. "Fine, we can walk down the street. I could use a drink."

Salar Tolazar grinned. His teeth gleamed under the halogen bulb illuminating the terrace. He stood up, and Minuit noticed how out of place the man appeared to be. He was wearing a Brioni jacket and pants over a light blue Tom Ford shirt. Everything was crisply starched. The Toscana loafers crafted from Baby Nile Crocodilian leather clicked on the concrete floor. Minuit couldn't help thinking that the man's attire cost more than most of the people in this city earned in a year.

Tolazar motioned for her to take the lead down the steps. She was grateful, given the awkward sensation the funhouse stairs created. In the lobby, Tolazar placed his hand at the small of her back, guiding her through the crooked security door.

The street in front of the hotel, Carrera 10, was busy. Nightlife in the neighborhood was in full swing, and the fact that it was a Thursday night—no, by now it was Friday morning—didn't affect it. Vendors hawking home-made jewelry, paintings, and second-hand clothing set up their makeshift shops along the curbs. Most were no more than a dirty blanket spread out over the sidewalk with the person's wares spread out. Minuit noticed a mix of people taking up those stations, from what she guessed were American or European hippies trying to scrounge enough pesos to continue their travels to local women selling off their baby's pajamas in order to size them up as they grew.

Minuit strolled alongside Tolazar down the middle of the cobblestoned street. At this point in the evening, cars gave way to pedestrians, and while a few still moved down Carrera 10 toward Trinidad Plaza, they moved slower than the people walking down the street. Horns honked, but no one paid attention.

"What happened tonight?" Tolazar asked as they walked past a fruit cart. The Arab let his eyes roll across the selection of fruit, and Minuit noticed the curl in his lip when he saw the wagon's owner slicing up mango on a piece of wood before scooping it all up in his hand and filling a plastic cup with the sliced fruit.

"Exactly what I was worried about. Not enough men." Minuit passed a man grilling kabobs over a charcoal fire. The aroma of roasting meats and vegetables mixed with the hints of marijuana permeated the night air. Crowds of people filled the street and plaza around the Iglesia de la Trinidad, a Catholic church in the middle of the neighborhood. Music from the midnight mass spilled out of the large open doors, and the droning melodies of Latin mixed with the thumps of bass from the speakers that some individuals set up in the plaza.

"Are you invested in killing Corsair?" Tolazar asked, turning his face to stare into hers. "My employer has made it abundantly clear that his highest priority is the death of the American agent."

Minuit cleared her voice. Someone shouted something in Spanish that she couldn't make out, but then a tall, thin man wearing a soccer jersey carried his ball into the center of the square.

"That is my number one priority as well," she assured Tolazar.

The man placed a hula hoop on the ground before stepping inside the circle. He had spread out a small towel with some shin guards and another old yellow jersey with a colorful football on the front.

Tolazar folded his arms across his chest. A six- or seven-year-old boy ran into the man's legs. The can of Coca-Cola the kid carried sloshed out onto Tolazar's pants. Minuit cringed at the thought of carbonated soda dousing the extravagant pants. Her companion didn't seem to notice the spill. Tolazar did sneer at the child as if such people should rarely be seen or heard. Minuit wondered if he had any children of his own. She hoped not.

The football player started bouncing the soccer ball off his foot. With his left leg firmly planted, he tapped his instep against the ball, keeping a steady rhythm.

"What happened tonight, then?" Tolazar repeated.

"He spotted my men approaching. Corsair hasn't lost his touch."

"The man's been domesticated," Tolazar commented. "He's been nonoperational for a decade."

Minuit shook her head. "You didn't know the man. If he's rusty or out of practice, that still leaves him as one of the deadliest men on the planet. What I saw earlier wasn't a broken pony. He was better than any of the men I had at my disposal. Hell, he was better than all of them."

Tolazar stared at the soccer player juggling the ball between his instep and his toe without losing the rhythm. He'd slowed the ball down to hit his foot with each thump of the bass emanating from the speakers mounted atop portable stands over the crowd.

"What do you need to kill him?" Tolazar asked.

Minuit didn't answer. Instead, she let the question linger in her thoughts. The former DGSE agent assured herself that in a one-on-one battle with Corsair, she'd come out on top. That was because she counted on the one weakness that she hoped domestication had developed in him—sentimentality. Minuit counted on the hope that there was more between her and Corsair all those years ago than just another mission. She suspected as much, otherwise the American would have killed her when he murdered Lefevre.

If that held true, then when the time came to face him, he wouldn't kill her. Of course, that didn't stop him from running. He proved tonight that he could evade her men with only slight effort. The only way to ensure a confrontation between them was to keep him in one spot. An effort like that would take manpower. A lot of manpower, she guessed.

"More men," she finally answered. "I need a force large enough he can't kill them all. We'll need to limit any escape routes, too."

"Give me a number."

"Twenty. Maybe twenty-five."

Tolazar nodded. "That will be enough."

God, I hope so.

She nodded. "It should do. Corsair is crafty and dangerous. And he can improvise, so he'll be looking for an escape before we even corner him."

Tolazar acknowledged that with a grim tightening of his lips. He'd been tasked with finding Corsair since the man's reemergence in Florida last year. If he didn't accomplish it, his boss, Mahmoud Abbas, might grow concerned with his abilities. There were plenty of Tolazar's subordinates who thought they'd like to have his position.

"I can arrange for the men," the Arab promised her.

She nodded and stepped back as the same kid with the Coca-Cola raced past her.

"*Cerveza!*" a man with a polystyrene cooler strapped around his neck shouted.

She gave the man a quick shake of her head, and the Colombian man gave Tolazar a brief glance before moving on to a more viable customer.

"You've lost him now," Tolazar remarked. "How do you plan to track him down again?"

"I have a few contacts in the city," Minuit assured him. "I have a very close relationship with a man on the Colombian police force. If anyone can help me track him down, he will."

Tolazar gave a curt nod. The soccer player shifted to keep the ball bouncing off the tip of his toe now. Across the plaza, the mass ended, and a hundred parishioners flowed out the entrance. The kids lined up along the front wall of the church as their parents filtered into the crowd in front of the church. A few teenagers forced to sit through the homily hurried over to the food stands to grab some *salchipapa*, a street dish made with sausage and potatoes.

"Mr. Abbas expects this to be handled in the next few days," Tolazar explained to her.

"As do I," she assured him.

"Good. I'll be in touch soon."

"Where are you staying?" Minuit asked, wary that he might try to stay nearby. She had no fear of the man, but what she didn't want was someone getting in the way. It reminded her of a statement her grandmother would say about extra hands in the kitchen create extra messes to clean up.

"At the Hotel Caribbean."

Good, near the hotel district. Given the wardrobe Tolazar sported, the Hotel Caribbean fit the man a little better than some of the boutique hotels or hostels in the walled city.

Without another word, Tolazar turned and left Minuit in the plaza. The football player gathered his ball and hoop and moved out of the center as a Michael Jackson impersonator stepped through the crowd. Minuit raised her eyebrows at the effort the man put into his outfit, including the sequined jacket, sunglasses, and black hat. When the first bar of Thriller started, he was joined by several zombies that were equally well-costumed.

Minuit spun her head around to see if Tolazar was still around. He'd disappeared from the street, and she turned to return to her hotel.

16

Cartagena de Indias, Colombia

The V-Strom rumbled between his legs, and Corsair twisted the throttle as he turned left at the next intersection.

What the fuck are you doing, Caleb?

The voice in his head scolded him. There was no exit strategy in place. He'd not only saddled himself with the girl, but in doing so, he assaulted two Colombian police officers and stole one of their motorcycles.

And the other one's gun.

This was an abject failure. He involved himself in a dynamic he should have walked away from. But he'd seen the fear in the vacant eyes. The girl was young—too young to be a part of what he suspected was happening.

Another voice in his head praised him. "She needed protection, Caleb," the dulcet sound of Audrey Harrod assured him.

Caleb's left foot briefly touched the asphalt as he leaned into the left turn. A blue and white tiled sign on the building claimed the street was Calle de Carlos Vélez Danies. The girl tightened her grip around Caleb's waist, and he wondered again what the hell he had been thinking.

The 645-cubic-centimeter V-twin engine roared as he sped up on the street. His left knee grazed against a blue Renault Logan that tried to pull out ahead of him.

"You okay?" he called back to Valentina.

She said something and nodded. He struggled to hear her affirmation, but felt the head bob against his back. It didn't matter because he couldn't stop now.

The breeze between the buildings gently flapped the yellow, blue, and red flag over the door of the Hotel Movich. A doorman standing on the sidewalk watched the pair intently as they sped past.

Caleb braked as he approached the next intersection. The street he was driving down ended abruptly at a cross street. He needed to distance himself from the two officers as fast as possible. He hoped he had at least two more minutes before either was able to alert their fellow officers that Caleb absconded with a police bike.

That idea died though in his head as he banked into a right turn onto the next street. A police officer leaned against a car, talking to a girl in her twenties wearing a gauzy dress. Corsair turned away as the officer straightened up.

In his rearview mirror, Corsair saw the officer dismiss the girl as he hurried behind the wheel. Blue lights flashed behind him, and Corsair twisted the throttle. As he sped up, Caleb focused on the park to his left. There were several stands still working at the late hour. A small crowd clung together around an old boom box, thumping with loud music that Caleb couldn't understand over the whine of the four-stroke engine.

The police car was now in motion and coming up behind the Suzuki fast.

"Hold on!" he shouted to Valentina as he released the throttle, braked, and jerked the handlebars to the left. Again, he dropped his foot down to help pivot into a ninety-degree turn.

Caleb pulled up on the handlebars as the front tire jumped the curb. Valentina let out a chirp and squeezed Caleb tighter. A couple dove out of Caleb's way as he ripped down the path through the trees.

He hadn't familiarized himself with this side of town since he'd only planned on avoiding surveillance during the scheduled rendezvous that Driver set up for him. Set him up for, Corsair corrected. This entire trip was becoming a disaster.

Corsair leaned to the right, extending his foot as he braked. The sole of his shoe pushed off a lamppost as he sped up. The V-Strom stood up as he raced down the short, straight path toward the opposite exit.

He needed to ditch the bike. The police logo painted on the side stood out, and Corsair suspected there might be a GPS transponder attached to the frame. Colombia might be behind the times, but he suspected that as cheap as the devices were, the local cops took advantage of it.

Caleb and Valentina flew through the next gate and dropped off the curb. Releasing the throttle and braking, Caleb brought the back tire into a skid to the left. It screamed as it skidded around, leaving a black streak on the pavement and a hint of smoldering rubber in the air.

He took a split second to survey the street. The pair came out onto a small one-lane road opposite the ornate stone doorway of the Museum of Cartagena de Indias. The steel security gates blocked the entrance, and a single guard stood sentry on the sidewalk.

Two of Caleb's right fingers lifted in a silent salute to the guard, who watched him with narrow, black eyes. Caleb twisted the throttle, and the Suzuki lurched forward. Valentina squeezed his waist.

A red umbrella with the word "Yupi" on it marked the next intersection. A man offered fresh juice from a plastic tank on his cart.

If Caleb went left, he'd be heading back the direction he came. Blue lights ricocheted off the walls from the cop car on the other street. He picked left, turning the handlebars. The bike blew past the juice man. The frills on the bottom side of the umbrella flapped in the breeze created by the rush of air behind Caleb.

White buildings loomed on either side of the one-way lane. The liquid-cooled V-twin engine screamed its high-pitch wail as Corsair gave the Suzuki full-throttle. A red needle in the speedometer on the top of the gas tank spun toward 152 kilometers per hour. Out of the corner of his eye, Caleb saw a short Latina woman in a worn, blue polo shirt and matching blue cap dive behind a Chevrolet Joy with a caved-in right fender. She shouted something after the bike; however Caleb couldn't distinguish the words over the din of the engine.

Ahead of him, the headlights of two cars crossed the street. A blue light bar strobed brightly as four police officers spilled out of the vehicles. Each pulled matching Jericho 941s as he charged toward them.

Corsair's eyes flicked across the street. There were several pedestrians still between the police and them. He banked the bike to the left, startling a trio of drunk white men shuffling down the sidewalk. The tourists hadn't registered the police presence or the scream of the motorcycle bearing down on them.

By the time one of them saw Caleb zipping down the sidewalk, he nearly got knocked off his feet by the passing bike. Caleb intended to bump them if they didn't move. It might put them on their asses, but he didn't intend to injure any of them. More importantly, he was counting on the officers at the roadblock's discretion. It would be insane to fire down the street where bystanders might be shot.

"Hold on!" he shouted over his shoulder. Valentina tightened her grip around his stomach like an anaconda.

Corsair accelerated as he pulled back on the handlebars. The jerk back lifted the front wheel off the concrete. One of the officers dove out of the way as the tire caught the hood of the car on the left. It wasn't a graceful jump, but it lifted the bike in a large bounce, and he managed to maintain his balance long enough for the back tire to get traction on the car, launching them past the back of the police cruiser.

The tires bounced, and Valentina's grip slipped. Caleb felt her slide back before she grabbed his shirt.

"They're going to catch us!" she wailed.

The girl was correct. If they didn't get off the street soon, they'd get pinned in. They were driving north, and over the rumble of the bike, Caleb heard the wailing of sirens. Behind him, the two cop cars were already trying to back up and follow him down the street. He pressed his heel down, braking fast, and turned right at the next corner. A small plaza in front of a church had a small group of college-age boys huddled around the statue of a larger woman reclining on a pedestal. The boys laughed as they fondled the bronze breasts of the naked woman. Behind the sculpture, three rows of bistro tables lined the space with a few people enjoying a coffee or late-night dinner from one of the handful of restaurants lining the plaza.

Again, the speedometer's red needle whipped up to about 160 kilometers per hour. Shuttered shops zipped past them, and Caleb was grateful that this street had closed up for the night, leaving only a couple of stragglers passing from one point to another in the old city.

A nearly identical Suzuki V-Strom pulled onto the street ahead. The driver locked eyes with Caleb before charging at him. The two motorcycles targeted each other in a headlong face off reminiscent of the childish games of chicken that Caleb played back in Georgia when he was a kid.

Corsair gritted his teeth as he flew down the middle of the road. The former assassin counted on his own determination over that of the cop. He was confident that the other man would peel off at the last moment, but if he didn't, then Caleb trusted his own reflexes were better than those of the policeman. Seconds ticked by as both Suzukis prepared to collide. The gap shrank to fifty feet. Twenty. The last second before impact found Caleb staring across the handlebars at the scared eyes of a young officer.

The cop on the motorcycle jerked the handlebars in order to dodge Caleb's bike. With a lean right, Caleb shifted the direction of the V-Strom to avoid the other man. The sudden change of direction by the cop sent the motorcycle into a skid. Unable to keep the bike up, the cop fell over, and the Suzuki skidded across the street before slamming into a parked Volkswagen Jetta. Caleb heard the crunch of metal on metal as the police motorcycle crushed the door of the Volkswagen.

Caleb never slowed as he slipped back into the center of the road, heading back toward the clock tower and what he guessed would be more cops trying to stop him.

17

Cartagena de Indias, Colombia

The room in the Hotel Monaguillo was smaller than the one Tolazar had in whatever four- or five-star hotel he was staying in downtown. That didn't bother Minuit. Much like her professional life, she found a fit in almost any condition. The room was sparse, having only a bed, a small flat screen television hanging over a rack that allowed her to hang up any clothes. The bathroom was only separated by a rolling door on a track.

With no chairs in the room, the former French agent sat in the middle of the bed with her legs crossed. She had gotten back to the room and showered. Now she held one of her burner phones in her hand. From memory, she dialed the phone number.

Despite the hour, or maybe because of the hour, she chose now to call the lieutenant general. Minuit insinuated herself close to Lieutenant General Alejandro Márquez years ago when she was working for one of the cartels operating in Colombia. At the time, Márquez was still a lieutenant in the police department, but Minuit recognized the ambition in the man.

Now, the older officer had been promoted up the ladder to lieutenant general. Minuit initiated an illicit affair with the married officer in order to glean some information from him. In the process, she connected Márquez with her contact in the cartel. Márquez found the new arrangement profitable for many years until the DEA in the United States broke the cartel and arrested the head of it.

However, Minuit knew the value of a respected police official, and given her work in South America, it struck her as prudent to keep him in her back pocket. Now was the time to pull that little toy out and make use of it.

The phone rang twice before a husky voice answered. "Hello?" the man responded in a sleepy tone.

"My love, this is Celeste," Minuit told him.

Márquez perked up on the phone. "Hold on," he told her. On the other end of the line, Minuit heard the movement as the lieutenant general probably got out of bed and left his wife alone to speak with his lover.

"Celeste, my dear," Márquez finally said into the phone in a hushed but gravelly voice. "Are you in Colombia?"

"I'm in Cartagena, Alejandro."

"You should have told me you were coming," he remarked. "I'd have cleared my schedule for you."

"It was a sudden trip," she explained.

"Uh, is our friend back from his trip to America?" Márquez questioned. The timbre sounded nervous.

"Not to my knowledge," Minuit responded. "This is a different matter."

"You didn't call me to set up a rendezvous?" he inquired.

"I have to close out the problem I'm here to handle first. However, the sooner I accomplish that, then the quicker I can find time for more entertaining activities."

The lieutenant general chuckled into the phone. "And something I can do will speed along the process?" The man wasn't dumb, Minuit noted. He didn't expect that a woman like her just popped in without a reason. However, he also knew they shared an understanding. His assistance came at a price.

"I'm looking for a man—an American. Dirty blond hair in his thirties."

Márquez asked, "Is this man deadly?

Minuit responded without thinking. "More than you suspect."

"I just took a call about an American that fits that description,"

Minuit straightened her back. "What do you know?"

"I'll need to call you back," he explained. "Perhaps I can help you faster than either of us thought."

"I'd certainly owe you for that," she replied coyly.

There was an excited grunt on the other end of the line that might have even been a giggle from the lieutenant general before he hung up.

Minuit laid the phone on the bedside table and stretched her naked form out on the top of the bed. Music along the streets of Getsemani penetrated the walls of her room. She thought about Corsair. The brief glimpse she caught of him filled her with rage. Minuit forgot the actual sensation. For years her anger had almost become a memory, but it flooded back along with emotions that Minuit hadn't sensed in a long time.

While the bass thumped from the Café Havana and Casa Palenque, she dreamed about killing Corsair. Her methodology changed for each fantasy, but her excitement swelled as she examined the different scenarios. While she was engrossed in thoughts of slipping a blade across his throat, the phone rang.

Minuit sat up and ran her right hand through her hair, smoothing down the strands out of place from the pillow.

"Hello," she answered in Spanish.

"Celeste, I may have found your man already," Márquez remarked breathlessly on the phone. "I had a call just before yours. Two of my officers were assaulted. The man might fit the description of the one you are looking for. Of course, it could match half the American men in the city."

"Where is this?" Minuit asked.

"It occurred in the old city. Near the San Pedro Claver," he explained to her.

Minuit removed the phone from her ear, switching it to speaker phone. She opened her map app on the phone while Márquez continued.

"The suspect stole one of their motorcycles, and we are in pursuit now. They are trying to keep him in that section of the city."

Minuit found the San Pedro Claver on the map and marked it with a pin. "I need to find this man before your officers do," Minuit told him. "Otherwise, I won't get what I need from him."

She didn't tell Márquez she intended on killing his suspect, but the lieutenant general knew the type of people she worked for and what she did for them. He would expect as much.

"I can put you in touch with the officer heading up the chase," Márquez offered. "However, I can't exactly give the man to you."

His implication was logical. The man couldn't assure that every officer she had contact with would be corrupt enough to turn his back while she gutted Corsair. A few of his police officers might be idealistic still. Or even incorruptible.

"I can handle your officers," she assured him.

"You'll want to speak with Captain Torres. His unit is the one that was attacked, and he's leading the officers in pursuit."

Good luck. Corsair will eat your cops alive.

"I can find him near San Pedro?" she asked.

"Yes, I'll alert him to expect you."

"Thank you, Alejandro," Minuit gushed into the phone.

"Where are you staying, my love?" the man asked her.

"In Getsemani," she answered. "If I can take care of my business tonight, I should have tomorrow free."

"That would be perfect. I will clear my schedule," he boasted with some satisfaction. Minuit envisioned the smirk that she thought she heard through the phone.

"Better clear the whole day," Minuit teased.

"I will," Márquez agreed before Minuit disconnected.

She rose to her feet and dressed in a thin dark blue blouse and matching pants. Her skin tingled under the feel of the lightweight fabric. As she slipped into a pair of flats, she dialed one of the men she had on hand.

"I have a lead. Bring the car to the front of the hotel," she ordered. When she hung up, she smiled. Corsair hadn't gotten away just yet. The image of his throat opening up under her blade played out in her head again, and she reveled in it.

18

Cartagena de Indias, Colombia

He skidded to the right. As his foot pressed down on the brake, the back tire slid across the street, leaving only a black mark on the concrete. Caleb's right foot dropped to the street to stop the Suzuki's momentum. A police cruiser drove toward him with its blue lights bouncing from building to building.

Caleb twisted the throttle, forcing the rear tire to spin the bike around with Caleb's leg as the needle point. When the motorcycle faced the opposite direction, Corsair pushed off with his foot. The Suzuki whipped down the street.

Without taking his eyes off the street ahead, Caleb noted that Valentina's arms still remained around his torso. He needed to get out of these narrow alleys and streets. If Caleb had a long straight path for the Suzuki to hit its top speed, he could outrun most of the cruisers. On these crowded and narrow city blocks, the bike's size gave him the flexibility the cop cars didn't have.

But that would only last so long. Eventually, the police would cordon off an area and Corsair would have no avenues of escape. With a bump, the bike jumped up on the curb. Caleb raced down against the traffic along the sidewalk.

He saw the opening ahead as Calle 35, the street he and Valentina raced up, butted into a green area he suspected was a park. In his mind, he drew out the lines of the street as he tried to imagine where he was. The multitude of turns could have confused him had he not placed each one on the imaginary map he was looking at. If he'd had a pen and paper, Caleb could have sketched out a rough approximation, although it would never be up to the snuff of even a mediocre cartographer.

However, he thought he was approaching the western point of the walled city. If he could get to the other side of the balustrade, the highway would offer him a shot out of town.

Of course, there was a thirty-foot-tall stone barricade.

The Suzuki never slowed as he whipped through the cross-street traffic. He banked behind a rusty white Toyota that was heading east on the street. Stealing a glance in both directions on the road, he spotted blue lights coming from both directions. The front wheel popped up on the curb and bounced Caleb and Valentina as they sped into the park.

The streetlights dimmed as the tree canopy blocked most of the ambient light. Only a few path lights illuminated the park. Caleb followed them like a trail of candy through the woods.

"They're coming!" Valentina shouted in his ear.

He checked the mirror to see two headlights wavering behind him. More motorcycles. The cruisers were easy enough to slip past on the bike, but motorcycle cops could follow him anywhere he could go. Any lead Caleb thought he'd gained just vanished.

Ahead, a sloping ramp climbed through a cap in the stone. Caleb sped up the ramp that led to the top of the wall, which offered a wide path around the city. Pedestrians strolled along the top, stopping at a few carts offering beer and sodas. Caleb turned right as he crested the ramp.

He twisted the throttle all the way. The Suzuki shot down the straightaway. The speedometer needle quivered around 160 kilometers per hour. In his mirror, Caleb saw the two police motorcycle cops appear at the top of the ramp.

While he had the space to run the bike as fast as possible, he had two pursuers who were equally capable of matching his speed. Worse yet, he had no alleys or side streets to dodge down. Effectively, he had nowhere to go.

A hundred feet ahead of him, there was a staircase leading down about six steps to a lower tier. Without slowing, Caleb flew off the top step and soared about eight feet through the air. He pulled his weight against the handlebars and leaned back a bit. The bike screamed as the engine continued to spin the back tire. It caught the concrete and fired forward.

The two police officers stopped at the stairs and turned to a steep ramp that had been added in recent years. Their slowdown gave Caleb a lead, and he didn't intend to squander it.

As he raced along the wall, he saw the flashing of blue lights reflecting below on the city streets. More police were responding, and it appeared they were in pursuit below. Now he worried he might have placed himself in a maze with every exit soon to be blocked.

The wall curved around the north side of the city. To his left, Caleb could see the moon hanging over the Caribbean Sea. Old cannons pointed through the embrasures toward the open sea. Below the barrels, Avenida Santander ran along the coast. If he could get to that road, the two of them could be out of the city within minutes.

As he raced past the next ramp that led back down into the walled city, Caleb saw two police cars blocking the path. They'd already started closing off his egress points. As soon as they did that, it would only take more motorcycle cops to join the pursuit up here to run him out of wall.

The speedometer now showed 150 kilometers an hour—over ninety miles per hour.

In his rearview mirror, Caleb saw the headlights of the two motorcycles back on his tail. He whipped past a small group of girls walking along the balustrade. The twelve eyes followed him as he ripped past. There should be another ramp coming up, and if he could stay ahead of the motorcycle cops, he might make it. Assuming that the ramp wasn't also blocked by the police.

His heart sank when he saw the sloping exit ahead. Two cruisers with their flashing lights barricaded the exit.

Caleb cursed to himself. He needed off the wall, or they'd just be running until he ran out of gas, or the cops took a more aggressive tactic.

Corsair twisted the throttle and sent the speedometer needle spiking toward 160 kilometers an hour.

He skidded to the right. As his foot pressed down on the brake, the back tire slid across the street, leaving only a black mark on the concrete. Caleb's right foot dropped to the street to stop the Suzuki's momentum. A police cruiser drove toward him with its blue lights bouncing from building to building.

Caleb twisted the throttle, forcing the rear tire to spin the bike around with Caleb's leg as the needle point. When the motorcycle faced the opposite direction, Corsair pushed off with his foot. The Suzuki whipped down the street.

Without taking his eyes off the street ahead, Caleb noted that Valentina's arms still remained around his torso. He needed to get out of these narrow alleys and streets. If Caleb had a long straight path for the Suzuki to hit its top speed, he could outrun most of the cruisers. On these crowded and narrow city blocks, the bike's size gave him the flexibility the cop cars didn't have.

But that would only last so long. Eventually, the police would cordon off an area and Corsair would have no avenues of escape. With a bump, the bike jumped up on the curb. Caleb raced down against the traffic along the sidewalk.

He saw the opening ahead as Calle 35, the street he and Valentina raced up, butted into a green area he suspected was a park. In his mind, he drew out the lines of the street as he tried to imagine where he was. The multitude of turns could have confused him had he not placed each one on the imaginary map he was looking at. If he'd had a pen and paper, Caleb could have sketched out a rough approximation, although it would never be up to the snuff of even a mediocre cartographer.

However, he thought he was approaching the western point of the walled city. If he could get to the other side of the balustrade, the highway would offer him a shot out of town.

Of course, there was a thirty-foot-tall stone barricade.

The Suzuki never slowed as he whipped through the cross-street traffic. He banked behind a rusty white Toyota that was heading east on the street. Stealing a glance in both directions on the road, he spotted blue lights coming from both directions. The front wheel popped up on the curb and bounced Caleb and Valentina as they sped into the park.

The streetlights dimmed as the tree canopy blocked most of the ambient light. Only a few path lights illuminated the park. Caleb followed them like a trail of candy through the woods.

"They're coming!" Valentina shouted in his ear.

He checked the mirror to see two headlights wavering behind him. More motorcycles. The cruisers were easy enough to slip past on the bike, but motorcycle cops could follow him anywhere he could go. Any lead Caleb thought he'd gained just vanished.

Ahead, a sloping ramp climbed through a cap in the stone. Caleb sped up the ramp that led to the top of the wall, which offered a wide path around the city. Pedestrians strolled along the top, stopping at a few carts offering beer and sodas. Caleb turned right as he crested the ramp.

He twisted the throttle all the way. The Suzuki shot down the straightaway. The speedometer needle quivered around 160 kilometers per hour. In his mirror, Caleb saw the two police motorcycle cops appear at the top of the ramp.

While he had the space to run the bike as fast as possible, he had two pursuers who were equally capable of matching his speed. Worse yet, he had no alleys or side streets to dodge down. Effectively, he had nowhere to go.

A hundred feet ahead of him, there was a staircase leading down about six steps to a lower tier. Without slowing, Caleb flew off the top step and soared about eight feet through the air. He pulled his weight against the handlebars and leaned back a bit. The bike screamed as the engine continued to spin the back tire. It caught the concrete and fired forward.

The two police officers stopped at the stairs and turned to a steep ramp that had been added in recent years. Their slowdown gave Caleb a lead, and he didn't intend to squander it.

As he raced along the wall, he saw the flashing of blue lights reflecting below on the city streets. More police were responding, and it appeared they were in pursuit below.

Now he worried he might have placed himself in a maze with every exit soon to be blocked.

The wall curved around the north side of the city. To his left, Caleb could see the moon hanging over the Caribbean Sea. Old cannons pointed through the embrasures toward the open sea. Below the barrels, Avenida Santander ran along the coast. If he could get to that road, the two of them could be out of the city within minutes.

As he raced past the next ramp that led back down into the walled city, Caleb saw two police cars blocking the path. They'd already started closing off his egress points. As soon as they did that, it would only take more motorcycle cops to join the pursuit up here to run him out of wall.

The speedometer now showed 150 kilometers an hour—over ninety miles per hour.

In his rearview mirror, Caleb saw the headlights of the two motorcycles back on his tail. He whipped past a small group of girls walking along the balustrade. The twelve eyes followed him as he ripped past. There should be another ramp coming up, and if he could stay ahead of the motorcycle cops, he might make it. Assuming that the ramp wasn't also blocked by the police.

His heart sank when he saw the sloping exit ahead. Two cruisers with their flashing lights barricaded the exit.

Caleb cursed to himself. He needed off the wall, or they'd just be running until he ran out of gas, or the cops took a more aggressive tactic.

Corsair twisted the throttle and sent the speedometer needle spiking toward 160 kilometers an hour.

19

Cartagena de Indias, Colombia

"Where are they?" Torres growled.

Daniel Ramírez responded, "Sir, unit twenty-seven reports that the suspect is driving on top of the northeastern part of the wall."

"Where are the barricades?" Torres barked.

"Setting up along the wall. It's taking a minute to get in place."

"Hurry them up," the captain ordered. "How is Carlos?"

Ramírez nodded. "The medic says he has a concussion but should be fine. He's refusing to go home, as ordered by the doctor."

"What?"

Ramírez shrugged. "You know Carlos. He doesn't want to leave the chase."

"Tell him I ordered him to go home."

"Captain, I think he worries that he let you down," the lieutenant explained.

"This guy got the drop on both of us. Who would have thought a fucking tourist would attack us?"

Ramírez nodded. "Did the girl know him?"

"Hell if I know," Torres replied. "Find them and I'll ask him and the little whore."

"Of course."

"You know, wait. Can you pass the word? I want them killed. Make it look like they fought back. After he put Carlos in the hospital, the men should have no problem with that order. Show this little whore-lover what happens when he fucks with us." Torres twisted his neck from side to side, trying to work a kink out in his spine. Stress-induced pain.

"Yes, sir," Ramírez agreed. "I'll pass the word."

"Not on the radio," Torres warned. "Wouldn't want someone to think we were putting out a hit on a tourist."

The lieutenant nodded before turning on his heel to carry out the order. Torres paced. The buildup of nervous energy needed to spill out. He felt the rage just below the surface. Now wasn't the time to allow it to show. This had become a fiasco, and if Torres didn't get a lid on it, the higher-ups in the Colombian National Police would start to raise questions. That was why this tourist and Valentina had to die. If someone arrested either of them, the prosecutors might uncover Torres's business with the girls. Valentina could show them where the apartment was. Had he ever put her at one of the other flats? He couldn't remember, but it was a good bet that she knew where the other girls stayed. Valentina could easily point out the whores working the streets.

It dug into his gut. Each passing thought bubbled the anger up to a frenzy. If the two of them survived, Torres's cash flow would die. At least for a bit. He'd have to move all the girls fast, and they'd all need to vanish from the streets. He'd still need to keep the palms of his men greased or all that work would be for nothing.

It will take six months or more to rebuild.

He offered a prayer up to some unknown saint that Valentina would meet her end. His phone vibrated in his pocket, and he removed it.

Torres paused when he saw the screen. Lieutenant General Alejandro Márquez's name read across the display. What was the regional supervisor doing, calling him at this time of night?

"Hello," Torres answered with some trepidation.

"Captain Torres? This is Lieutenant General Márquez. I understand you have a situation on your hands."

Torres stole a look at the time on his phone. It was thirty minutes past midnight. The lieutenant general should not have learned about this yet.

"Yes, sir, but I am getting it under control."

"I have no doubt, Captain. You are a capable officer."

"Sir, there's no need for you to step in. I have it in hand."

Márquez cleared his throat. "Of course you do, but I've been apprised of some extenuating circumstances."

Sweat bubbled on Torres's forehead. Had Márquez already learned about the captain's enterprise? Not possible, Torres decided. If Márquez knew about the girls, he'd have someone arrest him. Certainly, he wouldn't be calling him. Unless he wanted a piece of the action.

"What circumstances are you referring to?" Torres asked nervously.

"There is an American man involved," Márquez said.

"Yes, sir," Torres responded.

"This man is the subject of an investigation by some foreign operatives. I cannot divulge much about it."

Torres blinked. Relief hit him when he realized the lieutenant general wasn't muscling in on his money. By the time Torres processed what his supervisor wanted, the lieutenant general explained, "I'm sending a female agent to apprehend him."

"Sir, this man attacked one of my officers. I don't think we should let some woman outside of our unit in to handle this."

Márquez coughed under his breath. "I understand your concern, Captain. What this man did deserves our most severe punishment. In an ordinary situation, I'd turn my head while you and the men handled it. But this request comes in from above us."

Torres bit his lip. That red hot rage gurgled as it screamed for release. Everything was crumbling underneath him.

"Are you understanding me, Captain?" Márquez asked through the phone.

"Yes, sir. My concern is that this man has already attacked us. Are we supposed to allow him to continue to do so while we wait for this woman to show up and solve our problems?"

"Absolutely not," the voice on the other end told him. "If the suspect attacks our men again, respond appropriately. If not, wait until she arrives."

"Yes, sir." Torres ground his teeth as he responded.

"Keep me up to date," Márquez commanded the captain. Torres wondered if he actually cared or just wanted to sound supportive. Offering access to a female agent was unheard of. Even in the height of Colombia's struggles with the cartels, it was unusual for the government to offer what Torres consider *carte blanche* in an investigation.

Torres felt his predicament complicating. He dialed Ramírez.

"Daniel, we need to put a lid on this in the next fifteen minutes."

On the other end of the line, Daniel Ramírez questioned, "What changed?"

"I just got an order from Lieutenant General Márquez. He's sending a woman to apprehend the tourist. If she brings him in, she'll bring in Valentina too."

"Yes, sir. What do we do?"

"If we can't cordon them off soon and kill them, I want you to pass the order to men friendly to us. Even if they get orders from this female agent, I want their priority to be to kill the two suspects. I'll testify at any inquiry that the man was a threat."

"Understood," Ramírez replied.

"Daniel, thanks for stepping up. Let anyone know if they kill them, they will be rewarded."

Torres added, "I'm going to bump you up too, Daniel. If we can keep this from blowing up."

"Thank you, Captain. I'm always at your disposal."

"Let's keep the operation running then, so we all make money." Torres cut Ramírez off as he hung up.

The captain lifted his head to stare up at the side of the building. Whatever prayer he'd said earlier had only resulted in more complications.

20

Cartagena de Indias, Colombia

Racing along the top of the wall, Caleb ran through the scenarios that would get him off this wall. He needed to get ahead of the police force that was systematically blocking every access to the wall.

Behind him, the two motorcycle cops were joined by two more. He still had several hundred yards of lead on his pursuers. If he was running the bike at full throttle, and Caleb doubted he could squeeze any more speed out of the Suzuki.

He banked right, narrowly avoiding a woman wheeling her juice cart down the walkway. She shouted something at him, but Caleb ignored her. In his mirror, he caught the four motorcycles chasing him whiz around the woman.

Valentina tightened her grip on Caleb, and he wondered what he'd done by getting involved with her. Had he just walked on and minded his business, she'd likely have taken a beating, but walked away with only bruises and scars.

Now, he'd painted a target on her back, and even if they got clear of the city, she'd never be safe from that cop.

That thought dug into his gut. He'd run across his fair share of corrupt officials. Most were looking the other way for a quick payday, but those trafficking in humans like this policeman were the worst. He considered that this girl wasn't really all that much older than Amanda. Ten to twelve years, and he knew how fast a decade could slip past. He couldn't imagine Amanda being subjected to what he guessed Valentina had experienced. The girl behind him was nothing more than a baby. Where had her family gone?

In the time since his wife died, Caleb often found Audrey's voice to have replaced the one that used to be his conscience. As he flew across the top of Cartagena's fortifications, he heard her instruct him.

"You have to save her," Audrey whispered in his ear. "You're the only hope she's had."

"Lot of good I'm doing her now," Caleb pointed out.

"You're in action," Audrey assured him. "Nothing can stop you once you take action."

The last remark was a reminder of his training with his mentor at the OOC. Marcus David, who wore the code name Hood, took Caleb out into the Appalachian wilds of Virginia where he dropped the young man from a helicopter.

"You have twenty minutes before the posse comes after you," David warned him. "Don't sit still. Remember Newton's law—an object in motion tends to stay in motion. If you are taking action, you're already ahead of the enemy."

At the time, Caleb thought the sentiment was somewhat off. After all, Hood forgot the rest of Newton's law that said an object in motion can be stopped by an outside force. After three days in the forest where Caleb survived on puddling rainwater and juniper berries, he understood that he simply had to avoid the outside force. He eluded the hunters for two weeks before he found David at a roadside hotel waiting for him. The men who had been hunting him came out two days later after they lost his scent. Hood considered Corsair's survival training to be a success.

Those lessons stayed with Caleb, and as he raced at over a hundred miles per hour across this wall, he reached back in his training for anything that would help him.

Protect the girl.

He repeated the phrase in Audrey's voice to himself as if he were ordering Corsair to comply. Despite the odds, he believed he could do that. All he needed was to avoid the outside forces slowly corralling him.

That's exactly what they were doing, too. The Colombian police were eliminating all means of egress and funneling him to a point where the wall ended. Or at least he assumed as much. It couldn't go on forever. There were gaps in the structure for traffic at the least, and eventually he'd run out of road. Once that happened, the four cops behind him would be joined by more. Caleb would be surrounded by insurmountable odds.

Turn around. The voice belonged to Hood, not Audrey.

If he obeyed, he'd lose his lead and charge toward the four cops on his tail.

But they won't expect it.

Caleb wasn't so sure. After all, he didn't know if more police were behind those four. Probably some, but they were working him toward the end, and most of their forces would be trying to stay ahead of Caleb. They might not have enough manpower in place just yet, and if that was the case, they'd be moving pieces around on the board.

If he didn't do something, they'd run him down.

Audrey's voice suggested something. "Be the outside force."

Caleb blinked. He gripped the handbrake and pressed down on the foot brake. Tires squealed as the bike stopped suddenly with the smell of burnt rubber. His left leg hit the stone as he revved the engine. The back tire spun furiously, turning the Suzuki around with his leg as the fulcrum. When he'd made the 180-degree turn, Caleb raised his foot and shot forward toward the motorcycle cops who closed the distance in the split second it took for him to brake.

Stunned, they barely had time to react as Caleb flew through them. He drove his left leg out as he passed one, kicking the bike sideways. The police officer lost control, careening into the one on the far side. A loud crashing sound occurred, and Caleb heard the wreck over the whine of the engine.

In his rearview mirror, he saw the other two bikes recover and turn back around. Already, he'd had the bike up to over ninety and he sped back. Ahead, more lights flashed as other officers attempted to block Caleb and Valentina. Too many to plow through. So much for being the outside force.

He braked again, spinning the bike back around to face the remaining two motorcycles pursuing him. Both policemen reacted faster this time, braking before he came close. One even pulled a gun and fired it. The shot went behind Corsair, and he didn't flinch as he whipped past the cops.

"What are you doing?" Valentina called from behind.

"Just hold on," he warned her.

While he hadn't studied the maps of the old city as well as he had the area around Terraza Municipal, he still pulled up the map in his brain. He couldn't be sure, but he thought this section of wall ended on the far eastern side of the city where the *bovedas*, a collection of retail shops in the former dungeons of the fort, were.

He wasn't sure how far he had to go, but he suspected it wasn't far. Caleb slid to the left around the two wrecked bikes. One of the officers hadn't gotten to his feet, but the other was pulling at the bike, pinning the first down. Caleb hoped he hadn't killed the cop. That would cause some issues that he didn't want. Besides, while Torres had obviously been crooked, that didn't make all the police in Cartagena the same. In his operational days Corsair viewed collateral damage as par for the course, but since then Caleb didn't consider the ends to justify the means anymore.

He kept the throttle twisted all the way, and he and Valentina soared through the night. From their vantage point, he could see the moonlight glittering off the waves. There was almost a sensation of flying at this height. If he could have taken off and soared out over the sea, he would have done just that.

But that wasn't possible. Instead, he peered ahead to see the turn. The wall made a sharp turn just past the ramp leading down to the *bovedas*. Caleb released the gas to slow just enough to bank right. The top of the wall opened up, and a small group of locals crowded under a stone gazebo-type structure. Several men held guitars as they put on an impromptu concert. Children ran around playing, and Caleb braked as a three-year-old girl dashed into his path.

The bike skidded to a stop. Valentina pressed into his back as he leaned over the handlebars to maintain his balance. The young girl froze less than a foot in front of the Suzuki's front tire.

"Carmen!" a woman shouted as she ran over and scooped the girl up.

Caleb gave the motorcycle gas and felt his heart sink. As he feared, the wall came to an abrupt end only a hundred feet ahead. A ramp led down to the street level, but a police car blocked the bottom.

He checked his mirror to see the two remaining cops coming up fast. Corsair stomped his foot onto the ground and spun the bike back around. Both cops charged at him with guns drawn. Corsair gunned the engine and prepared to either ram them or slide past them. Both officers held fire—likely because of the musical performance now at Caleb's back.

"Hang on!" he warned Valentina as he turned hard just before the two motorcycles collided with his bike. The cop on Caleb's right clipped his back tire, and Corsair struggled to regain balance before he and Valentina went into a skid. Once he recovered, he flew toward the turn he'd just made.

More police bikes raced toward the same junction, and Caleb realized he'd run out of road. In the distance, he stole a brief glimpse of the black sea in the distance. The city lights only reflected a few hundred feet off the beach.

"Do you want off?" he asked Valentina over his shoulder.

"What do you mean?" she asked.

"We're out of places to go. I can let you off and try to lead them away."

He felt her shake her head. "He'll kill me, or worse."

Caleb braked again, bringing the rear tire in a sweep to his left. "You sure? Last chance."

"Before what?" she questioned.

"We either die or get away."

The girl squeezed tight around his waist. Caleb swept his head from left to right. Five motorcycles converged on him.

"Fuck it," he muttered. "This is going to suck."

The Suzuki screamed as he revved the engine while holding the brakes. He released his left hand, and the stolen bike flew forward toward the edge of the wall. For a brief second, Caleb thanked the government of Colombia for not installing handrails and safety measures everywhere. It was a fleeting thought as the front wheel came off the wall.

Valentina screamed when the Suzuki went airborne. Like the steps he'd jumped down earlier, Caleb pulled back on the handlebars as he tried mentally to raise the front wheel, so it didn't dive to the ground.

Don't fall off. He willed Valentina to not let go. The free fall felt like it slowed in his mind. Corsair felt the wind on his face, the girl's nails digging into his flesh, and the force of gravity in his gut.

The top of the wall was only about thirty feet from the top to the grass below. When the back tire hit the grass, he throttled up and let inertia push him over the handlebars again. Flecks of grass and mud flew up behind the bike as he recovered from the jump.

He ripped up the greenery as he aimed for the street. He glanced back to see three headlights stop at the top of the fortification. His Suzuki hit the pavement, and he turned toward the ocean and gasped with relief.

21

Cartagena de Indias, Colombia

"Follow them!" Minuit screeched at the man driving. His name was Taylor, but at the moment, she couldn't pull it from her memory. Instead, she fumed that he wasn't reacting as fast as she thought she would have when the police car zipped past them.

In her hand, she held the portable police scanner that reported Corsair's current whereabouts. Well, it should, but the Colombian police force had misjudged the former American assassin. She should have felt some sympathy for them since earlier in the evening she'd done the same thing.

From what she'd heard, the pursuit led to the top of the famed wall surrounding the old part of the city. Now she was on the coastal highway, running along the outside of the stone fortification. Three minutes ago, a shocked motorcycle officer announced that the suspect had jumped off the wall while still driving the motorcycle stolen from another officer earlier in the evening.

Minuit might have smiled when she heard that if it hadn't reminded her of how Corsair escaped in Marseille. She realized that she'd miscalculated Corsair. Any edge she thought he lost in matrimony was still there. He was far more formidable than the local police force could handle. Although she knew that wasn't completely true. The Colombian Police had enough men to throw at the assassin until someone killed or caught him. Corsair thrived on luck as much as skill, and eventually all the abilities in the world couldn't compete with the sheer numbers they could throw at him.

But she didn't get paid for the local law enforcement to take her prey. For now, she'd use them, though.

"Stay on them!" she shouted again at the driver—Taylor, she remembered.

"Yes, I'm trying," the African announced with some frustration as he sped up to stick to the bumper of the police cruiser racing east on Avenida Santander.

The police cruiser made a sudden stop, sliding to the side to block the street. Taylor braked as a Suzuki V-Strom ripped past the hood of the cruiser. Minuit saw the face of Corsair as he flew past.

"That's him!" she yelled, motioning for Taylor to turn around.

The driver was already making a fast three-point turn to give pursuit before Minuit alerted him. Smugly, he gave pursuit without being ordered to do so.

There was a girl on the back of the Suzuki. Minuit caught a glimpse of her and thought she was only a teenager.

Who the hell was she?

She'd heard that when Corsair surfaced a few months ago in Mexico, it had been with another woman. Minuit was thorough, and when she first got the call that Corsair was still alive, she started digging. The girl, Khloe something, had crossed paths with organized crime and had a target on her. Corsair saved her, and, in the process, eliminated the mob threat.

But the girl she just saw was Latina and far too young to be the same woman from Mexico. Beyond that, why was he involved in a police chase? Corsair avoided Minuit and her men in Terraza Municipal earlier. How had he done that only to fall afoul of the local constabulary? That didn't make sense.

Unless the girl was involved. When she knew Corsair in France, she might have thought the man had enough empathy to help out people in need. Yet, after he assassinated Lefevre, Minuit realized it had all been a ruse. The American didn't feel anything except some sense of duty to his bosses.

But he'd run from that too. Perhaps something changed.

Minuit pulled her pistol, one of the Berettas she took from the dead men Corsair left in the alley. She stuck the barrel out and fired as Taylor changed lanes.

"Dammit, keep it straight," she cursed.

"Sorry," he rasped as he shifted up a gear to speed up.

The little Toyota she'd stolen from a long-term parking lot whined as Taylor closed the gap between them and the Suzuki V-Strom. Minuit leaned out the window to take another shot. She leveled the barrel at the rear tire. The girl on the back of the seat might shield Corsair from a round, but the tire would render the motorcycle useless.

The Suzuki swerved and braked. As Taylor compensated, attempting to ram the police motorcycle, Corsair turned 180 degrees.

"Fuck!" Minuit cursed as she shifted her aim at the bike and squeezed the trigger. The V-Strom raced past her. For a split second, she locked eyes with its driver.

Quickly, she turned to fire back at the bike when Taylor braked too late. The impact threw Minuit into the dash. The airbags deployed, tossing her back into her seat. Stunned, she lost her grip on the Beretta as the Toyota spun around three times, skidding across Avenida Santander.

"What the hell!" she shouted at Taylor.

When she turned to look at the driver, she sucked in the words. The driver's head left a bloody concave indention in the windshield. His lifeless head lolled to the left, and she saw his left eyeball dangled loose from the mangled face.

Minuit found the door handle and pushed it open. With little muscle control, the dazed assassin spilled out of what remained of the Toyota and onto the asphalt.

"What the fuck are you doing?" a voice shouted at her in Spanish.

She rolled onto her back and tried to sit up. As the seconds passed since the impact, the shock of the accident wore off. Minuit felt the side of her face swelling. She blinked a couple of times to take in the scene.

The Toyota, whose left fender now curled under as if it had been an aluminum soda can someone crushed with their foot. A police cruiser going the opposite direction had similar damage. Minuit realized that Taylor had a head-on collision with the cop car.

"I am speaking to you," the voice continued, screaming at her.

Her attention turned to the man in the street berating the woman. Minuit lifted her hand to signal for him to be quiet. The officer stared at her, dumbfounded that someone would defy him that way.

Silenced, the uniformed officer stood in the street staring at her. Minuit pulled herself to her feet, where she did a quick self-evaluation. The skin on her cheek strained as her face swelled. She'd have a black eye in the morning, but unlike Taylor, she'd escaped mostly unscathed. Nothing was broken. Perhaps because she was twisting around to take another shot at Corsair, she'd been thrown with her back to the dashboard instead of through the windshield.

"If you can point me to the officer in charge of this chase," she told the man in front of her. "I'd like to speak to him."

The cop put his fists on his hips. "That's me."

Minuit gave him a closer inspection, reading the name "Torres," on his uniform. "Officer Torres, if you will contact Lieutenant General Márquez, he'll tell you to help me."

"You're the agent?" Torres blurted out.

Minuit gave a curt nod.

Torres responded with a mumbled curse.

"Officer Torres, can you give me any information on the suspect?" Minuit asked, brushing her hair over the swollen cheek.

The Colombian officer corrected her. "It's Captain Torres."

"Whatever," she muttered, turning to walk along the street to the Beretta. "Captain, can you tell me about the suspect?"

"He attacked me and one of my officers before stealing my officer's motorcycle."

Minuit holstered the pistol and gave the captain a long look. She cocked her head to the left and asked, "Who's the girl?"

The police captain's pupils widened for a brief second before he said, "I don't know. She was some hooker with him in the square."

Minuit nodded, but she let her gaze stay locked on the captain's.

"Your friend is dead," a second officer announced as he approached from the wrecked police car.

"Yes, it's tragic, isn't it?" Minuit noted. "He should have been a better driver."

"Who is this man?" Torres asked her.

"A suspected terrorist," she lied.

Torres's left eyebrow lifted. "That seems unlikely."

Minuit didn't respond. "Did the lieutenant general tell you to offer me your assistance?"

"Yes," Torres responded in a begrudging tone.

"Then offer it," she told him. "You'll need to take care of this." She waved her hand over the wrecked Toyota.

"Your vehicle doesn't look like it's going anywhere, either. Maybe you could arrange to get us back to where the chase started."

Torres grunted and turned to the other officer. "Ramírez, call a car for me and Señorita—I didn't get your name."

"No, you didn't," Minuit replied to the officer.

Torres's face flashed with rage. "Ramírez, just call a car."

"Yes sir," Ramírez answered. "Do you want me to stay until they haul this off?"

Torres nodded as Minuit walked to the car and peered through the driver's window at the mangled Taylor.

"Should have been better," she scolded the dead man.

Two minutes later, another police cruiser pulled up. The officer climbed out.

"I'll be taking your vehicle," Torres told the new officer. "You stay with Ramírez until he can clear the scene."

"Yes, sir," the new policeman answered.

"I'm guessing you and the driver weren't close," Torres remarked.

"No," she confirmed.

"I'm sure someone will be looking for his family," Torres said.

"Don't look at me," Minuit explained stoically. "I didn't know him, and I wasn't in that car."

Torres pursed his lips and marched toward the cruiser. He opened the back door for Minuit, but she walked around to the passenger side and slid into the front seat. She heard him whisper, "Bitch."

He had no idea.

"Where did it start?" she asked Torres when he got into the car.

"We were patrolling the square around the clock tower," he explained.

"Is your partner dead?" she asked.

The captain shook his head. "He has a concussion."

Minuit said, "He's lucky."

"Who is this guy, then?" Torres asked.

"I can't say," she informed him. "Why don't you tell me who the girl is?"

He shook his head. "Just some hooker."

"She hang out at the—where did you say? The clock tower?"

Torres nodded as he pulled away from the wreck and made a U-turn.

"You patrol the area regularly," she wondered.

"Yes," he answered, while turning to pass through a gate into the walled city. They drove for a few minutes in silence until he stopped behind a horse-drawn carriage.

The square was packed, and Minuit stepped out of the police cruiser. Immediately, she saw three women or, really, girls wandering around the crowd. They had the look of a streetwalker making eye contact with potential johns.

"Let me understand, Captain Torres," Minuit asked. "You are telling me that you—a captain in charge over there—don't know the prostitutes working your area?"

"I think she's new," he lied again.

Minuit started rolling pieces around as he drove. Corsair wasn't careless enough to pick up a whore and fight a cop, let alone two cops, for no reason. Torres was a terrible liar, too.

What the hell was Corsair up to and how did Torres fit into the puzzle?

22

Mexico City, Mexico

The phone danced across the nightstand. Lee rolled over to find an arm draped over her back. She struggled to remember his name. Was it Luis? She wasn't sure. He'd been in the hotel bar last night. While they'd had lots of tequila, she remembered he was an attorney from Merida. The gold band on his finger reminded her that he was married.

He groaned a little as she moved his arm off so she could sit up. Picking up the phone, she expected to see Angie's name. Instead, the switchboard number for the Office of Compliance showed on the screen.

With some relief that she wouldn't have to pretend for Angie's benefit that she was alone, she answered.

"Agent Hubbard?"

"This is Hubbard," she replied.

"It's JW," he told her.

"Oh, JW, yes," she said, as her brain put the face to his name. JW Collins worked in the Basement at the OOC.

"Sorry, did I wake you?" he asked. "I wasn't sure what time it was in Mexico."

"Yes, but it's okay. I was up late working," she lied.

"I'm sorry then," he repeated.

"What's going on, JW?" she asked as the attorney stirred more. He lifted his head to see Lee. A wry grin appeared on his face.

She started to tell JW that she'd call him right back when she remembered that the man hadn't spoken any English. Lee gave him a smile back. He did have a striking face and even with all the tequila, she recalled he had some better uses for his tongue than learning English.

"We received a phone call last night," JW explained as Luis ran his fingers up her inside thigh.

"What are you talking about, JW?" she asked. He was a good analyst, but JW lacked some of the communication skills he needed.

"Sorry," he apologized again. "It was an anonymous call about Corsair."

Lee's spine straightened. Suddenly, she wasn't aware of Luis's fingers anymore. "Tell me," she insisted.

"It was a male and I estimate he was in his thirties or forties. Hard to iron that down yet."

"Get to the point, JW," she ordered. Luis now pressed his palms against her inner thighs to spread them. Despite his talent, Lee wanted to tell him to stop right then. However, he wasn't listening to her and if she dissuaded his attention, he might focus on her conversation. Even if his English was virtually nonexistent, she didn't trust that he wouldn't understand something.

"This man said he thinks Corsair will come after him."

"What makes him say that?" Lee asked.

"He only said that Corsair might think this guy double-crossed him."

"Double-crossed Corsair?" Lee clarified.

"That's what he said," JW confirmed.

"Did he tell you where he was?"

"Corsair?" JW asked, a tone of confusion in his voice.

"No, JW," Lee said with some frustration. "The informant."

"Oh, right? I'm sorry."

"Don't apologize, JW. Just tell me what I need to know."

"He's in Belize."

Lee sucked in a gasp as Luis focused his attention a little deeper.

"Can you confirm that?" Lee asked after catching her breath.

Through the speaker, she could hear JW typing. After a few seconds, he answered, "Yes, the call came from Belize. He wasn't on long enough to get a trace, but I can at least confirm it came from Belize. But he did try to route the call through several points. Ukraine, Hong Kong, and, huh, Mexico City? Ironic, isn't it?"

She didn't really think that constituted irony, but she didn't want to discourage JW, so she didn't say anything.

"I have Blake working on finding out where in Belize," JW explained. "That might take a little time, but by the time you get to Belize, we should have something more concrete."

"Why didn't this guy give us his location?" she asked. "If he thinks he's in danger, what did he expect us to do?"

"I suspect he's done something illegal for Corsair. He hid his location but not very well. In fact, Blake suspected that he made it look like he was trying to hide it, knowing we'd break it."

"Why?" Lee asked, letting her head lean against the wall and her free hand reach down and stroke through Luis's hair.

"Well, it was too easy to trace it to Belize, but not to get a more detailed location. It's like he wanted us to know to look for Corsair in Belize, but this guy didn't want to give up his location, even if his life was threatened."

"Smart, JW. Let me know as soon as you hear something else."

"Roger that, Agent Hubbard."

She hit end and let the phone drop to the bedside table as she pulled the naked figure of the striking attorney up to her lips so that he was right between her thighs.

When Luis left an hour later, Lee stretched out naked on the bed. Her mind was on fire. This was the first hint of Corsair since he was in Mexico City. She picked up the phone and dialed Carl Winston's office number.

"Winston," the weasel answered.

"Carl, it's Lee. Have you heard we have a lead in Belize?" She knew the answer to that. He shouldn't know anything unless she gave him that information. Despite being the head of the Office of Compliance, Carl Winston now preferred to keep his hands clean. Lee suspected this was because he wanted the perception of separation from the dirty deeds the OOC performed. Since Corsair went underground, Lee thought Carl had worked to stay clear of anything that might blow back on him. That fact was what made finding Corsair alive so important. Lee was certain the former agent held the key to Carl Winston's demise.

"Belize? Is it a sighting?" he asked.

"No, someone who thinks Corsair might be coming for him."

"Oh, that's rich," Winston mused. "We could catch him in the act."

Lee didn't think it was likely. An asset like Caleb Saunders didn't stay off the grid by making mistakes. Still, it was the only substantial lead they'd had, and it needed to be investigated.

"I'm going to head there now," she told her boss. "I think I might eventually dig up something here in Mexico City, but most of the leads are all dried up now."

"The team can be down there in a few hours," Winston told her.

"Let me get there first," she said. "This might be nothing."

"I don't want another incident like in Puerto Vallarta," he warned. "By the time you confirmed he was there, you lost him. If the team is there, they can react faster."

She couldn't disagree with him, especially since her reasoning was that she wanted Corsair alive while the company line was to terminate the former agent.

"I have the company plane here," she reminded him. "As soon as I get to Belize, I'll send it back to D.C. to retrieve the team."

"Good. Let's not waste time," Winston said. "I want this traitor taken off the board."

"Roger," she replied, but Winston hung up.

She dialed Angie's number. It rang twice before her girlfriend answered.

"You aren't coming home, are you?" Angie asked.

"Sorry, got a lead. I'm going to Belize."

"You know, you could take me to places like that," Angie whined.

"Since we are a secret, it might be hard to sell me taking an analyst with me in the field."

"Ugh," Angie groaned. "I was hoping we could go catch a movie and dinner."

"You can always go without me," Lee reminded her.

"That guy at the coffee shop asked me out yesterday," Angie told Lee in the hopes it would spur some jealousy on Lee's part.

"Oh, the cute one with the lumberjack beard?"

"Yeah," Angie replied.

"Don't get beard burn," Lee told her.

"Ugh, fuck you," Angie growled before hanging up.

Lee rolled off the bed and walked into the bathroom, where she turned on the shower. While the water warmed up, she called the OOC pilot who was on standby. Once she ordered him to prepare to leave for Belize, she stepped into the shower to rinse off the attorney from Merida.

23

Cartagena de Indias, Colombia

Caleb's stomach grumbled, and he slowly opened his eyes. He felt the sway of the thirty-eight-foot sailboat and heard the muffled sound of an engine passing through the marina. He sat up on the settee of the Hans Christian boat that he'd broken into early this morning.

After escaping the police, he and Valentina ditched the motorcycle in the parking lot of a Wyndham Hotel near the airport. Caleb stole a lime green Hyundai mostly because it was in the darkest corner of the lot—and weaved through the city. Since the little compact car had such a distinct color, he swapped it an hour later for a Kawasaki Ninja. He'd noted the prevalence of bikes throughout the city, and another nondescript black one wouldn't be noticed as quickly as a police-issue bike or a bright green car.

He wanted to avoid the walled city section of Cartagena de Indias, choosing to drive toward the marina district. During his operational years, he'd often use boats as temporary safe houses. The vessels tended to be left unattended for days, weeks, or even months. Strangely, boat owners didn't take the same precautions in securing their yachts as they did their homes. It amazed him that more things weren't stolen from them, but he chalked it up to a perceived inaccessibility to the thieves.

He found the boat about halfway down the pier. When he saw the buildup of grime on the hull, he thought it made a perfect hideaway. Add in that the only thing securing the cabin was a hasp with a wire twisted through it, and he knew that, at least for tonight, he'd found a place to sleep. Even if the owners hadn't come by to clean it in a few months, Caleb didn't want to stay long. While security can be lax in a marina, the people tend to merge into something of a community, and new people on a boat that no one uses might draw some attention.

As long as they stayed in the cabin, he didn't think anyone would notice them. Besides, the toilet worked—bonus. Valentina used it before he had a chance to check its functionality, but thankfully, it flushed with ease.

The girl was curled up in the V-berth where she huddled beneath a blanket and passed out. After the chase last night, the sudden crash of adrenaline had been too much for her. They'd barely spoken once they got on the boat, and prior to that, he'd been more concerned with keeping them safe and out of sight rather than striking up a conversation.

Besides, his mind was already spinning too fast for even him. Corsair had grown accustomed to having things thrown at him from out in left field, but last night shocked him.

Camille.

He thought the only thing that might have surprised him more was if it had been Audrey in the passenger seat of that Toyota he passed. Camille Dubois. Caleb hadn't seen her in over ten years.

As he crossed his legs on the settee, Caleb thought back to the last time he'd seen Camille. Marseille. She was wearing a black-and-white-striped shirt and tight jeans.

"I'll be here when you get back." Those were the last words he heard from her lips. If that had been the last time he saw her, he might feel different.

But it wasn't. Only a few minutes after she said that farewell, the DGSE agent charged onto the rooftop to see him standing over the corpse of her mentor. Her eyes held a mixture of shock and betrayal. In that instance, Caleb saw her heart break. Not just for the loss of her friend, but also she saw the lie that existed between them.

It wasn't all a lie.

Over the years, Caleb thought about Camille often. In his life, he was certain he only loved two women. Camille Dubois was the first. Yet he betrayed her. His training taught him to push missions out of his mind once they were done, but that morning atop the Tower of King René lingered with him. Camille's eyes stared at him in the dark every night after that.

It was only two months later that Winston sent him into Turkey, where he found his target wasn't a high-level political threat but a young boy and his mother. After that, he walked away.

Last night, it all flooded back.

What was Camille doing here? Hunting him, obviously. Was she after Corsair specifically? It made sense. He could only imagine what she thought of him. Had she been biding her time?

No, that didn't make sense. She, like the rest of the world, thought Corsair died in the explosion in Konya. Just like the OOC, Camille learned Corsair was alive when those two motorcycle thugs murdered Audrey and Jackson. He'd painted a target on himself that day, and now the debt collectors were lining up for payback.

Voices outside pulled him from his thoughts. He rose and moved the vinyl covers, blocking the light from the portholes. He saw four feet standing on the main pier. Once he shifted his position, he could see the two men. Both were Latino and dressed like some of the local fishing guides. He relaxed. They were just regular dock people heading either to or from the water for the day.

A shuffling from forward turned his attention. The mound of blankets in the berth shifted and a pair of feet slid from beneath them. Valentina appeared a second later. Her near-black hair pressed against her head, leaving the girl disheveled. She stared at Caleb for a second before slipping off the bed. Her bare feet hit the deck and she seemed to waver as the Hans Christian rocked to the side.

Without a word, the girl vanished into the head and closed the folding accordion-style door. Caleb tried to hum to himself, to no avail. The steady stream of her urine echoed through the door. There was a pumping sound as she flushed the toilet and pulled in sea water to refill the bowl.

When she reappeared, Caleb gave her a reassuring grin. "Did you sleep okay?" he asked.

Valentina nodded.

"We didn't get to talk last night. How are you holding up?"

The girl lifted her shoulders.

"How about we start with a proper introduction? I'm Caleb."

"Val," she said warily.

Caleb nodded. "And Torres is your—what? Pimp?"

"I guess," she answered.

"What's he going to do?" he asked.

Valentina shook her head. Tears welled in her eyes, but they didn't flow. "He'll probably kill me."

Caleb sighed. "I won't let him do that."

"He's the police," the girl argued. "How can you stop him?"

A smile crept across his face. "He didn't get us last night," Caleb pointed out.

"I've never been so scared in my life," Valentina said. "You jumped off the wall. How did you do that?"

"Sometimes you just have to do things," he explained.

"You're American?"

"Yeah."

"Like FBI or something?"

"No," Caleb answered. "Nothing. In fact, America wants me dead."

Her eyes widened. "What?"

"That's a bit of an exaggeration, I suppose. It's only one man, but he runs a dangerous organization that is after me."

"Now the Colombians are after you too," she suggested.

"It would seem they are after us," he corrected.

She nodded.

"How long have you worked for Torres?"

"I don't know. Months, now."

"Are you from Cartagena?" he asked.

She shook her head. "My father was bringing my family over from Venezuela when the Colombians raided the house where we were staying. I don't know if they got my family or not. My aunt lives in Bogotá, but I don't know her name or anything."

"You never met her?"

She shook her head again. "I don't think I'll see them again."

Caleb listened.

"Torres found me and promised to help. But he was a liar." At that, the girl's eyes lifted to study Caleb. He guessed she was wondering if he was going to do the same.

"I think child prostitution is still illegal in Colombia. Why don't you report him?"

"To whom? The only police I see in the city all work for Torres. If I try to go above him, how do I know those men won't do worse things to me?"

Caleb inhaled through his nose. He thought of his daughter back in Belize with Khloe. Again, he was struck that Valentina and Amanda were about ten years apart in age. The idea of Torres trafficking and presumably raping and torturing Amanda gnawed at his gut. It infuriated him that someone like this captain could abuse any girl, much less one Valentina's age.

"How old are you?" he asked.

"Thirteen."

He cursed to himself. Corsair's mind began formulating strategies. If he could get Valentina to safety, it might do the world some good if Torres vanished from its surface. He'd done the same thing to men with far more humanity than this child-raping pimp.

But there was Camille to deal with. When he worked with her before, the DGSE agent had been skilled. In the decade since, she might have honed those abilities.

Suddenly, he recalled the voice speaking in French in the alley last night. Damn, he'd already walked into her trap once.

Cut bait and run!

Corsair's inner voice shouted at him. If Camille and the entire police force in Cartagena de Indias were after him, it wouldn't be smart to stay in the country.

But the girl?

It was his conscience, and it sounded just like Audrey. But it wasn't just the girl. There was Camille. What could he do about her?

He owed her something. That didn't mean he intended on letting her kill him, but he also realized that she deserved something. Could he explain to her? What would he even say?

The next thought he had was to wonder who she was working for. He'd tracked her after that day in Marseille. She'd been ousted from the DGSE and gone underground. Now, he assumed she was freelancing for someone. There was a long litany of people who would pay to capture and kill Corsair. She'd planned on taking him alive at the park, but he caught the fire in her eyes as they passed on the street. If she'd had the shot, she wouldn't have hesitated to kill him.

Either taking him alive was only optional or she let her fury push her past her mission objective.

With almost anyone else, he wouldn't have cared about their motivation, desires, or plans. It would only matter that he put the threat down. This time, he couldn't just do that. That left him two choices: Avoid her at all costs or, if it came to it, meet his fate with her.

There was still Amanda. He knew she was with Khloe, and that was somewhat safe. But even Khloe, who he knew would care for his daughter, wasn't in a position to do so. She might not have as big a target on her, but there were factions of the Cincinnati mafia along with the cartel that might want to exact revenge on her. When she joined them in Mexico City, Caleb gave her the address of Audrey's parents with the instructions to make sure she reached them if something ever happened to Caleb.

He wasn't quite ready to die, and if he didn't intercede, Valentina would fall back into the grasp of Torres. He sat in the cabin of that sailboat staring at the young prostitute, knowing that he wasn't going to cut and run just yet.

But beneath that silent urge to help the Venezuelan girl escape, her captor was a nagging, lingering command to face Camille Dubois and close that circle.

24

Cartagena de Indias, Colombia

He threw the half empty paper cup from a Juan Valdez at the Venezuelan refugee in the street, asking him for money for a coffee.

"Get out of here, you son of a whore," Torres barked as the black liquid spewed from the top when the drink smashed into the sidewalk. Droplets of coffee splashed over the refugee, who shrank away from the captain.

Fucking trash.

Torres fumed as he marched toward the cruiser where Ramírez waited for him. He hadn't been home yet, and his muscles ached from the long night on his feet. When they lost the American last night, he found himself babysitting this French bitch who refused to even give him her name.

"Talk to the lieutenant general," she retorted when he pressed her for more information.

He assumed she had something on Márquez, but it didn't matter. He had to tread carefully about how he handled this situation.

His phone buzzed and he saw Márquez's number.

"Torres," he answered begrudgingly.

"Captain, tell me what happened last night?" Márquez asked.

"This Frenchwoman you sent not only interfered with our pursuit, but her driver crashed head-on into my cruiser when we were on top of the suspect." Torres understood the nuances of bureaucracy. If he could pin the failure last night on the Frenchwoman, it would, in turn, put Márquez in a tight spot and keep the spotlight off not only the failure to capture the suspect but also the fact that one of the suspects was Torres's whore.

"She expressed it differently," the lieutenant general commented.

"I'm sure she did," Torres remarked, trying to keep a steady demeanor in his tone. If he devolved into accusations, it would only serve to enrage his superior. "However, her driver is dead, and we have one police cruiser totaled."

Márquez grumbled something inaudible into the phone. Then he said, "What is the situation now?"

"The motorcycle was recovered near the airport, but it was at the Wyndham. We suspect they stole another vehicle, but so far, no one has reported anything stolen from the hotel."

"It's still early," Márquez advised. "Did you question the staff?"

Of course he did, Torres wanted to say. Did Márquez think he was a rookie? It was generally known that the lieutenant general's commission was largely political. He'd spent a year in uniform before being put on the rising track to command. Torres had more police work this year under his belt than Márquez had in his entire career. It took a lot of control for Torres not to snap that at his boss.

"Yes, sir," he finally answered. "The manager will alert the guests to let him know and inform us if anyone finds their vehicle missing. Once we know what he's in, we can search for that car."

Torres didn't note that by now any competent criminal would have changed vehicles a few times. If Márquez didn't know that, then Torres didn't think he needed to be the one to instruct the lieutenant general.

"Who is this Frenchwoman?" Torres asked.

"She's an agent with a keen interest in the man you are pursuing."

"Am I supposed to let her destroy my investigation?" Torres asked, pushing the lieutenant general.

"She will be working in cooperation with you," Márquez stated plainly.

"Sir, I would have the suspects now if she hadn't been working in cooperation," Torres pointed out as he leaned against Ramírez's police car. The other officer watched Torres as he gestured with his hands in frustration.

"I understand your situation, Captain. However, I expect you to comply with my orders."

Dammit.

Torres kept that thought to himself, though. Instead, he answered, "Yes, sir."

"Thank you, Captain," Márquez said. "I'd like you to contact her as soon as you get any new information. Do not hold it or investigate it without her."

"Yes, sir."

"Good. Have you been home yet?"

Shaking his head, Torres replied, "Not yet."

"Get some rest. It will be a few hours at least before any information comes in."

Torres almost hoped not. If this American took Valentina and left the country, then it would be the next best thing to killing them. That situation might be preferable. He wouldn't have to arrange it to look like a justified killing. The two could just be gone.

When he hung up with Márquez, Torres tapped the top of his cellphone against the bridge of his nose. Several of the girls were nearby when Valentina escaped with the man, and word would have spread quickly. He needed to contain any issues before the others decided to rebel.

He slid into the car next to Ramírez. "Let's go to the apartment on Carrera 3."

Lieutenant Daniel Ramírez nodded, knowing from the captain's expression not to ask about the phone call.

Torres used his key and pushed through the front door. The apartment was only a two-bedroom that housed six girls. The front room remained cluttered, and Torres reminded himself that these women weren't paid for their housekeeping skills. Most were under eighteen, and they didn't care what kind of filth they lived in. Empty food containers and plastic cups littered the small kitchen where no one ever cooked.

A girl stretched out across an old, ragged couch in a t-shirt that she'd gotten from a street vendor that read "Colombia" in the red, yellow, and blue of the national flag. Gabriella slept with a half bottle of rum. The bottom of the shirt rolled up over her bare hips. At fourteen, the girl was the second youngest one in his harem. Now, she'd be the youngest if Valentina was gone.

Torres lifted his foot and nudged her with the sole of his boot. The girl stirred but didn't wake up. He kicked her this time, jarring her up with wild, frightened eyes.

"Get up!" he growled.

Ramírez stood behind the captain and surveyed the scene. Gabriella stared at the captain with an open mouth.

"Where's Valentina?" he demanded.

"Uh, I don't know," Gabriella whined. "Let me sleep, please."

"Get the fuck up!" Torres shouted, and the girl realized he was on a rampage.

His torrential anger was known, and every girl in the house knew to avoid it no matter what. Despite her youth, Gabriella was quick to understand the situation. She'd learned from the other girls what was normally needed to appease one of the officers coming through. She came off the couch, sliding to the floor in front of Torres.

"Not fucking now," he snapped, pulling her up by the shirt and ripping the seams in the cheaply made material.

"What?" Gabriella stammered as she pulled away from the furious captain.

"Where is Valentina?" he screamed.

A door to one of the bedrooms opened and Isabella, the oldest girl in the flat, emerged wearing only a bra and panties. She'd been working for Torres for almost two years, and while she'd never sacrificed herself for one of the other girls, she did try to look out for the younger ones.

"Izzie, get out here," Torres demanded.

"Captain, what's wrong?"

"Valentina," was all Torres said.

Izzie shook her head. "She never came back last night."

"Where did she go?" Torres asked.

"She didn't say," Izzie told him. "But her stuff is still here."

The girl pointed to a small bag in the corner containing everything that Valentina considered important. Torres stared at the blond seventeen-year-old whore before turning to the duffel on the floor. He tore it open as the other door opened and Sofia peeked out.

Torres found a picture of a man and woman. He recognized the man as Valentina's father. He'd found the man after taking Valentina under his wing. It hadn't been difficult when a woman from Bogotá came searching for a missing girl named Valentina. Torres traced the woman, who was a Colombian citizen, to Diego Pérez. Instantly, he recognized the girl's features in her father, and with a phone call, he had the man picked up and deported to Venezuela, where a colleague on that side of the border would ensure Pérez never left Venezuela.

Besides the picture, Torres found a small stuffed dog whose fur was worn thin. None of the items had any value, but Torres wondered if young Valentina would have left them had she planned to run.

He didn't think so. The girl took the leap when the opportunity presented itself. The American only stepped in out of some chivalrous duty.

Torres threw the bag across the room. He turned to stare at the three girls standing in the room. "If Valentina shows up, I better hear about it," Torres demanded.

Izzie responded first, stepping forward with a bobbing head. "Yes, Captain. I'll call you."

"Don't let her leave!" he ordered. Three heads nodded in unison.

Torres motioned for Ramírez to follow him out. He caught the lieutenant's lingering eyes staying on Izzie. "Ramírez!"

"Yes, Captain," the man replied as he turned to follow his superior out of the apartment.

"Do you think she ran?" Ramírez asked.

Torres cut his eyes over to the man without a word. He marched down the steps to the street, where he slid into the passenger seat of the police cruiser. Ramírez took his position behind the wheel.

"Take me home, Daniel," Torres ordered with a cracking voice.

25

Cartagena de Indias, Colombia

Corsair sat in the front window of the Juan Valdez, watching out the window as Captain Torres stormed from the building. Another officer scurried after him in a rush to beat the man to the car. There was a defeat in his face when the captain got to his door first, but the other officer didn't speak, even when the captain mouthed something in the front seat.

Valentina gave Caleb the address of Torres's hideaway apartment. She had spilled as much information as she seemed to know, but Caleb had been careful to press her gently. Interrogation techniques varied depending on the situation. Valentina would be a friendly witness, and those were often better for getting honest answers. She had no motivation to lie. In fact, once she understood that Caleb wanted to help, she spilled all the details she knew.

Unfortunately, she didn't know much. Unlike a hostile witness holding something back, more pressure wouldn't bring that information out. If Camille's car hadn't smashed into the police car carrying Torres, he wasn't sure he'd have gotten away last night. While there wasn't a lot of logic to it, Torres seemed to Caleb to be the best lead to Camille. Even if all he did last night was get whatever alias she was working under, it would be a start.

If, however, it turned into a dead end, then Corsair intended to shut Torres down completely. From the details that Valentina shared, there was a cadre of officers working for him. A few had branched out with their own girls as they built up this small empire built on human slavery.

Caleb waited until the police car pulled away before rising from his seat and tossing the remainder of the coffee into the trash receptacle. He climbed on the Kawasaki Ninja. This morning he'd stolen plates off a different model of Kawasaki. He hoped that would buy him several hours.

He straddled the bike and started it. Over his head, Caleb slipped a full-face helmet that he lifted off a different bike after he swapped the plate. Keeping the police car two blocks ahead of him, he puttered along slower than most of the other motorcyclists who weaved through stopped traffic with no regard for the rest of the cars.

As he idled behind a taxi, Caleb thought more about Camille. She used to have a way of getting close to assets that might help her. Torres made the perfect mark. He was vested in catching Caleb and Valentina, and with his resources, that made him the perfect person for Camille to partner with. Or, at the minimum, to take advantage of.

The woman he remembered, though, had scruples. If she learned that Torres was operating a network of under-age prostitutes, would she be willing to go along with the captain?

Corsair began building a plan, albeit somewhat simple for now. If he planned to kill Torres, he needed a strategy to escape the city first. If he didn't, he might find he had to take out more than Torres if the man had set up an entire unit of corrupt cops. Somehow, a citywide manhunt might intensify if the target was suspected of killing several police officers.

Caleb needed a minimum of an hour head start before the police force descended on him. The airport would be locked down, and there wouldn't be much of a chance of getting through it before the police showed up. He considered the Hans Christian. It would be easy to sail out of the harbor, but it wouldn't be fast. Panama was the safest port for him, not to mention the closest. Yet, it was still a three-hundred-mile trip, and the Hans Christian would take over a week. There was a ferry that took six days to circumvent the wilds of the Darien Gap, but like the airport, it might be on their watch list.

No, he preferred the idea of taking a boat, but he wanted to be on his own. He wouldn't need to get to a major city, just close enough to one to make landfall, hike out of the jungle, and find transport back to Belize. From anywhere in Panama, he could drive north and avoid most people. The border crossings shouldn't cause him a problem as long as the Colombians didn't know his aliases.

Torres's car turned toward the clock tower, and Caleb twisted the throttle and followed the cruiser. Torres passed the square and turned to drive through the arches. When the cruiser crossed Avenida Venezuela, it sped up. Caleb watched Torres heading southeast along Centennial Park. Caleb turned left down an alley and gunned the Kawasaki's engine. He raced to the next right and made a sharp turn before accelerating down the street. He traveled two blocks before turning right again to take him back toward Torres. When he reached the cross street, the police cruiser was pulling away from the red light and traveling into the Getsemani neighborhood.

As Caleb turned to follow, he caught sight of the car making a right just past an arepa stand. When he reached that intersection, he glanced down the street. It was filled with pedestrians, and the cars barely moved. Torres's cruiser appeared parked in the middle of the street, but on closer inspection, Caleb distinguished the outline of two heads in the front seat. They were just inching forward.

If he pulled in behind them, it would be noticeable. He moved to the next block, where the street was much clearer. Colorful *papel picados*, the traditional paper decorations, were strung across the street and danced in the breeze. Caleb sped beneath them as he hurried down the street. At the end of the block, he turned back toward the street Torres was on. He pulled the Kawasaki over and left it on its kickstand. Caleb considered leaving the helmet on his head, but then thought it might draw more attention than simply slipping through the crowd.

As he walked toward the street, he passed a busy square in front of a plain church. Gigantic wooden doors swung open to reveal the inside of the cathedral. While simpler than many other Catholic churches, it still had a regal quality to the sanctuary with gold embossed figures and etchings that he could see hanging on the wall even from across the square.

The police cruiser turned next to him, and he saw that only one officer was in the front. It wasn't Torres. He'd gotten out of the vehicle on this block. Caleb scanned through the crowd. There was no sign of Torres. He strolled down the sidewalk, slowing to peer inside open doors of stores. There was no sign of the cop.

When he reached the other end of the street, he turned back again. Somewhere along this section, Captain Torres was inside a building. Caleb glanced over at the arepa stand and dug into his pocket for some pesos. He bought two fried beef arepas. The vendor wrapped them individually in butcher paper and handed them to him. Caleb crossed to a doorway where an old white five-gallon paint bucket sat overturned. He settled on the makeshift seat and ate the one of the arepas while watching down the street.

Wherever Torres went, he'd have to come out sometime.

26

Belize City, Belize

The air conditioning in the Toyota Corolla rental blew directly in Lee's face. It wasn't until she got out of the parking lot at the airport that she noticed the controls were messed up.

At least it's blowing on high.

Better that she's getting too much cold air than none, given that the temperature outside at one in the afternoon was pushing ninety-six degrees. Somehow, she thought that the air felt cooler than Mexico City had. More than likely, the breeze off the sea made it manageable.

Collins had texted a location to within a thousand yards of where the phone call into the OOC last night had originated. Unfortunately, it was right in the middle of a neighborhood. At least the Belizeans spoke English. That would make a door-by-door canvas easier.

She'd considered the best way to approach it. In the States, people still showed up to make cold sales calls to random homes, but the occurrence was rare enough that now residents were uneasy. No one was inviting any strangers into their homes. That culture of suspicion didn't translate to other countries quite the same. Lee counted on the hope that this community was welcoming enough to not alert the neighborhood watch of some American woman going house to house.

The neighborhood was a twenty-minute drive from the airport. Here, that seemed like quite a distance since it was a twenty-minute hike on foot across Belize City. She turned into the neighborhood with rows of single-story homes on both sides of the street. She drove the block before braking in the middle of the street when the sun glinted off something to her right.

Once she saw the small camera attached to a small post, she started looking for more. After she drove around the block, she had counted eighteen cameras. JW said the guy bounced the phone signal around the world. Someone that does that would be paranoid enough to place his own cameras around his house.

Lee cruised through the neighborhood, examining each house as she did. She slowed in front of a blue and white single-story home. The curtains were drawn, leaving it with a lifeless look. There was something about vacant homes that she couldn't pin down. Even a home that had a trimmed lawn and was taken care of had a "not lived in" vibe to it. In contrast, this little blue and white house appeared to be unoccupied, however, it had an occupant. Unlike the houses next door to it, this one had what appeared to be two power lines coming into the house.

There was no parking area in front of the house, so she left the car on the edge of the street. When she rapped on the wooden door, she marveled at the thickness. This wasn't a standard door. It was a solid mahogany security door. Not impenetrable because nothing was, but short of a battering ram, no one was coming through this. More confirmation that this was the house where the phone call originated.

No answer to her knock. Lee turned to look up and down the street. The neighborhood looked like many in the middle of a business day—quiet. Lee walked around the house. The rear door was as heavy as the front. Still, she knocked again.

After several minutes with no sounds from the house, Lee lifted a small rock from the yard and broke the window. After unlatching the catch, she slid the pane up and crawled through the opening.

The inside of the house was dark. When she took a second to look around, she saw the cameras covering the inside of the house. Whoever lived with her now probably knew she was here. She wasn't armed, having left her Kel-Tec in Mexico City. Even with the right credentials, getting a gun across the border took more time than she wanted. Besides, she didn't want to kill Corsair, and after their encounter in Puerto Vallarta, she doubted he would kill her if she offered no threat.

Of course, that was the challenge—ensure that she presented no threat to the assassin.

That thought, though, followed with the one that pointed out this wasn't Corsair's house. It was an unknown subject that preferred to maintain their privacy.

"Not much I can do about it now," she mumbled under her breath.

Lee walked through the house. The living room looked like it had been designed in a gamer's wet dream. A seventy-inch television hung on one wall. In front of the screen was one of those immersive gaming recliners with built-in speakers and controls. Along the wall under the television, this gamer installed shelves that held several gaming systems. She recognized the original Nintendo and its successors, along with an Xbox and the latest rendition of the PlayStation. A computer tower with a clear composite outside and a pink LED light inside showed off the guts of the PC. Lee assumed she should be impressed by the setup.

There were three bedrooms in the house, and the first was nothing more than that. The second had been converted into a storage room, filled with boxes of things still new-in-the-box. The range of products varied from laptops to leaf blowers, and Lee wondered if it was somehow all stolen.

In the third bedroom, Lee thought she walked into the control room at NASA. There was a U-shaped desk in the middle of the room, with eight monitors curving around the surface. She counted four keyboards arranged so that whoever sat at the desk could rotate around from screen to screen.

Lee sat in the chair and tried to turn on the computer. All eight screens came to life asking for a password. This guy didn't leave his password lying around. No one with this type of security was lazy enough to jot it down and leave it. She removed a device that resembled a USB flash drive. It was a small piece of tech designed to circumvent most encryptions.

She inserted it and immediately the screens flashed red.

"Fuck!" she cursed, yanking the drive out. It was too late. The hard drives were self-destructing.

She pocketed the USB, noting she needed to ask the tech guys in the Basement about it. Lee didn't know enough to be sure the subject couldn't have some virus waiting to infect anything attempting to intrude.

This was fruitless. It seemed she'd alerted the house's occupant, and he was already skittish about Corsair. If he didn't bolt now, she'd be shocked.

Lee worked her way around the desk. The surface was almost empty, holding only a few scraps of paper with doodles of fish on them. Lee pulled on the center desk drawer. It had a hoard of Werther's caramel hard candies and some pens.

The second drawer she tried was locked. Lee leaned over to look at it. The lock was the cheap latch that came on the desk. She went to the kitchen, returning with a butter knife. It slipped in the crack and pried the catch open. When she finished, the drawer was open, and the knife was bent.

Inside was a small manila envelope. Lee poured the contents on the desk. A stack of hundred-dollar bills fell out with several documents and some pictures. When she flipped over the first picture, she stopped.

Lee stared at the smiling face of Khloe Evans. More pictures of Khloe were taken as the woman walked through the streets of what Lee guessed was Belize with a little girl. Amanda Harrod, Corsair's daughter. On a piece of yellow legal pad paper, an address was scrawled at an angle.

27

Cartagena de Indias, Colombia

Corsair moved down the street when a small crowd of people passed him. As he slipped along with the group of English-speaking guys, he smiled and laughed when the rest did. From their accent, he guessed they were from Northern England. Under his breath, he rattled off a non-sensical phrase to approximate the natural patter of their speech. If someone approached him now, he'd come across as the older friend of these English tourists.

It was a practiced habit that he hadn't regularly practiced in years. During his OOC training, Caleb learned dialects from a coach who taught him to listen to the speech patterns and the best practices to imitate them. The techniques were similar to musicians who performed songs from just the chords. A layman wouldn't notice the difference, but a linguist might.

As the group continued toward the end of the street where the church stood, Caleb stepped into the open door of a gelato shop. He ordered a scoop of raspberry gelato on a freshly made waffle cone and sat in the open window overlooking the street.

He had a clear view down both sidewalks except a small blind spot on the south side of the street. That shouldn't matter. If Torres happened to come out of a building where Caleb couldn't directly see, the officer would have to pass through his line of sight at some point.

A cop on foot patrol ambled along the sidewalk. From the familiarity the officer had with several of the shopkeepers and vendors, Caleb guessed this was his regular beat. When the fruit vendor offered the policeman cold water from a dirty white foam cooler, it further confirmed his suspicion.

Caleb ate on his gelato and waited. When he was halfway through the cone, he spotted Torres walking out of a double iron security door diagonally across the street from Caleb. The foot cop saw the captain and gave him a courtesy nod, as if to acknowledge the officer he either was only familiar with or didn't personally know.

Torres returned the gesture and walked over to the beat cop. The two exchanged words before Torres walked away, putting his phone to his ear. Caleb wondered if he should follow Torres or learn where he'd just been.

He swallowed the point of the cone and rose to his feet. When he came out on the street, he saw Torres already walking down the block away from Caleb. He was almost to the cross street. Caleb followed a distance back.

He stopped when a police cruiser pulled up at the corner. Torres climbed into the passenger seat, and the car pulled away. The Kawasaki was on the other block. It would be impossible for him to get back to it in time to pursue the police captain.

A man on a handheld loudspeaker appeared behind. "We have hot pizza, *cerveza*, and rum," his voice blared through the speaker.

Caleb saw the sign over his head advertising pizza. It stood across the street from the building Torres had exited. Next to the double doors, the sign read, "Hotel Monaguillo." He walked past the security door and peered through the glass. A single desk faced the door in the tiny lobby. Behind it, a girl in her twenties posted herself to greet guests entering. He tested the door to find it locked, and then he crossed the street. They were monitoring who came and went, likely to ensure no extra guests showed up.

Inside the pizza joint, Caleb ordered a mojito and settled in a seat next to the open window. The open-air quality in this neighborhood made surveillance easier. He was just above street level, so he could watch with ease, but most of the pedestrians didn't turn their heads up enough to see him. Even if they did, he chose the seat against the wall, making it easy to lean back in his chair and disappear from the window.

The beat cop returned, and he seemed to pay special attention to the same building Torres had left. Had the captain asked him to watch the hotel? That piqued his attention.

He studied the policeman. His black tactical vest combined with the sweat bubbling on his forehead and, Caleb assumed, the rest of him, made him look hot. He had a Jericho handgun on his hip and three grenades strapped to his vest. The grenades felt like overkill, and Caleb wondered how often a police officer needed one of those. Likely, they were only stun grenades. Maybe even smoke. Still, it felt more like window dressing than a functional necessity.

Caleb watched the cop stroll down the street and step into the corner *tienda,* where he came out a few minutes later with a large bottle of water. Again, he moved down the same street, passing underneath Caleb's window.

The officer was definitely watching the Hotel Monaguillo along with Caleb, who continued to sip on the mojito and wondered if Camille was in that building. If she was, he expected her to be prepared for anyone surprising her. It wouldn't matter. There only appeared to be one entrance, and the building was narrow, so it would be like charging down a tunnel.

His best hope was to wait and learn what he could. He ordered a second mojito, knowing that he needed to sip it slowly. He probably should have gone with coffee, but he'd had his fill earlier at the Juan Valdez while he waited on Torres to show up.

An hour later, Caleb had ordered and dumped two more mojitos. As long as he was buying drinks, the staff wouldn't care how long he sat there. Now, he ordered a water and a slice of pizza in a slightly slurred voice.

He'd counted eight times that the beat cop walked the street. At some point, he must have decided to make the block, or he was distracted by something because he disappeared for an extended time. But he'd reappear a bit later.

Caleb straightened in his seat and leaned back as the door to the Hotel Monaguillo opened. Camille Dubois stepped onto the sidewalk, pausing to look up and down the street. If she spotted Caleb, there was no indication.

For a brief moment, Caleb felt his stomach do a flip as anxiety washed over him. He could have been a thirteen-year-old boy talking to his first crush, or he could have been back in Camille's flat in Marseille. She didn't appear to have aged at all in the last ten years. Her hair might have been longer, but it was pulled back and curled into a sort of bun. She wore a simple cotton dress with blooming red and yellow flowers on a creamy background. He thought her skin tone was tanner than he remembered, but that could be so easily changed, he discounted it.

But she was beautiful, and her walk was filled with confidence. Suddenly, waves of guilt collided over him. He thought back then that he had been in love with her, but his duty overpowered that. Right now, he didn't have to suspect it. Those feelings rushed at him, and he wondered for a second what would his life be like if Marseille had been the breaking point with the OOC and Winston instead of Turkey.

The answer disturbed him. There'd be no life with Audrey. No Jackson. No Amanda. But he wouldn't have lost Audrey or Jackson, either. That pain wouldn't exist. Again, a new flavor of regret struck him. Even considering for a second what life without Audrey would have been made him nauseous.

He tried to shake the feeling off as he watched the Frenchwoman cross the street to a restaurant.

28

Cartagena de Indias, Colombia

The inside of Doña Lola was dimly lit, with flickering candles on every table. Camille Dubois sat at a corner table by herself. She sipped on a Morandé Pionero Rosé, a Pinot Noir from Chile. The purplish liquid appeared black as she put the glass to her lips. Today had been quiet besides that useless prick of a police captain coming to her room.

The officious fool despised her, and he didn't have the good sense to disguise it. The man leered at her as soon as she opened the door to her room. She'd considered seducing him to ensure his cooperation, but the tiny advance she made was rebuffed without a thought. The captain was too preoccupied with her interference. It was tunnel vision on his part.

The man didn't have anything useful to add, either. He'd come under orders from Márquez to report to her. However, the man didn't offer her much concession. It was obvious that Torres didn't think much of women, and his demeanor showed that clearly.

The server brought out a plate of ceviche with some homemade wafers.

"Can I bring you anything else?" he asked her in Spanish. His eyes widened when he spoke to her. He hadn't overtly flirted with her, but she could see he found her attractive.

"No, thank you," she replied.

The server nodded and moved to another table.

"Mr. Abbas would like to know of your progress," Salar Tolazar remarked as he approached the table. The man pulled out the chair opposite Minuit and sat down.

Camille Dubois scooped a dollop of the citrus-cooked fish onto a wafer and took the bite. She chewed slowly, staring at the man who'd interrupted her dinner without an invitation.

"We lost him last night, thanks in part to the local police force."

"I do not understand," Tolazar remarked. "Corsair engaged the police. What was his purpose?"

Minuit lifted the wineglass, putting it to her lips, and sipping it. When she set it back down, she said, "I can't say." It was an answer she hadn't figured out yet, either. However, Minuit suspected it centered on the girl that was with Corsair.

"It appears he was traveling with a street whore," Minuit explained further. "I'm not sure to what purpose."

Tolazar's face contorted. "That is bizarre for a man like Corsair. His history doesn't suggest he'd get involved with a woman like that."

Minuit didn't remark. She wondered how much of Corsair's history he thought he knew. It might not be as accurate as Tolazar thought. However, she wondered how much of her relationship that he knew about, too.

"Why did the police get involved?" the man asked.

"Corsair assaulted two officers and stole one of their motorcycles," she explained to the man.

"Would you like a drink?" the handsome server asked upon approaching the table.

"Water, please," Tolazar requested.

Minuit stared at the man who was intruding on her dinner. She didn't comment, knowing he was the emissary for her employer. When the server walked away, Tolazar continued the conversation. "Corsair might not be the man he was. He had always been one to move completely in shadows. Now, he is bringing the attention of the local law enforcement. I believe he might be losing his edge."

Minuit didn't disagree. At least, not completely. Tolazar was correct, though. This involvement with the prostitute and the police was uncharacteristic of Corsair. But she was comparing him to a man she knew over ten years ago. According to the reports, Caleb Saunders restarted his life. Domesticated himself. That's how Tolazar referred to it. A twinge of envy filled her. If he'd have asked her all those years ago to leave the DGSE and start a life with him, Camille thought she might have accepted. Instead, he moved on to some middle-class American woman who probably had her Starbucks every morning.

But Minuit didn't think he'd softened completely. Or at all. He'd escaped a city-wide manhunt last night and vanished. From the mouths of officers under Torres, the chase across the city was unlike anything they'd seen.

"Mr. Abbas is paying you a hefty sum to catch this fiend," Tolazar reminded her.

Minuit took another drink of her Pinot Noir and held her gaze on him. "I'm well aware of my responsibilities to Abbas," she said flatly.

"He has certain expectations," Tolazar droned on with an accusatory tone.

Minuit leaned forward. "Abbas hired me for a reason," she reminded the man. "If he's unhappy with my performance, then we can part ways. You can track down Corsair on your own."

"You cannot quit our partnership," Tolazar snapped sternly.

She shook her head slowly. "Salar, do not presume to tell me what I can and cannot do. I do not mind taking Abbas's money, but that does not sequester my control. Your insistent nagging about how I should accomplish my task grows tiresome."

Tolazar sat back. His face paled. Most people deferred to him due to his rank with Abbas. When he cleared his throat, he replied, "I do not think this is a task for a woman. However, Mr. Abbas felt you were the right—er, um—person for the job. I'll respect his opinion, but if you fail or in some way double-cross Mr. Abbas, I'll make sure this is the last job you have."

The server appeared with a plate. He set the dish in front of Camille. A purplish octopus splayed over the plate. Black grill marks marred the flesh.

"Would you like to order?" the server asked Tolazar, who shook his head as he stared at the entrée in front of Minuit.

"If you don't mind, Salar," Minuit remarked. "I'd like to enjoy the rest of my dinner in solitude."

Tolazar pinched his face and glared at the insolence of this woman. "I will speak with Mr. Abbas, but this matter needs to reach a resolution soon."

"It's been one day," Minuit pointed out. "What is the saying, 'Rome wasn't built in a day'? If you want it done fast, send in an assault team. Although, I don't think you'll succeed in doing anything except getting your team killed. This is delicate work. Either leave it to me or find another professional who will fail much harder."

He sneered at the Frenchwoman as he pushed the chair back. His eyes lingered on the plate of octopus before he turned to leave.

Camille picked up the knife and fork and cut into a tentacle.

29

Cartagena de Indias, Colombia

The police officer had seen Camille's exit. He'd been farther down the street, but his gaze followed her from the Hotel Monaguillo as she crossed the street to the restaurant. As soon as she went through the entrance, the cop pulled a phone out and made a call. It was short, and Caleb presumed he was alerting Torres to the woman's activities. He nodded as he talked, obviously agreeing to something. Then he hung up and pocketed the phone.

Caleb watched the officer return to his regular patrol. He stopped for a minute to chat with a man selling beaded jewelry. The vendor offered a couple of pieces for the officer to inspect. His facial expression brightened after having gotten off the phone, and he smiled at the man.

Caleb stepped out onto the street and started down the sidewalk. He paused in front of a tiny gift shop that advertised currency exchange through Western Union. A squat table with brochures featuring tours and destinations around Colombia sat beside the open door of the store. Caleb picked one up for the Rosario Islands, a chain of islands about ten miles out in the Caribbean Sea. Charters offered to pack forty to fifty tourists on a boat built more for thirty-five and drive them out to the islands where they could snorkel for fifteen minutes before the crew carried them to a few prearranged destinations for alcohol. Caleb thought the whole thing sounded terrible. It was the fastest way to see nothing of the islands and spend hundreds on overpriced cocktails.

He carried the flyer, opening it to feign reading as he walked down the street. The cop was coming the opposite direction, now talking to two young women dressed in tight-fitting Lycra dresses that only came a few centimeters down their thighs. The officer's eyes struggled to meet theirs instead of drifting down to their cleavage. As the trio almost crossed paths with Caleb, he shifted on his feet to pass between the group. With his face in the brochure, he ran into the officer.

"I'm so sorry," Caleb muttered with his faux English accent.

The officer gave him a smile, having barely understood the man's English. "*No problema*," he assured Caleb before turning back to the two women.

Caleb continued down the street. He slipped his hand into his pocket, depositing the grenade he'd lifted off the officer's tactical vest. He hoped the man didn't notice the missing armament for a few minutes.

He continued down the street to the intersection and turned onto Calle 30. He paused at a shop where he entered and found a cheap button-down shirt and a straw fedora. When he bought the items, he changed in the store, leaving the shirt he'd been wearing in the garbage bin. Attired in an almost completely new wardrobe, Caleb came back out onto the street and returned down the street.

He saw the panicked police officer hurrying back down the sidewalk. The cop rushed past him without giving him a look. Caleb assumed he'd realized he was now missing a grenade. He might even suspect the English fellow who ran into him, but as he came by Caleb, he didn't recognize the assassin.

Caleb mentally smiled with satisfaction that his ruse worked. The police officer would likely get into some trouble for losing his weapon, but it was his own fault for allowing his situational awareness to be hampered just because he was flirting.

Now Caleb had the means to initiate his plan. If he was going to confront Camille, he needed a way to keep her in check while they talked. He just needed to get into the restaurant without being spotted.

Most of these businesses, even the nicer establishments like Doña Lola, were constricted into small spaces in the buildings. When the neighborhood grew up, construction put each building right next to the other. Often, they shared walls, or they were so integrated that one wall was literally added to the adjacent one. Space was at a premium, and most businesses only had one entrance. Doña Lola was in part of a building with a small hotel, but there were no alleys on either side. It left two entrances: one for the restaurant and one in the hotel.

Caleb entered the hotel first. The lobby was small but ornate, with a plush red couch and a carved wooden desk. The young woman lifted her head from something she was reading. Caleb smiled at her with a curt nod that told her he belonged in the hotel. He counted on her seeing a regular carousel of faces pass through here. If he appeared to belong, she wouldn't say anything. The woman returned his nod with a "*Buenas noches.*"

He went to the door leading into the restaurant and paused. Cracking the door, he peered through. The dining room was dark, lighted mostly with candles. There were twelve tables in the dining room that was divided into a split level to accommodate more guests.

On the upper level, Camille sat alone at a table. She was speaking with a server who seemed more attentive than some of the others. He couldn't blame the guy. Camille was an elegant woman dining alone.

Caleb started through the door to make his approach when another man appeared. He was tall, and there was something familiar about the man. He didn't fit, even in this fine dining establishment. Everything about him stood out. He was Middle Eastern, but Caleb couldn't tell from where exactly. Caleb couldn't recognize the suit's designer, but it was definitely a tailor-made one, and it fit him to a tee.

This wasn't one of Camille's hired men she had last night in the park. The high-dollar shoes probably cost him two grand, and Caleb couldn't guess what the suit ran him. He was important, and Camille reacted to him.

Surprise. That was the look she had. Caleb decided it wasn't utter shock, but more of an inconvenient surprise. There'd been no sign that Camille intended to eat with anyone. The extra place setting had been removed, most likely by the server when she sat at the table. If she'd expected company later, they would have left the silverware for him.

No, he just showed up, and it annoyed Camille. While she didn't hide her disdain, she tolerated the appearance.

She's working for him.

Now he was torn. He needed to talk with Camille, but if he could find out who this man was employing Camille to find Caleb, it would answer a few questions. He took a seat at the bar and ordered a martini. He chose his seat so that she didn't have a clear line of sight on him. Still, he kept his head down as he sipped.

After a few minutes, the man rose from the table and walked out the front door. Caleb considered following him, but it meant postponing his planned talk with Camille. Somehow, it didn't seem as important to find out who wanted him dead as much as trying to reason with his former lover.

He drank the rest of his martini, and while he didn't plan to chase after her employer, he did commit the man's face to memory. Later, he could work to discover who this man really was and why he was after Corsair.

He pushed the glass across the bar with some cash before he slid off the barstool and swallowed hard. This was about to be the most dangerous interaction he could remember.

30

Cartagena de Indias, Colombia

She was on her third bite of octopus when a figure slid into the chair across from her. Minuit lifted her eyes to stare into the blue eyes of Caleb Saunders. She straightened up suddenly, having expected it to be Tolazar returning to the table. Her eyes darted around for one of her hired muscle, but she'd come to dinner alone.

Corsair raised his hand to stop her from making any sudden moves. He dropped something on the table next to her fork. Minuit's gaze shifted to the black ring on the white tablecloth. She recognized it for what it was, but Corsair flashed the grenade he had hidden in his palm.

"I thought we could have a civilized discussion," he suggested.

Minuit leaned back in her seat and lifted the Morandé Pionero Rosé. She let the liquid slip past her lips.

"It's been a long time," she finally said as she set her glass back on the table.

"Camille," Caleb began.

"Don't." She stopped him. "You do not get to come in here and use my name with any affection. You don't deserve that."

Corsair nodded. "You are right. Can I apologize though?"

"Apologize?" she snapped. "For ruining my life? For killing the only father figure that I ever knew? For leaving without saying goodbye? Or for coming back from the dead?"

"All of it," he admitted. "I knew when I killed Lefevre that it didn't feel right."

"Didn't feel right?" Her voice escalated, and she realized her emotions were sliding through. After restraining her feelings, she continued, "You didn't feel right?"

"It was a mission," he explained. "You know how missions go. We obey without question. You know that's how it works."

"Did that make me the mission too?" she demanded.

"At first, yes," he said. "But that last day—I almost didn't go through with it."

"We were in bed together that morning," she reminded him.

Caleb gave a small bob of his chin. She watched his face. It was softer than she remembered.

"I think about that morning a lot," he told her.

"Even when you were with your wife?" she quipped with a sneer spreading over her face.

The man across from her let out a huff that was akin to a chuckle. "Probably especially with her."

"Your wife must not have been much in bed if you thought of me often."

"My thoughts were remorseful," he told her.

"Great, you regretted being with me?"

Caleb shook his head. "No, Camille, I never regretted it. If it hadn't been for you, I'd have never left the OOC."

Minuit picked up her fork and stabbed a tentacle before slicing a bite off.

"Sir, would you like something to drink?" the server asked Corsair.

"No, he wouldn't," Minuit informed the man in a curt tone. The server nodded and vanished.

"Why did you leave?" she asked him.

"Carl Winston, my boss, had been sending me on questionable missions. But I was a dutiful public servant. I didn't question my orders. When he sent me to kill Lefevre, I trusted those orders. But then there was you."

Minuit didn't respond. She stared across the candlelit table at the former assassin.

"Camille, I fell in love with you."

She dropped her fork, and it clanged against the china. "You fell in love with me? You know what you do when you fall in love? You buy flowers. Chocolates. Take romantic trips. You don't ruin the person you love's life and kill their friends and family."

Caleb dipped his head.

"I took you straight to Marc. You, the damned wolf. And I carried you into the paddock with the sheep."

"Camille."

"Don't use my name," she snapped.

Caleb didn't answer.

"Do you know what I had to go through?" she asked. "I had to defend myself against treason claims. My career ended that day. I doubt I'll ever be able to step foot in France again. But all that's okay, because you fell in love with me."

"I'm sorry."

"Don't apologize again or I'll take that fucking grenade and shove it down your throat."

"I made a lot of mistakes," Caleb told her. "I've always thought betraying you was the biggest one."

"Oh, it was," she said coldly. "I'll make you pay for it. When the news came that you weren't dead, I jumped at the chance to fix that miscalculation."

"I deserve it," he told her.

She fumed. How dare he come in here and expect to apologize and grovel? He didn't deserve it.

"I'm going to kill you," she promised. "And I'll make a ton of money doing it."

"You do what you have to," Caleb said. "I'm not going to roll over. There are people counting on me."

"It's going to be me or you?" she asked.

Caleb shook his head. "No, if it comes down to me or you—I can't hurt you."

Minuit flew forward, driving the fork toward Caleb's forearm. He moved back in time to let the tongs stab into the table.

"I said I'm not going to roll over," he repeated. "You're working with that cop, Torres."

"What about him?"

"He's a pimp. The girl that was with me last night was held hostage by him. She's only thirteen."

"So what? Are you some kind of babysitter now?"

"I'm a father."

Minuit glared at him. "So was Marc. Is that supposed to make me want to spare you?"

"No, but you need to understand what I have to fight for."

"You didn't fight for your wife?" she asked.

Caleb closed his eyes for the beat of a second. "I didn't."

"I don't understand you. Why was she enough to stop you?"

He shook his head. "She wasn't. I'd already ran from the life when I met her. She changed me, for sure, but she wasn't the impetus to leave. That was probably you. After I left Marseille, I couldn't get you out of my mind. I knew I'd betrayed you."

Caleb tapped the table in a slow, rhythmic beat. "But I'd betrayed people for years. It's part of the job, right? We get close to people, no matter how, to perform our missions. None of them lingered with me after the job was done."

"Lot of good it did me," she retorted.

"You're right. But when I confronted the next questionable mission, I knew I couldn't do it anymore. After I was 'dead,' I wanted to come back to you."

"I'd have killed you," she informed him.

"I expected as much," he replied with a wry grin. She recognized the smile from the man she'd fallen in love with, and it irritated her more.

"Listen, Camille—Minuit? I mean, is that still the codename you use?"

She gave a quick nod.

"This girl that Torres has been raping and pimping out. She needs help."

"Not my problem," Minuit replied.

"It's not fair, but I'm asking. If you succeed, someone needs to help her."

"Shouldn't you be concerned for your daughter instead?"

"I'm always concerned for Amanda."

"Amanda?"

Corsair nodded. "She's three, and I'd love to see her grow up. That's likely not going to happen. If not, I have someone who can care for her. Valentina doesn't have anyone."

"Valentina's the whore?"

"Valentina is the girl who's being tortured by your new friend."

"Torres isn't my friend. He's a means to an end."

Caleb sat back. "I really am sorry. It doesn't help, I know. You won't stop hating me, and I deserve it. But I'm different now."

"So am I," she reminded him. "Betrayal tends to scar beyond recognition."

"When you kill me, please save Valentina."

"When I kill you, I'll be reveling in your death. I'm not about to cross the police force in this country for a whore."

"I guess we don't have anything else to say then."

"You don't want to show me pictures of your honeymoon?" she remarked snidely.

Caleb laughed. "Audrey would have liked you."

"Fuck Audrey," Minuit blurted out, but she sucked in as if she realized she said something wrong.

Caleb only chuckled more. "She knew about you," he explained.

Minuit straightened in her seat.

"She knew everything about me, and I'd talked to her about you. About how I'd wronged you."

"Yes, so what did she say?"

"She told me you'd hate me for it, and there's nothing I could do about that."

"She seems like a smart woman," she remarked in a softer tone.

"See, you two would have been friends."

"Did you love her?" Minuit asked wistfully.

"More than anything I've ever loved," he told her.

"More than me then?"

Caleb nodded. "I've only loved two women, Camille. I'd have never loved her the way I did had I not loved you first. I know that's not fair, is it? I could lie to you and tell you how I longed for you. That's not entirely a lie, because I never stopped loving you. I just knew there are certain things you can't get back from."

"No, you can't," she said, biting her bottom lip.

"Camille, you'll have to come at me yourself," he told her. "I'll kill every man you send after me, but I swear, I'll never hurt you."

He tossed the grenade toward her. Minuit reached out to grab the explosive but knocked it onto the floor. She dipped down, scooping it up. With both hands, she twisted the top hard. The fuse system turned, and she rotated it three times in quick succession before yanking the fuse out of the base. As the top came free, she flung it across the room. It clattered on an empty table where the detonator ignited with a sharp pop.

She breathed in relief before dropping the explosive base on the table and grabbing her phone. She dialed a number.

"He's here in the restaurant," she barked into the phone. "Kill him now."

31

Cartagena de Indias, Colombia

Corsair pushed back through the door leading into the boutique hotel. There had been no explosion. That was good. He had no intention of killing Camille, but he knew relying on her to disarm a grenade carried some risk. Corsair felt some relief that he'd trusted she could do it.

The girl behind the front desk looked up again as he came past. Whether she wondered why he hadn't stayed so long was never voiced. She gave him a smile as he exited the building onto the street. The sun hadn't set yet, but the sky was already gaining that tint of orange that came at the end of the day. It would be dark soon, and he hoped to use the night's shadows to slink back to the boat.

Caleb didn't know if he'd reached Camille. Based on her reactions, he actually had a difficult time knowing. For the sake of caution, he assumed that nothing he said helped his situation. Still, despite the fact that she wanted to gut him at the table, it had been nice to see her. During the many sleepless nights he spent thinking about her, he never expected to see her again.

Lost in his thoughts, he didn't see the man come away from the wall. A meaty white hand caught him by the forearm. Corsair pulled back, stepping his right foot behind his left as he caught the wrist of the man who grabbed him. The guy was about six feet tall and white with grayish blond hair.

By grabbing the man, he used the other guy's momentum against him. Corsair jerked the blond man down and, having stepped back, now used his left leg to sweep into the man's ankles. With his feet suddenly knocked out behind him, the blond fell forward, releasing Corsair's arm to catch himself before he landed face-first on the sidewalk. Once freed from the goon's grip, Corsair pivoted counterclockwise on his left foot to cock back his right knee before driving into the man's shoulders. The impact slammed the man down faster, and he didn't shield his face this time as it smashed into the concrete.

Caleb turned to dash down the street toward the church and the intersection where he'd left the Kawasaki. Two men focused on him as they hurried down the sidewalk in his path. When he changed directions, Caleb spotted two more men coming from the other way.

With both avenues of escape blocked, Corsair scanned the street. He broke into a sprint, leaving the blond man to get to his feet on his own. Corsair crossed the one-lane road and leaped onto the hood of a royal blue Nissan March idling on the curb. He ran up the windshield to the roof, where he jumped toward the building.

Caleb caught the wooden dowels serving as burglar bars on the building. As he climbed, he saw in the open window a mother and her two children watching some cartoon. All three heard the man slam into the side of their building and turned to look. He gave them a two-finger wave without letting go of the dowels before he started ascending and praying that the *rejas* remained attached to the window frame.

He swung over and caught the edge of an awning jutting out from the rundown building. After pulling himself up, he glanced back to see the four men converging beneath the window below. Caleb scaled up the wall to a ledge about five feet over the metal roof. A four-by-eight piece of sheet metal hung loosely over an opening. Most of the screws holding it in place had rusted, leaving only three of the original twelve. With little effort, Caleb pulled the metal back, wincing as its screech echoed off the building across the street. Caleb ducked and clambered into the dark gap.

A second later, he was crawling on his hands and knees through thick layers of concrete dust covering the floor. He stood up to find himself in a small room. There were three walls and a door. Where the fourth wall had been was now an opening that looked out over the neighborhood. This apartment or hotel, or whatever it had been, was long gone. Now the building was in ruins, and with an entire side missing, it resembled a Barbie mansion that was opened up to display the interior.

Caleb stood up and brushed off his hands and knees. Turning back, he saw a trail behind him where he'd crawled through the dust. He moved away from the gaping hole in the building and into a corridor. Everything was concrete, with all the furnishings and accoutrements stripped, leaving cinder block walls and concrete floors. Massive holes in the floors and ceilings were left when the ventilations systems were removed.

Caleb stifled a cough from the dust he'd stirred up while crawling into the building. The sheet metal on the side of the building screamed to announce someone entering the ruins. Caleb climbed what remained of a set of stairs leading up to the next floor. The concrete-formed steps crumbled under his feet. Missing steps were replaced with jacked pieces of rebar metal sticking out of the stone. Caleb stepped carefully over the gap, thankful the waning bit of daylight allowed him to see. Once it got dark, the hallways and empty rooms would become more dangerous, with the open pits leading to lower floors.

When he turned back, Caleb realized there was little chance to hide. He was leaving fresh footprints that would lead his pursuers after him. When he reached the next level, he ran down the hallway, entering each room before backtracking carefully out. It took too much time, but when the first man emerged on this level; he had four different paths to choose.

Caleb crouched in a room away from the open section of the wall. Without the direct sunlight, the room was dark, with only bits of light seeping in through the door. It was enough for Caleb to see the black mass on the floor two feet from him. He kicked a pebble toward the dark blob, and the *tink tink* of the pebble dropping below sounded.

He heard the footsteps in the hall, and Corsair counted them. Two sets. Where were the other two men? Maybe they hadn't made the climb and were looking for other exits to the building. Or they could have stayed on the lower level waiting for Caleb to come back.

The first figure appeared in the doorframe as he tried to peer into the darkened room. Caleb grabbed him by the front of his shirt and swung him into the room. The man stumbled forward before he caught his footing and turned toward Caleb. The former assassin's foot caught him in the chest, and the man instinctively stepped back to balance himself. His back foot didn't touch the floor, and, even in the dark, Caleb saw the flash of panic across his face as he rocked back.

"Aaah!" Then a *thunk*.

"Emil! Are you all right?" a voice shouted in German. "Emil!"

Caleb heard the footsteps running down the hall, and he lunged out at the German dashing toward his room. He hit the man like a running back, and the two slammed into the dusty wall, sending plumes of swirling concrete powder into the air. The German recovered, and Caleb realized he outweighed the American by at least fifty pounds, none of which were fat. An elbow cracked Corsair in the chin, and the German cocked his arm to hit him again. This time, he pummeled him with four blows to the face, and Corsair stepped back.

The German lowered his body and charged at Corsair, who had a split second to prepare for the blow. It was like getting ready to be hit by a freight train. There's only so much one can do. When the German rammed him, Corsair let him knock him off his feet. If he'd tried to stay standing, it would give the man a more solid target to hit. Instead, the man wasn't prepared for the lack of resistance, and the pair tumbled together with the German's inertia.

Corsair crashed onto his back as the German fell on top of him. The air rushed out of his lungs when he landed, but he jabbed his right fist into the man's kidneys. The German scrambled up, trying to pin Corsair down. He shifted enough that the former OOC agent fired his knee up between the man's legs. He didn't think the blow was strong enough, but he heard the man let out an "Ooomph" and slump forward in pain.

With a snap of his neck, Corsair drove his forehead into the German's face, smashing his nose. At the same time, he delivered two more kidney punches while his left arm came up between the two men's faces. Rotating to the left, he caught the big man across the neck. There wasn't much force behind it, but he used the arm to lever the man into a roll.

Enraged, the German exploded out, throwing both arms forward and knocking Corsair away from him. The smaller man scampered back and onto his feet as the German pushed up off the grimy floor.

The sun was setting, and now a gray dimness filled the space where sunlight had been streaming a few minutes earlier. Caleb heard voices below, and he knew the other two men would be joining them soon. A three-against-one match wasn't going to end well for Caleb, certainly if compared to how the fight with this German was going.

The German, now on his feet, straightened up to his full height, and Corsair estimated he was six feet, five inches tall and easily 270 pounds. He sneered at Caleb as if to taunt him into an attack. If Corsair went at him straight on, the man would reach out with his massive arms and swat him away like a fly long before Corsair got close enough to do any damage.

Instead, he bolted to the right as if to run around the man. A long German arm swiped out toward him, barely missing his shoulder. Corsair leaped up, placed the soles of his shoes against the wall, and sprang off the cinder blocks. Surprised, the German wasn't prepared for the attack, and Corsair rocketed into his torso, sending him staggering back. The man had a second to lock his stance, and unlike Corsair, he fought to stay up, resulting in a more solid object for Corsair to strike.

His feet stayed under him, but the German shuffled back, trying to catch his balance. It was long enough for the American to fly up off the ground into the man's abdomen. Still off balance, the German now took several steps to absorb the blow.

"Friedrick's got him," a voice shouted in French from the stairs. Corsair didn't have time to look back, instead digging his feet in to keep the German rocking back.

A gunshot echoed in the corridor, and Corsair buried his head into the man. The German realized that his comrades were shooting at both of them, and he raised a hand to order them to stop when Corsair planted his left foot against the wall and shoved. Two hands wrapped around Corsair before he could disengage from the German.

Corsair tumbled after the German, who fell back down a gaping black hole in the floor.

His opponent hit first with a wet thunk, and Corsair felt a jab in the chest that knocked him back. He rolled out of control and felt gravity fail him again as he dropped through another opening in the floor.

He slammed into the concrete floor on his back. Again, the wind rushed out of his chest, and he gasped for air. After the sticky, powdery air filled his lungs, Caleb rolled to his side and pushed off the floor. Everything hurt, but it was a good pain that told him he'd be sore, but nothing was damaged.

He was on the second floor, and this hallway was pitch black. Any light that filtered through the opening above was stifled by the time it got here. He could look up at the hole in the ceiling and see the light. The German dangled above him, and Caleb saw the black streak of blood on the man's chest. A metal rod protruded from the man's chest.

Caleb shuffled his feet back until he felt the wall behind him. He slid his feet sideways, feeling for any openings in the floor he couldn't see. Above him, he heard the voices in French, but they were unintelligible by the time they reached him down here.

It wouldn't take them long to come downstairs to find him. Now, it was only a two on one fight, and he had no qualms about that. Providing they weren't built like that German boulder he'd just dropped down the chute.

He'd reached the steps, and while he could see up, the stairs themselves were poorly lit. He tested each one.

"I found Friedrick. He's dead."

"Motherfucker!"

"Find him. They both fell down the hole."

"Maybe he's dead too."

"We aren't that lucky. He crawled away."

"What if he fell the rest of the way down?"

"Go check. I'll clear this floor."

Corsair backtracked down the stairs. He kept his hand on the concrete steps and sidled around until he was under the staircase.

A glow danced around in the dark, and he realized the man was using his cellphone's flashlight. Its beam was spread out and weak, barely illuminating more than five feet around the man. He moved down the corridor with the phone held over his head.

The view Corsair got was a surreal figure following a light. In any other situation, he might think it looked like a tomb raider or an elf following a fairy into a tunnel. Here, though, it looked like a scared, dangerous man.

Corsair moved out from beneath the steps and started slowly behind the tomb raider. As long as he remained in his path, Corsair trusted there were no holes to tumble down. When he was within ten feet, he picked up the pace without making any noise. In fact, the only sound echoing in the darkened tunnel was the man's labored breathing.

Corsair took a long stride forward and wrapped his arm around the man's throat. He dropped his phone, which clattered to the concrete floor. His hands came up to pull at Corsair's arm until the American dragged the man to the ground and twisted his head around. The crack of vertebrae resounded in the dark.

The lifeless figure slid out of Corsair's arms, and he reached over to pick up the phone. With the flashlight, he searched the man, removing a Beretta nine-millimeter handgun. He slid it into the back of his waistband and climbed the steps.

He emerged at the top and stepped over to the nearest doorway. Corsair looked back and saw the footprints in the dust. He hoped the final man didn't see them until it was too late.

Corsair waited, listening.

"Leon, you find him?" the man asked in French.

There was no answer. Caleb heard the footfalls as the man returned to the stairs.

"Leon!" he called.

Corsair stepped out, leveling the Beretta at the man.

"He's not answering," Corsair told the man in French.

"Shit," the other muttered, turning slowly to face the American.

"Do you want to live or die?" Caleb asked.

"Live," the man responded.

"Tell Minuit it has to be her."

The man nodded and swallowed. His hand swept back for his own gun, but the Beretta bucked in Corsair's grip. The bullet hit the Frenchman in the chest, knocking him backwards. He vanished down the stairwell. Caleb heard the man rolling down the steps until he came to a stop.

He blew out his nose, trying to chase the smell of dust and sulfur away.

32

Belize City, Belize

Lee sat in the sweltering car on the side of the road. Despite the sun going down, the air hadn't cooled much. She could have kept the car running to blow the cold air, but a running vehicle on a small dead-end street might attract attention.

The address she'd gotten from the hacker's house led her here. There still wasn't an identification on the informant who called the OOC, but Lee followed procedure, calling in the forensic team to sweep the home. Perhaps they'd find a fingerprint or some piece of data to link to a name. Quinn, the computer tech from the Basement, was going through the hard drives. So far, his outlook was grim. It appeared when she entered the house and maybe when she tried to access the computer, it went into a self-destruct mode. Quinn couldn't tell if the self-destruct was triggered remotely or on the premises. Given the cameras in and around the house, it seemed reasonable that the hacker knew she was at the house.

"He's probably out of the country already," Quinn told her after spending a few minutes in what he donned "the control room." He surmised from the intricate setup that this guy was a top-tier hacker, which must mean he had an escape plan in place for this kind of incursion. "Why didn't you wait until you knew he was home? We might have gotten something from him."

Lee didn't argue with him. She knew he never did field work and wouldn't understand. She was already approaching an unsub in a foreign country without backup. It would have been nice to wait, but once she spotted the external cameras, Lee assumed time was of the essence.

Quinn assured her he would get her whatever he found as soon as he had it, but her hovering wasn't going to help. Lee hadn't included the manila envelope she found. Once she realized what it was, she returned it to the drawer and continued her search. Then she disconnected the cameras. Her excuse was to limit the unsub's ability to watch them search the house. Once the cameras were off, she removed the manila envelope, leaving the cash behind. There was a big difference between reviewing evidence and misplacing thousands of dollars.

Now she stared at the little bungalow-style house in the cul-de-sac near the shore. The neighborhood could almost pass for a lower-middle-class one in Daytona Beach. However, while she waited, she perused a few of the local listings in Belize City to find most were in the mid to high six-figure range.

She waited until she saw some life in the house. Corsair was careful, and it would be logical for him to implement his own surveillance. The last thing she wanted to do was spook the man, who might well be the most dangerous person she'd ever encountered. After all, she only wanted to talk to him. If she could come to some understanding, then Caleb Saunders might help her wrest control of the Office of Compliance from Carl Winston.

The street was quiet. The only people she'd seen so far appeared to be American tourists renting a vacation house for a week of tropical sun. There was a beach, albeit a rocky one, on the backside of the house. A path wide enough to accommodate golf carts, ATVs, or just wagons, was cut into the hillside leading down from the houses.

Lee considered making an approach on the beach. If Corsair or Khloe Evans went down to the water, they might not balk at a curious stranger approaching. Of course, now that she'd had two run-ins with Corsair, he'd recognize her instantly. But Khloe wouldn't. That might be Lee's best chance to make contact with Saunders.

The girl came from Ohio, and according to her records, her parents were still living up there. Initially, she was hunted by the Cincinnati mob, but the organized crime there had been sent into shambles after Corsair killed the de facto leader in Mexico. Perhaps there was more information that their sources didn't have, or Khloe might be playing it safe by staying away from home until things settled down. Lee wondered though if there was another reason she was staying with Caleb Saunders. Corsair didn't strike her as the type to keep a girl around just because.

From all accounts, he was madly in love with his wife, and it would take more than just some girl to replace her.

Her phone buzzed in her pocket, and she looked at the screen. Winston.

"Have you gotten confirmation?" Winston asked, without offering a greeting.

"Not yet," she told him. "Quinn's tearing through the computers right now. I have a team at the closest airports reviewing footage, too."

"Corsair won't be using a commercial airline," he scolded her.

"Not likely, but if we ignore it, then it leaves him an avenue to escape."

Winston grunted. "Lee, we need to close this up."

It was Winston's way of deflecting the blame to Lee. He'd make a snide remark here or there about how she let him get away in Mexico. Lee bit her tongue. She'd replayed the night in Mexico over in her head, and she admitted that she miscalculated her approach to Saunders. Although, she walked away from the encounter, and that kept her thinking that perhaps it wasn't as large a misstep as it appeared.

"Carl, you trained this guy," she reminded him. "He's the best there is. You know there's no easy way to wrap this up."

"I'm not sure he's the best," Winston retorted, without a lot of resolve. She knew she was playing to his ego. By labeling Corsair as Winston's handiwork, it put her boss in a tight position. Winston knew how skilled Caleb Saunders was, and denying it implied that Winston wasn't as skilled a handler as he'd like everyone to think. It also shifted the blame off Lee. After all, how could she be expected to outthink one of the OOC's craftiest assets?

"Come on, Carl. Who can you send up against him? I'll track him down eventually, but catching him will be a different task altogether. He's got a decade of rust on him, but he's still better than anyone we're training now."

"Hmm," her boss mused.

"If he's here, we'll confirm it. There's always the possibility that Corsair instigated the call to throw us off his scent." Lee didn't believe that at all, but it was best to keep Winston in the dark.

"True," he agreed. "Just keep me apprised."

Winston hung up without a farewell. Before she could return the phone to the console where it had been sitting, it buzzed again.

"I accessed the security footage," Quinn told her when she answered. "I'm sending you a screenshot."

Lee pulled the phone away from her face to see a text come across the screen. When she opened it, a picture of Caleb Saunders appeared. He was standing on the street in front of the blue and white house.

"That's him, right?" Quinn asked.

"Yes," Lee acknowledged, feeling a mixture of elation and disappointment. Mostly, she didn't want to call Winston back with this update. That was inevitable. Quinn would include the image in his report, which Winston would get in the morning. That gave her the rest of the day to investigate before she alerted her superior.

She turned her attention back to the house at the end of the cul-de-sac.

Are you inside, Caleb?

The better question was how long could she wait before approaching the house? By this time tomorrow, she'd have to release the fugitive team to hunt for Corsair, and she'd lose any control she had over their actions.

She still had a few hours to wait in hopes that Corsair or Khloe Evans showed themselves. Lee leaned back in her seat and wiped the sweat off her brow.

33

Cartagena de Indias, Colombia

Minuit stood in the middle of the street. A uniformed officer was talking to one of the Germans that Tolazar hired. The man held his right arm and dried blood caked along his temple. By the time Minuit disarmed the grenade and exited Doña Lola, Corsair had escaped.

"Can you contact Captain Torres?" she asked the officer as she approached him.

The policeman eyed her with some familiarity before nodding.

That was easy.

As the cop stepped to the side to call the captain, Minuit turned to her hired muscle. "Which way did he go?"

The man motioned across the street. "He climbed into that building. Friedrick and the others followed him. I think he dislocated my elbow, though."

Minuit scowled. She'd completed missions in far worse shape than that, but she didn't point that out. After all, she'd just been sitting face to face with Corsair, and he escaped.

Now she struggled with that conversation. She hated Caleb Saunders with every fiber of her being, but it made little sense for him to show up like that. It was reckless and dangerous. At best, Corsair had fifteen minutes to survey the restaurant before making contact. There'd be no way to ensure that every exit hadn't been covered by Minuit's crew.

The fact that they weren't fell on her. She hadn't expected Corsair to find her or even attempt to talk with her. It surprised her, and it made no sense. What did it gain him? Of course, he tried to manipulate her by playing with her emotions. Minuit could normally read a person, but Corsair had similar training. He could easily appear to be genuine while lying through his teeth.

"Captain Torres is on his way," the officer told her.

"Can we get into that building?" she asked, pointing across the street at the dilapidated structure covered with murals and posters.

"We should wait on the captain," the policeman replied.

"Call him back," she insisted. "I'm going in one way or the other."

"I can't just allow you to trespass in there."

"You can stop me, but first I'd call Lieutenant General Márquez. It might save your job."

The officer stammered, staring back at the Frenchwoman. Minuit walked toward a boarded-up door.

"Get over here," she shouted at the German.

"My arm?" He waved his limp forearm.

"Get the fuck over here! Your other hand works fine, doesn't it?"

The man obeyed, and the police officer followed along, trying to figure out how to stop the woman. She counted on his reticence. After all, she'd dropped a few big names, and presumably Torres already confirmed her importance by telling the officer he was on his way.

Minuit reached behind the plywood and pried with her fingers. The screws holding the wood in place allowed some movement, but not enough.

"Give me some help!" she insisted of both men.

The German slid the meaty fingers of his left hand behind the plywood while he held his elbow close to his torso. The two gave a sharp pull. A wrenching of metal on metal sounded as one screw pulled out of the door frame.

"You! Give us a hand!" Minuit demanded of the officer.

Reluctantly, he came over and grabbed the bottom and heaved.

"Together," Minuit scolded.

The three pulled again, and the weight of the plywood came loose, dropping to the ground. Behind the sheet, an open doorway loomed. Minuit started into the building.

"You don't need to go in alone," the German advised.

"Are you going to protect me?" she asked him, eying his wounded arm.

The German looked over at the police officer, who gave an exasperated sigh. "I'll go with her."

Minuit didn't wait on the policeman as she charged into the darkened building. Inside, the smell of mold and dust filled her nostrils. She waved her hand in front of her face as if it would disperse the particles and relieve her senses. Minuit began to slow her breathing, knowing that inhaling too much dust might create a coughing fit.

"Do you have a light?" she asked the policeman.

"Yes," he replied, pulling a small tactical flashlight from his belt. When he turned it on, white light washed over the corridor, revealing piles of trash, puddles of what she hoped was water, and feces, both animal and human. The stench overpowered the cop, who covered his nose. Minuit seemed unfazed by what she saw, and she continued through the building.

"What's your name?" she asked the officer.

"Rafael Garcia," he responded.

"Good, Garcia. Keep the light on. We're going up the stairs."

"Miss, shouldn't we wait on Captain Torres or some backup?"

Without turning back, Minuit replied, "There is no time for that."

"Who is this man?" he asked nervously.

"He's a killer, but I want to get him alive. If you see him, don't engage."

"Why?" Garcia asked.

"He'll kill you," she told him. Minuit heard him suck in a breath.

On the second floor, Garcia shined the light around. "What's that?" he asked, directing the beam on a mound on the floor.

Minuit approached the figure and nudged it over with her foot. It was one of the French guys, but she couldn't remember his name.

"His head," Garcia noted. Minuit didn't need to get closer to see the awkward angle the neck made. Corsair snapped the man's neck.

"Come on," she urged. "We can't help him."

"Look at the floor," Garcia said, shining the light on a trail of footprints. There were signs of scuffling near the body, then a single set walked away toward the steps behind them.

"He went upstairs," Minuit deduced before returning to the stairs.

"What if he's up there?" Garcia asked.

"We stop him," Minuit explained, although she had a sinking sensation that all she was going to find were three more bodies. None of which would belong to Corsair.

"Oh, shit!" Garcia exclaimed, shining the light above their heads. The body of Friedrick hung through an opening in the ceiling like he'd been pinned to the concrete with a tack.

Minuit stared up at the figure for a full second before turning back to the stairs again. "Let's go."

Garcia pulled his police-issue Jericho 941 from his holster. Minuit glanced back at the nervous officer who trailed behind her. She started to remind him not to shoot her in the back on accident, but the Frenchwoman thought Garcia might take the remark to be demeaning.

She stopped below where another body splayed across several steps. The front of the man was stained with blood where a bullet pierced his chest. To Minuit, it looked like the shot hit him in the heart. He was probably dead before he fell down the stairs.

"Who is this man?" Garcia asked again.

Minuit ignored the question this time. At the third floor, she knelt down to study the footprints. Dried blood on the floor indicated where this latest victim had been standing when Corsair shot him.

More footprints went up the next flight of stairs. Minuit followed them as they led her and Garcia to the back of the building, where the prints ended at the edge where an entire side of the structure no longer existed. From her viewpoint, she stared down over a view of a treed courtyard below.

The sun had gone down, but the last bits of daylight clung to the sky in a red-orange hue. Minuit leaned over the edge to peer down the side of the building. The climb down would have been easy for Corsair. Her eyes scanned the ground for any sign of her former lover. A few people milled around the courtyard, but all of them appeared to be locals doing ordinary chores.

"Is that him?" Garcia asked, pointing through two large banyan trees. A figure passed through the opening, and Minuit recognized Corsair casually walking away from the building. The man stopped and turned back to the building. Despite the distance, Minuit held his gaze for several seconds before Corsair lifted his hand to wave at her.

"Damn!" she cursed before turning back to Garcia. "Call Torres and tell him where to find..." She paused, considering how to identify Corsair. She added, "the subject."

The police officer pulled his radio out as Minuit vanished into the dark, leaving the officer alone on the ledge over Getsemani.

34

Cartagena de Indias, Colombia

Caleb took brisk steps as he passed a pair of women pulling clothes off a clothesline made from what appeared to be an old copper wire. He was surprised that some entrepreneurial spirit hadn't tried to recycle it for cash. Perhaps anyone who might do that knew they were stealing from these specific women. They both had the wizened faces of grandmothers. What monster would steal the clothesline of someone's grandmother?

Caleb glanced back to see no one following him. He was certain that only four men entered the old ramshackle building, but he didn't openly accept that. Such suppositions might get a man killed. He still needed to get out of the neighborhood before anyone spotted him. Plenty of people on the street would have seen him escape up the side of the wall, and once they found the bodies, there'd be another manhunt for him. Corsair wanted to be out of the neighborhood before that happened.

He chanced another look over his shoulder at the face of the building he'd just descended. It hadn't been a difficult climb, but it took him longer than he wanted. Every second put him in more danger.

His eye caught a movement at the upper floor where he'd been. Two shapes appeared on the edge. One wore the uniform of a police officer, and the other's shapely figure identified her as Camille.

Caleb stared at the woman whose bed he shared so many years ago. She was staring down at him as the officer pointed his direction. So much for getting away unseen. He'd lost precious time.

Despite the rush, he paused long enough to wave at the woman standing atop the neighborhood. He couldn't see her face clearly, but he imagined the reaction wasn't congenial.

Caleb turned and sprinted under the trees. It would take them several minutes to get down from up there, but the cop would call in reinforcements. He needed to get on the street and into a crowd.

Of course, that's what they'd expect him to do. There weren't a lot of options, but he cut down a passageway leading out of the courtyard. Ducking his head beneath a stone arch, Caleb found himself on a cobblestone street next to a wall covered in canvas paintings. He turned to hurry down the road, trying to put some distance between himself and Minuit.

When he looked into her eyes earlier, he felt the same pang of regret he had when he thought of Audrey and

Jackson. Only he realized in this case, the pain wrought upon Camille had entirely been his fault.

He could shift the blame to Winston some, knowing now that the man had been using him as his own hit squad. But Caleb didn't do that. Winston had his part in this for sure, but Caleb made choices that he should have never made.

One of the questions that plagued him was why he'd never verified what Winston had told him. Some part of him didn't trust the orders, but the training taught him never to speculate about the mission.

Follow blindly. That's what he'd been taught. All that did was ensure Corsair was nothing more than a weapon. Only a weapon doesn't give a shit how it affects people. Caleb did.

He hadn't been lying to Camille either. The murder of Marc Lefevre might not have been the first crack in his devotion to Winston and the OOC, but it was the first moment he wondered if his actions had been true. Like a defect in a levee, it only took the right pressure at the right time for the levee to break. Marseille widened the break, and Turkey gushed through that opening, washing any allegiance he had to Carl Winston away.

Why couldn't he have realized that before Marseille? He could have avoided the pain he caused Camille. Even if he'd just waited long enough to hear Lefevre out on that rooftop. He'd been planning to inform Corsair of corruption in the OOC. If he'd have listened, Corsair might have taken a different tack. Perhaps he'd have refocused his efforts on taking Carl Winston down.

Why didn't you then?

It had been over a decade. Not once in that time had it crossed Caleb's mind to go after Winston. Since Caleb faked his death, how many lives had Winston taken through his own intermediaries? He could argue that he had a family to take care of. What kind of excuse was that? He knew soldiers and agents with families who dedicated their lives to the service of America.

Caleb knew the answer. He'd been frightened. Not of what would happen to him. No, Caleb was scared to find out all of it had been nothing more than a house of cards. If every life he'd taken in his career had been for Winston's profit, then he'd be staring at the face of a traitorous murderer every morning in the bathroom.

At the end of the street, Caleb turned left, heading toward the bay. This section of the city sat along the shoreline. He'd have to cross the waterway to get to the marina district. Even if he circled back to Centennial Park, he'd have to come back over to the bridge.

After turning, Caleb found himself on a quiet block with no businesses. A young teenage couple walked toward him on the other side of the street. The lovers held hands and laughed as they meandered along the sidewalk. Caleb watched them for a second as they strolled along.

He'd seen Camille now. There wasn't anything else he could do. Her eyes told him everything—she wasn't forgiving anything. Not that he expected it.

He chuckled as he thought about a fight with Audrey. Now, he couldn't recall what it was about. No doubt something he was at fault for. But it had been one of their first big fights after getting married. Caleb, who could kill a man with a toothpick, found he struggled with understanding relationship dynamics. He got hung up on who was right and who was wrong until it didn't matter. He'd dug himself so deep in a hole with Audrey that he was certain he wasn't cut out for wedded bliss. He smiled, recalling what she told him after the third day of fighting. "I don't give a shit if you think you are right. I want to be listened to."

It wasn't something he thought he was ever good at, but after that, he endeavored to listen to what was wrong. It rarely worked, because inevitably he'd go from listening to trying to fix it—something Audrey hated, and he never understood.

Now, ten years later, Caleb thought he had a better grasp of those emotional roller coasters. He thought he owed Camille the courtesy of a face to face. Now that he saw her, he wished he'd done it years ago.

It didn't matter if Camille had a change of heart. In fact, he expected her to only be angrier. Not that he was an expert in such things, but his decade of marriage often showed that those emotions don't always do anything but scar over. Despite how this turned out with Camille, he hoped she healed.

Caleb also knew if she came at him directly, he'd let her kill him. Not because he wanted to die. He just didn't want to kill her to save himself.

Of course, it didn't have to come to that. He could get Valentina and leave the country. Camille could continue her hunt for him. But hopefully, he'd disappear with Amanda completely this time.

At the next intersection, he took a right and froze. A motorcycle cop was leaning against his bike and talking to a young girl in her teens. The police officer locked eyes with Caleb for a split second before drawing his weapon.

"Stop right there," the cop demanded, aiming his weapon past the girl. She let out a shriek and cowered in front of the officer.

35

Cartagena de Indias, Colombia

Torres rode down the narrow streets of Getsemani. His head ached from lack of sleep. Garcia woke him up when he called, and Torres wasted no time running out of the house. His wife, used to his nightly jaunts, didn't question where he was going. She'd only done that once, and he reminded her that they lived in a much finer home than most of the other officers. If she'd prefer to go back to the village where her father lived, she could question him again. Now she just waited for him to leave before heading to bed alone.

Garcia reported that the American killed four foreigners, leaving their bodies in a rundown apartment building in Getsemani. He wondered if the man had been in the area when he'd visited the French bitch earlier.

Less than fifteen minutes after getting the call from Garcia, he got a follow-up. Another officer confronted the American on Calle 25 near the waterfront. The officer whose name Torres didn't know apparently had the suspect at gunpoint. When the officer tried to cuff the man, the American disarmed the officer, breaking his arm while in the process. At least he hadn't killed the idiot.

Torres pulled up behind another police-issued Suzuki to see a pretty little girl bending over a uniformed officer. The captain thought he recognized the young rookie's face, but he wasn't positive. All these kids start to look alike.

The girl turned to Torres. "He broke his arm!" she blurted out.

Torres knelt beside the cop. His forearm jutted out at an odd angle. "Did you call for a medic?" Torres asked.

The rookie nodded, trying to maintain his composure.

"You had your weapon drawn?"

"Yes, Captain. I thought he was complying when he caught my wrist. It happened so fast."

Torres listened without making a gesture. He'd been a victim of the same man last night, and while he didn't want to gloss over the mistake this rookie made, he felt some sympathy for him.

"Did he take your weapon?" Torres asked.

"No, sir. He took out the bullets," the girl explained. "He threw the gun on the roof." She pointed at the building across the street.

"We'll get someone to retrieve it," he assured the officer. "What's your name?"

"Herrera," the cop moaned, pulling his misshapen right arm closer to his body as if he was worried the captain might try to touch it.

"He was crazy," the girl told Torres.

"Which way did he go?"

Herrera motioned down the street with his head. "He ran that way, but I lost sight of him."

"He did, Captain," the girl repeated, putting her arm around Herrera.

"Are you his girlfriend?" Torres asked.

She shook her head. "I was just here. He was trying to protect me."

Torres reached to put his hand on the young cop's shoulder but stopped. Instead, he clapped his hand down on the boy's leg, hoping not to jar the injured arm. "You're lucky. I understand the suspect killed four men just before he encountered you."

"He told him he was sorry," the girl said.

"What?" Torres asked.

"He said he didn't mean to break the arm," Herrera answered.

"How nice of him," Torres remarked. His comment laced with thick sarcasm.

Both Herrera and the girl stared at the captain.

"Officer Herrera, I'm going to pursue. When the medic arrives, have them send units to follow me."

"Yes, sir," Herrera replied. "I'm sorry, sir."

"It's a lesson," Torres reminded him. He gave the girl a leer before adding, "At least you have a pretty nurse to care for you. Be sure to get her number."

The girl blushed, but cast her eyes at Herrera. Torres stood up, thinking that the broken arm might not be as tragic for the young rookie as it could be. The little girl saw him in action, and Torres bet it wet her panties a little.

If he'd had the time, he might have given the girl more attention. Instead, he'd let Herrera score with her.

As he started down the road, an ambulance pulled up, followed by a police cruiser. The captain waved at the officers from the cruiser while the medics focused on Herrera.

"Our suspect is nearby," Torres explained. "I want a full sweep of the neighborhood. Stop every American you see. Interrogate them and send me a picture before you let them go."

The two officers saluted and hurried to facilitate the search.

"Captain Torres," a feminine voice called.

Torres turned to see the French bitch coming down the sidewalk. She was walking with one of his officers, Carlos Gutiérrez.

"Captain, I found the lady over on Calle 33. She demanded I bring her to you," Carlos told him.

"She seems good at demands," Torres noted. "Your man assaulted another officer. Broke his arm."

"He killed four men," she reported.

"I've heard," Torres said. He wished he'd just let the fucking bitch Valentina go at this point. It was a struggle now, keeping ahead of this while this fucking *gringo* ran around killing people, even if they were foreign operatives of some sort.

"Captain, I've got a good idea why you are so invested in finding the suspect and the girl. Valentina's her name, right?"

"I don't know that we have that information," Torres stated.

"I do," she explained. "My understanding is that you are running a brothel, of sorts."

Torres puffed out his chest. "Accusations like that are unfounded."

The Frenchwoman smiled broadly as if she didn't have a care in the world. "The thing is, I don't need a foundation to make these accusations. I'm not bringing any charges against you. That's not my responsibility. All I want is the American agent."

"Agent?" Torres questioned, and he saw in the woman's face her error. She'd been careful not to reveal too much to the captain, but her enthusiasm in yoking Torres gave her a slip of the tongue. "Who is this agent?"

Her smile returned. "Doesn't matter, and it's above your pay grade. I already spoke with Márquez. He's given me *carte blanche* to capture the American."

Torres folded his arms. "We are dealing with the situation as we speak."

"How?"

"We are conducting a complete search of this neighborhood. I have officers coming in to speak with every American male."

"Where are they sleeping?" the woman asked.

Torres shook his head. "We don't know. Carlos, do you have thoughts?"

"Captain, we've circulated the American's description to every hotel and hostel in the city. We can't cover every home rental or boarding house, as so many are unregistered."

"Anything?"

"One hostel in the old city reported a man that might fit his description. He checked in for three days, but he hasn't been seen since the first night."

"That fits," the woman interjected. "He's on the run and hasn't gone back."

"It also means he can be anywhere," Torres advised.

"Can we spread his description on the media?" she asked.

Carlos nodded. "I'll get the details to the local news. It'll take a little time."

The Frenchwoman considered that before regarding Torres. "Will that work?"

The captain nodded. "Do it, Carlos."

"Sir, he could be sleeping in the street somewhere," Carlos suggested.

The French bitch shook her head. "I saw him. He hadn't been on the street. I don't think he's changed clothes, but he certainly was able to wash up and look presentable."

"Why is he still here? He and the girl could have left town. It would make it easier to disappear."

The woman didn't respond, but her face tightened.

"It is curious that he showed up so close to where you are staying," Torres remarked. "Did you say you saw him?"

"He approached me while I was at dinner," she admitted, somewhat begrudgingly.

"Indeed." Torres fought back a smile. The French bitch was surprised by the American too. She hadn't prepared for him to approach her.

Why would he do that, anyway?

"How did he know where you were eating?" he wondered.

The Frenchwoman folded her arms across her chest. Something crossed her mind, and she didn't share it.

"What?" Torres asked.

"It's nothing."

"Look, I don't like working with you, but I certainly can't do my job and help you if you hold things back."

"The only person who came to see me was you," she noted.

"Are you suggesting I told him where you were staying?"

She shook her head. "No, but I'm wondering if he followed you."

Torres furrowed his brow. He was operating on a little over an hour of sleep, and his head still throbbed. He tried to remember if anyone followed him. The captain hadn't noticed. He'd been driven by Ramírez. How would the American follow him?

Then it clicked with Torres. He'd gone to the apartment, searching for Valentina. She must have told him where it was. Torres hadn't paid attention at the time, but it made sense.

Not really.

There was little about it that seemed logical. Why follow Torres at all? This American agent had proven himself to be capable and dangerous. What had been his endgame with Valentina? In fact, why would an American spy, for now Torres suspected the man was just that, want anything to do with a thirteen-year-old street whore?

Suddenly, Torres felt a sick feeling in his gut. Was he the target of this man? That didn't make sense. At best, he'd be arrested by his own police force for trafficking underage prostitutes. That wasn't something the Americans cared about.

Torres wondered if it was Valentina the man was after. But why? And how did this secretive French cunt have anything to do with it?

"Carlos." He waved the other man to the side as he raised a finger to signal the Frenchwoman to wait. Under his breath, he asked Carlos, "Call Daniel. Send him over to Valentina's flat. If this guy shows up there or even if Valentina does, he needs to pick them up."

Carlos nodded and hurried off.

"You have something planned?" the woman asked, stepping forward.

"No, I'm just covering my bases."

Her face widened into a grin. "You think the whore is the key?"

"You're smart," he said. "For a woman."

"I'll rip out your spleen too," she retorted.

36

Cartagena de Indias, Colombia

The boat had gotten dark, and Caleb told her not to turn on any lights. He didn't want her to attract any attention from the harbormaster, who might know the boat was supposed to be empty. Caleb had been gone for hours, and Valentina wanted off the cramped boat. She never cared for tight places, and after nearly twenty-four hours in this cabin, she was growing anxious.

Caleb promised to get her out of the city. While she was happy at that prospect, she thought about her little duffel bag in the flat. All of her possessions were in that bag, and while none of them were worth anything, she really worried about only one thing—the picture of her family. It was all she had in this world to remember them. If she didn't have at it, the girl worried she'd forget what her father or mother might look like. Even now, she wasn't sure that the voices she remembered were actually theirs or a figment of her imagination.

It won't take long to sneak in and get it.

After all, it was late. The girls would all be in the square turning tricks. She could take the long way around the city and come in from the north. Five minutes to slip in, grab the picture and maybe a change of clothes, and get out. Captain Torres would be in the square, wouldn't he?

It took her over an hour to skirt the clock tower and approach the building from the north. Her flat was on an upper level above the square, and Valentina lingered by the sculpture of Gertrude, a popular tourist site where it was considered good luck to touch the bare breasts of the rotund, naked woman. She could see the statue from the apartment, and somehow it was the only thing that made her smile since arriving in Cartagena de Indias. The artwork reminded Valentina of an aunt's home in Venezuela. It wasn't the nudity or likeness, but the sculpture triggered some nurtured emotion in her and made her feel safer.

Now she hung next to the figure and stared up at the window of her flat. Anxiety twisted in her chest. Was this a bad idea? She thought about the picture of her family. Her heart longed to see the face of her father. After these months under Torres's thumb, Valentina found adulthood faster than she should have. The realization that she would never see any of her family settled in an acceptance of facts.

That meant the only thing she had was that photograph.

"Fuck him," she mumbled to herself. Torres took enough from her, and she'd be damned if he took her family, too.

The girl straightened her back with a rush of bravado. Five minutes. She needed to get into the unit and leave. Valentina, emboldened by this determination, strode across the street to the building.

At the door to her apartment, she paused for a brief second, placing her ear against the cheap door to listen. No voices came from the other side. She opened the door and walked inside.

The girls might have picked up a little. That usually meant Torres had come by. He'd almost always scold them for the mess they left. After he was gone, Izzie would push everyone to straighten up and, at least, throw away the trash and old food. They took turns doing laundry, with one taking the task every week. Since they basically shared the clothes, it made some sense to them.

Hurry up.

She marched across the room to the area she deemed her corner. Her bag was upside down. Its contents spread over the floor.

"No!" she gasped, reaching down to pick up a wadded paper.

Unfolding it, she found the crumpled image of her family. Valentina spread it out on the edge of the kitchen counter and tried to smooth the wrinkles away.

It had to be Torres. If the girls went through her stuff, she didn't think they'd damage the picture like that. Every one of them had some weird memento that reminded them of the time before, and it was sacrilege to mess with another's prize. Clothes and other things were all fair game, but memories were sacred.

The picture would never be perfect, but it would have to do for now. She stuck in back in her bag.

Her stomach grumbled, reminding her that she'd only eaten a few stale crackers the boat's owners left on the sailboat. She opened the fridge to see a few Manzana sodas and some questionable leftovers. She grabbed one of the canned drinks and opened a cabinet. Valentina found a small bag of plantain chips.

As she ripped the bag open, she crossed the apartment and picked up her duffel bag. Sweeping across the room, she gathered a few articles of clothing and threw them in the bag.

When she had enough to last her a few days, Valentina stood in the middle of the flat. Slowly, she rotated around, surveying the room. A sensation of relief coursed through her. The place was barely livable, and even though the sailboat Caleb had them hiding in was small, it revealed how much of a dump she'd been residing in. It wasn't some kind of enlightenment. More than that, over the months here, she'd just accepted that this was what life looked like. While she'd started making plans to run away, those always felt more like pipe dreams than a reality she'd ever see.

But at this moment, freedom seemed to be right there. Caleb promised her he'd get her away from here. She wanted to trust him. He wasn't like the men that pawed her and stripped her naked every night. No, he reminded her more of her father. Or, perhaps, a better example was an older brother.

Part of her was wary. Torres promised to take care of her, too. But then she'd not seen the depth of men's depravity yet. She'd known boys who wanted to get between her legs, but they'd mask it with sweet talk and platitudes. Here she was regarded as garbage. Valentina developed a better sense of people now, knowing the johns who were easy targets versus the ones who were dangerous. Caleb didn't come across as either, though.

What other choice did she have? If she stayed here, Torres would either make her miserable or kill her. Anything had to be an improvement.

Valentina worried that Caleb might only get her out of the city and dump her. On the other hand, it concerned her that he'd just take her with him. While he didn't strike her as a threat, Valentina suspected he didn't really want to drag her back to America. Could he even do that? She only had a little schooling when she was little, but she'd read that too many Latinos were driven back over the borders because the Americans didn't want them. Everyone she knew saw America as a pipe dream.

If he did take her, could she go back to school? When Valentina was little, she remembered her mother watching a show about a lawyer. The idea of becoming a lawyer intrigued her. She'd need to learn English too, though.

Yes, she could do that. The very thought of Americanizing herself gave her some hope. She hoisted the duffel bag over her shoulder and started for the door.

Before she made it across the room, the door swung open. Daniel Ramírez stood in the frame.

Valentina let out a scream as he came at her.

37

Cartagena de Indias, Colombia

C aleb's back ached as he stumbled along the sidewalk. He silently praised the twenty-four-hour pharmacy he found near the marina. Armed with some muscle relaxers and some off-brand ibuprofen, he hoped that the meds would allow his body to forget the two-story fall he'd taken. It would have been worse if the German hadn't been under him for the first drop.

He swallowed two ibuprofens and a cyclobenzaprine without anything to wash it down. Caleb bought some guava-filled pastries, and a few bottled waters at the drugstore. It wasn't an ideal dinner at this time of night, but the high sugar content would sustain them a little longer.

Once he got away from that cop, he felt some guilt. When he took the officer's gun, he applied too much pressure to the man's arm. Caleb released it as soon as he felt the bone break, even apologizing for it. In the past, Corsair would consider that collateral damage. Anyone interfering with the mission became a target. He might have even killed the man if it progressed the mission.

That he ever thought like that disturbed him. After confronting Camille, he was now more acutely aware of the damage he'd done at the OOC.

When he approached the marina, he stopped across the street, pressing himself against the building. In the shadows, he watched the dock. There didn't seem to be anyone living permanently on their boats, but that didn't mean someone hadn't come for the night. Along the dock finger where the Hans Christian had been berthed, there was only one boat with lights glowing from the portholes.

The night air drifted off the water. A gentle breeze tussled his hair. Under different circumstances, this evening would be a nice one to enjoy in the cockpit of a sailboat with a cold beer. Instead, he lingered in the dark like a sentinel on watch. In the distance, he heard a motorcycle scream in the night, and he waited as the bike eventually zipped past him with a solitary rider silhouetted against the water and purple night sky.

Once he was confident that no one was watching the vessel, he pushed off the side of the building and strolled casually down the walkway. He boarded the darkened Hans Christian sailboat to find it empty.

"Valentina?" he called as he came down the companionway.

He'd warned her not to turn on the lights lest they alert their boat neighbors that someone was squatting aboard. When he didn't get an answer, he stopped on the steps, listening. In the pitch black of the cabin, someone could be waiting for him. He held onto a breath, waiting. The boat felt empty. No breathing or moving sounded from the dark, and after a full two minutes, he proceeded into the cabin.

Valentina wasn't there. Caleb instructed her to wait here for him, but he hadn't forbidden her from going anywhere. That might have been smart, but Caleb assumed she understood the gravity of the situation.

She's a teenager.

For only being thirteen, Valentina often presented herself as older. Her life sentence was responsible for that, and Caleb, whose experience with teens was nonexistent, forgot that she was actually far from being an adult.

Did she get hungry? Or did Torres find her?

He broke his own rule and found a light switch. The cabin showed no signs of a struggle. There was a scrawled note on the counter.

"I'll be back. I need to get something."

Stupid girl.

Where could she possible go? He'd been gone a long time, but he warned her that might happen. There's no reason she should have given up. He promised after he did what he had to do, they'd leave in the morning.

Caleb realized the only place she would go—her apartment. He hadn't asked her if she needed anything because it was simply too dangerous to go back to get it.

By now, Torres would have responded to the run-in he had with Camille's guys and the motorcycle cop. It meant Torres might know that Valentina wasn't with him. Just like how Caleb found Torres, her apartment was the best link. A man like Torres had subordinates he could station on the building in case Valentina showed up.

He flipped over the note that Valentina left him. "If you get back, stay here. Remember my instructions." he wrote.

It was risky, however, Caleb thought if Valentina returned alone then she'd succeeded and hadn't been coerced to disclose their hideout. Or Torres was smart enough to only watch her and tail her back.

If Torres did find her, then he would likely use any means necessary to find Caleb. Even if he wasn't inclined, Camille would waste no time coming for him.

He had to assume the boat was no longer viable for him. If he waited here, it left him open to an assault. He'd have limited room to mount any defense, too. As if Camille would give him a chance to fight. She'd surround the boat and wait him out. Or Torres could storm the vessel with a tactical team. Could Caleb fight off ten to twelve armed men boarding the sailboat? Not likely.

But he'd come back nonetheless to find Valentina. Caleb needed to trust his instincts and pray that Valentina returned safely. He left a light on, hoping Valentina obeyed the note and followed his previous instructions to turn out the lights. It was far from failsafe, but if Camille came aboard to lie in wait, she'd leave the lights the way she found them. He guessed Torres's men would do the same thing so as not to alert Caleb that anything was amiss. Of course, this was a thirteen-year-old girl, so pinning everything on her following instructions was quite a gamble.

Disappointed, he didn't have time to sleep off the aches in his body. Caleb crossed the walkway again to the shore.

He'd get to the apartment and find Valentina. If she was still there, they'd leave tonight. While he wanted to get some rest, Caleb worried that every minute he stayed in Cartagena kept him in Camille's crosshairs a little longer.

38

Cartagena de Indias, Colombia

The front door slammed open. Captain Alejandro Torres stepped in the door. His eyes fell on the girl seated in a wooden chair in the middle of the room.

"I haven't touched her yet," Ramírez reported. "Not much, at least. She tried to run, and I hit her to stop her."

Torres cocked his head to the right, maintaining eye contact with the young girl.

"I didn't mean to," she blubbered.

"You didn't mean to?" the captain repeated. "What? Run away? Help some American attack me and Carlos? Who is he?"

She shook her head. "I don't know. We never met."

"Are you telling me some stranger risked his life to help a useless fucking whore?"

Valentina's head bobbed as he talked. "I was scared, and just reacted. You were hitting me."

"You are right. I was hitting you, whore." Torres made three strides across the room and struck her in the face with the back of his hand. The blow split the girl's bottom lip on the right. A ribbon of red appeared on her mouth. "You're mine to do with as I want."

Her head twisted from side to side. "No, I'm not."

This time, Torres balled his fist and punched the girl in the face. He felt her nose break under the blow, sending a dribble of red out her left nostril.

"Just kill me," she begged.

"Kill you?" Torres questioned. "I'm going to make you wish I killed you."

"Fuck you," she spat a glob of blood from her mouth.

Torres chuckled. The red splatter covered his face in tiny droplets. He turned and walked to the kitchen counter where a pile of napkins sat. He wiped this face, clearing most of the blood away but streaking a few of the thicker drops.

"Valentina, why have you been so difficult? I try to take care of you. You have a nice apartment, clothes, food. What do you want?"

"This isn't taking care of me," she snapped. "It's hell."

Torres turned and leaned into her face. "It's not hell. Not yet."

Valentina's eyes welled as she fought back the tears. "I'm not scared," she stated boldly, even if it was a lie. Torres could see the fear in her eyes. Her hands quivered with the energy dumped into her system from the adrenaline. The girl was on the brink of losing control.

"I want to know where the American is," Torres told her.

"He dumped me."

"I think that's a lie," he retorted. "If you do it again, I'll let Daniel take you in the back. You know he likes it when you scream."

Her head twisted back and forth.

"Val, tell me where he is. I can bring you back in the fold. There'll be some punishment, but nothing too severe. We want to keep you pretty for the men."

"He really left me. That's why I came back. Where else was I going to go?"

Torres leaned over and picked up the duffel bag filled with clothes. "Daniel said he found you with this on you. Looks like you thought you weren't coming back."

"Uh, I thought you wouldn't take me."

Torres narrowed his eyes. "You have no desire to come back," he said. "Let me tell you a story. When I was a younger man, I found a dog on the street. She was a pretty little bitch, but she had sharp teeth. The first time she bit me, I took a stick to her. The second time, I kicked her down. Do you know what I did the third time?"

Tears slid down her cheeks now, but she held her tongue.

"I took another stick to her. That time I broke her leg, and I felt badly. I nursed that dog back to health. Fed her by hand and cared for her until she was back on all four legs. It took months for her to recover. I thought I'd finally tamed her. But you know what?"

Valentina shook her head.

"The fucking dog bit me again. I shot her dead because after a while I had to recognize that some bitches can't be broken. I don't think you can learn. In fact, I'm certain you aren't capable of it."

"I am, Captain. I promise."

Torres squatted on his haunches.

"I learned my lesson from that mutt. You've started trouble, so I punish you. Yet, you don't learn, do you?"

Valentina nodded furiously.

"Where is the American?" he asked again.

The girl opened her mouth as if to speak, but nothing came out.

"Daniel, make her talk."

"Gladly, Captain," Ramírez snarled. His lecherous yellowed teeth gleamed as he turned to the young girl.

"Is that necessary?" a voice came from behind the pair of officers.

Torres spun around, surprised by the intrusion. The French bitch stood in the doorway.

"What are you doing here?" Torres demanded.

"I followed you," she answered, walking into the apartment. Valentina lifted her head to see the French agent approaching.

"This is none of your concern," Torres told her.

"You're investigating my suspect," the woman replied.

"I was going to call you when we had his location."

The woman brushed the captain aside and knelt in front of Valentina. The girl's face was turning a dark purple. The agent reached forward and stroked her bruised cheeks. The woman's head twisted around to glare at the two men.

"How old is she?" she demanded.

"I don't know," Torres lied.

The agent returned her focus to Valentina. "Thirteen," the girl replied.

Standing up, the woman held her palm against the prostitute's face. "Captain, while I appreciate your efforts to bring in my suspect, I do not care for your methods."

"Look, you don't give us any information. How we run our investigation is none of your concern."

"Is she your whore?" the Frenchwoman asked, spinning to face the two men.

"Of course not."

The woman looked back at Valentina, who seemed to understand the importance of not talking at the moment. "Captain Torres, what would Lieutenant General Márquez say about this?"

"Captain," Ramírez started, but Torres raised a hand.

"I don't know who you are, but I don't take kindly to threats," Torres said. "I don't care if you're fucking Márquez or not, I'll kill you if you get into my business."

The woman stepped closer to Torres without breaking her gaze. Nothing in her demeanor indicated she was scared of the two men. She gave the captain a coy grin. "Why don't you do that, then? But let me explain to you who I am and what I do. Just so you understand who you threatened. I kill people. A lot more people than a limp-dick shithead like you has done."

Ramírez reared back and swung a fist at the woman. She stepped back, letting the arm flash past her head. With both arms, she clapped them down on his arm, pinning them together like a vice. Before Torres registered what happened, Ramírez hit the ground on his back. The Frenchwoman drove her heel down on his throat.

"If you move, Captain, I'll crush his larynx and possibly those vertebrae in his neck. Either way, he's going to suffocate. It only matters whether he's paralyzed for those last few seconds."

Torres stepped away. "Fine. What do you want?"

"I want to talk to the girl without your masculine bullying."

"Let him up," Torres said.

The woman's head tilted to the right as if waiting for Torres.

"Please," Torres added.

"Manners are important," she told them as she lifted her foot off Ramírez. The officer rolled to his knees, struggling to get up. Neither the woman nor Torres offered him a hand.

"What's your name, child?"

"Valentina."

"You know the man who helped you, yes?" she asked the girl.

A nod.

"Did he tell you his name?"

"Caleb."

A strange look passed over the French agent's face. Torres thought it was a surprise. Was this not the man she was looking for?

"What did he do to you?" she asked.

"He stopped—he stopped me from being hurt."

The agent glanced back at Torres with a determined countenance. "Was the captain hurting you?"

Valentina cast a wary eye toward Torres. Then she nodded. Torres stifled a growl under his breath.

"Captain, do you plan to hurt this child again?" the woman asked while holding her face level with Valentina's.

"Of course not," the captain lied.

"Valentina, I promise he isn't going to hurt you."

The girl didn't seem convinced. She moved her gaze between Torres and the Frenchwoman.

"Captain, you are telling me you aren't pimping this girl out, correct?"

Indignant, Torres replied, "Of course not."

"Good, Valentina. When I've finished with my business here, you can come with me."

The girl turned to Torres as if searching for an answer.

"Captain, do you have a problem with that, or do you plan to arrest a thirteen-year-old girl?"

"We just want her to have a safe, happy life," Torres remarked through nearly gritted teeth.

"See." The woman smiled at Valentina. "But I need to find Caleb first."

"Are you going to kill him?" she asked, concerned.

The Frenchwoman continued to beam at the girl. "No, but my employer wants to speak with him."

"He really did leave me," Valentina told the woman.

"I'm sure, but where did he leave you?"

"It was a boat over on the other side of the bay. A big white and blue sailboat."

The woman reached up and touched her face gently again. Valentina winced. "Don't worry, no one else will strike you. Do you know where Caleb went?"

"He asked me where I lived."

"You told him here?" the woman asked.

Valentina nodded. "He wanted to know if the captain came by the flat much."

Again, the French bitch turned to look at Torres. Her face was pinched, casting a warning at the captain.

"Valentina, when did he leave you?"

"Early this morning. He promised he'd be back."

"But you left on your own," she asked the girl.

"He said we'd be leaving town, and I thought I could sneak in and get the photo of my family. It's all I have."

The Frenchwoman listened. "Did you tell him you were coming here?"

Valentina shook her head. "I just left a note saying I had to get something."

The Frenchwoman stood up and faced Torres. "I meant what I said," she told the captain. "When this is done, the girl goes with me."

Torres curled his lip, but nodded in agreement.

"If he doesn't find her in this boat, he's going to come for her."

"We can wait for him here then," Torres said with some satisfaction.

The Frenchwoman glanced between the two officers. "He'll kill you."

"I'll bring in more men," Torres countered.

"He'll kill them too," the woman explained. "Do you have another place to keep her?"

"Yeah, I have an apartment two blocks from here."

"Let's take her there," the woman told him. "Valentina can give me the details of the boat on the way."

"I'll come along," Torres suggested.

The Frenchwoman cast a disgust-filled look at him. "No, you'd only get in the way. Besides, he's still going to come for her."

"What makes you say that?"

The woman didn't answer, but she had a reposeful expression on her face.

39

Belize City, Belize

After sleeping in her car, Lee's neck felt like someone tried to twist her head off. She stretched, feeling exhausted. She'd slept on and off, watching the house where she suspected Corsair might be hiding.

So far, there'd been no sign of him. In fact, there'd been no sign that anyone was in the house.

How long would she wait before giving up and leaving? That answer came immediately. She wouldn't just leave, but she couldn't just wait here. In the next few hours, Quinn's report would reach the OOC, and Carl Winston would see the screen grab that Quinn took from the hacker's security feed. At that point, she'd have to answer for not calling in the fugitive retrieval team.

Fuck it.

Lee got out of the car and walked toward the house. She searched for any evidence of cameras. There were two mounted on the front of the house. They were not high tech, and they looked like models one could find easily on Amazon. A cheap do-it-yourself setup. Not something Corsair would do. More like surveillance for the home-owner who rented the place out. They likely got the feed online so they could check on their property from Chicago or Dallas or wherever they lived full time.

That didn't mean Corsair didn't hijack the feed for himself. Lee assumed as much. Once she showed herself, he'd know who she was. Hopefully, he didn't come out shooting.

Stay calm. Just knock on the door.

She did. *Knock. Knock. Knock.*

It took a minute before someone asked, "Who is it?" The voice belonged to a woman.

"I live next door," Lee lied.

"What do you need?"

"We just arrived, and I was hoping you had some bat-teries. AA. Of course, I came all the way down here and forgot them."

"Hold on," came the reply.

The sound of bolts turning in the wood came from the door. Then a crack appeared, and Lee stared at the face of Khloe Evans.

"How many batteries do you need?" she asked.

"Two," Lee said.

Khloe said, "Wait."

When she turned from the door, Lee stuck her foot in the crack. "Khloe, is Caleb here?"

The woman spun around, grabbing the door to slam it. Lee's foot prevented it from closing.

"Wait, Khloe, I'm not here to hurt you."

The girl backed away quickly with wide, fear-filled eyes. Lee put both hands on the door, swinging it open. She stepped inside. The girl hadn't called for Caleb, and if he'd been home, he would have come to the door instead of Khloe.

"Where is he?" Lee asked. "I just want to talk to him."

"You're with the OOC?"

Lee lifted both hands to show she was unarmed and to signal that she meant no harm. "I am, but I need his help."

"He said you want to kill him."

"No, Khloe, I don't."

The girl pressed her back to the wall. "He said you tried."

"No, my boss wants to," Lee explained. "I need Caleb's help to prove my boss is a bad guy."

"He's gone," Khloe repeated.

"I assume he is, but you can talk to him."

She shook her head. "No, he set me up here, but he left. He said if he stayed, it would be too dangerous."

Lee nodded along, but she didn't believe the girl.

"Fine, but you're the closest thing I have to him."

Khloe's eyes widened again. "Are you arresting me?"

Lee shook her head. "No, but you have to get a message to him. The OOC knows he was here just a few days ago. Within the hour, I have to report to my boss that he is in Belize. At that point, a fugitive retrieval team will be sent down to find him. I can't control them."

"What do you want?" Khloe wondered.

"I believe Caleb performed jobs—kills, that is—for Carl Winston. I think Caleb realized he was being manipulated and dropped off the grid. If I can work with Caleb, I hope we can prove that Carl was murdering people with government resources. We can remove him."

"I don't know," Khloe said. "I'm not sure if I'll ever talk to him again. He was pretty adamant about no communication."

Lee nodded again, still not believing the girl. Although she did admit that Khloe Evans lied quite proficiently.

"He can't run forever," Lee pointed out. "Corsair is the best in the world, but he's still human. And he has his daughter with him. It will be disastrous if something happens to him. What will she do?"

Khloe didn't answer.

"Listen, remember my name, Lee Hubbard. I'm the deputy director at the OOC, so Caleb can email me or call me through there."

"He won't trust that," Khloe reminded her.

Lee chuckled. "No, he won't, but he's smart enough to get in contact with me. Explain to him what I want."

"Khloe?" a child's voice came from the other room.

"Stay in there, sweetie," Khloe announced loudly.

Lee smiled. "Amanda?" she asked.

Khloe shook her head. This time, the lie was obvious, and the girl knew Lee saw it.

"I'm not going to hurt her or you," Lee promised. "You'll have to take me at my word."

"He's really gone, Ms. Hubbard," Khloe told her. "I'm protecting her so that what you say won't happen."

That part Lee believed. At least that Khloe was protecting Amanda.

"Here's a freebie then. It might help you trust me." Lee handed the manila envelope to Khloe. "I found this at the house of someone who reported that Corsair was going to come kill him. The guy only lives about fifteen miles from here. I'd suggest you find a new place to hide out before the rest of the OOC finds a strand of evidence leading them to you. They will take you and Amanda as collateral for Caleb. There's nothing I can do to stop that."

Khloe took the envelope and pressed it to her chest.

"Tell him I helped," Lee said. "I'll leave you alone."

Without waiting for the woman to let her out, Lee exited the house. She swept her eyes over her periphery in case Caleb Saunders actually was waiting to pounce. She made it back to the car when her phone buzzed.

"Hubbard," she answered.

"It's JW Collins."

"JW, what's up?"

"We have a Corsair sighting. The news in Cartagena, Colombia, has issued a warning about an American fitting Corsair's description."

"Colombia?"

"Yes, ma'am. Mr. Winston has ordered the fugitive retrieval team down there."

"Shit, can you get me on a flight there?"

"I'm already working on it," Collins told her. "Next flight out of Belize City is in three hours."

Lee sighed. Maybe she could sleep on the plane. She shifted the rental car in gear and drove away from the house where Khloe and Amanda Harrod were hiding. She hoped Khloe took her advice about leaving. It might generate some goodwill with Caleb Saunders. Assuming Winston's kill team didn't get to him first.

40

Cartagena de Indias, Colombia

Corsair trudged back across the city. He'd slept sitting up on a park bench for about an hour. Long enough to clear his mind, but not near enough to stave off the exhaustion. Valentina's apartment was empty when he got there. While waiting across the street, he counted three girls who were obviously younger than eighteen returning in the early morning hours. They dressed like they'd been partying in some of the local clubs, but their demeanor reminded him that they were like Valentina, only serving out a sentence with no end in sight.

He needed to get to the boat to see if Valentina returned. He could have missed her if she came back to the flat. It was possible that whatever she wanted to retrieve wasn't here, but Valentina had few options and, from her own mouth, no possessions. While he understood why she'd choose the time she did to return to the flat, he would have advised against it. The girls might not be home at that time, but it was still an obvious location to watch. After all, he'd done that exact thing yesterday when he trailed Torres to Camille.

He hoped the girl returned safely to the boat, but he wasn't going to risk it. If she'd walked into Torres, it was inevitable that she'd report where they'd hidden out. The girl was brave—she'd have to be to survive her life—but Torres displayed how brutal he could be for a small infraction. If he wanted information from her, he might get a lot meaner and bloodier to get it.

If she was safe at the boat, they'd waste no time getting out of the city. He'd been working on the best route. He thought he could trek down to Medellín or Bogotá where they could find a private plane, ideally back to Belize, but anywhere out of Colombia would be a start. Valentina said she might have some family in Bogotá. If so, he could ensure she was safe and maybe enlist some help in getting transport north.

If she didn't show up though—something Caleb worried would happen—he couldn't leave her to a fate with Torres. Somehow, Corsair thought he needed to deal with this Captain Torres. Nothing about the man made the city or the world a better place. After watching the girls Torres kept locked in that apartment make their defeated return to their less-than-gilded cage, Caleb knew the man needed to be eliminated.

For now, he'd worry about getting the girl to safety. He stopped at a Juan Valdez to fuel up on coffee. He sipped the black coffee, relishing the flavor as he walked back.

It took an hour to hike back to the marina. Morning traffic picked up, giving the city a different vibe from only a few hours earlier. It seemed like Cartagena never slept. Music pumped through the streets at all hours of the night, and even in some of the less populous areas in the wee hours, there were small clumps of people moving about the streets.

He settled on a bench with a direct line of sight on the bow of the Hans Christian. He couldn't see the light on the boat, but since he'd let the sun come up, it might make it more difficult. Caleb watched the vessel for forty-five minutes. There was no activity on it. If Valentina came back and used her common sense, she'd stay below deck and out of sight until he returned.

Finally, he gave up. The only way to know if she returned was to take a look. He approached carefully, watching for anyone who was out of place. If Valentina gave up their location, Torres or Camille might be waiting in the cabin. But it couldn't be more than two or three people at the most. There simply wasn't enough room, and Camille certainly wouldn't want to find herself in a confined space with Caleb even though he vowed he wouldn't fight her. He knew her well enough to know that she wouldn't take that promise at face value.

Caleb reached behind him to touch the gun in his waistband. The Beretta he'd taken off one of Camille's goons comforted him. He swept his head from side to side. Nothing seemed amiss.

He climbed aboard, trying unsuccessfully not to rock the boat. As he opened the door, he didn't see anyone.

"You've been out all night," Camille said, stepping out of the head as he climbed down the companionway.

"Fuck!" he murmured, staring at the barrel of her own Beretta 92.

"Are you going to fight it out?" she asked, staring at him with a softer gaze than he expected.

"Where's Valentina?" he asked.

"Right now, she's with Torres."

"Dammit, Camille, he's going to kill her," he complained. "Or worse."

She shook her head in disbelief. "You really do care, don't you?"

"I did a lot of bad stuff before," he explained. "I guess I'm trying to make up for it wherever I can."

"Unbelievable," she muttered.

Caleb pulled the Beretta from his waistband and set it gently on the counter. "I don't care what you do to me, but you can't leave her with that asshole."

"I'm surprised you haven't killed him yet," she remarked.

"It's on my to-do list."

She smiled. It had been a long time since he'd seen that smile. It was genuine, and he wondered if it was just because she'd finally gotten him.

"Here's the deal," she told him. "I'm going to deliver you to my employer. I did ensure that Valentina remain unharmed by Torres."

Caleb lifted an eyebrow.

She responded, "Under threat of death."

Now Caleb smiled. "Who's your employer?"

"Soon enough. If you try anything, and I can't go back for Valentina, her safety is in Torres's hands."

"I promised you I wouldn't hurt you," he told her.

"Your word doesn't mean much," she pointed out. "You told me plenty of things that turned out to be false."

"I am sorry for that," he told her.

"If I have to kill you, I will," she said.

Caleb shrugged. "I thought you'd do that, anyway."

"My client pays no matter what, but he offers a bit more if I deliver you alive. Personally, I think you'd prefer I do it."

"You know, Camille. I actually would. If it ends with us, I'd be okay with that."

Camille motioned with the barrel to the companionway. "Unfortunately, you don't get what you want."

Caleb climbed into the cockpit, with Camille pressing the barrel against his back. It was actually a mistake, and one he didn't think she'd do on purpose. If he wanted to escape, she gave him the opportunity by staying too close. Corsair could disarm most people in that position. Was it a test? Did she want to know if he meant it when he said he wouldn't fight her?

He waited as she climbed into the cockpit. Three men stood on the dock. All of them looked like clones of the ones he'd fought yesterday. A fourth man stood back nearer to the shore. Caleb recognized the man from the restaurant yesterday. Now that he had a clearer view of him, his brain flipped through a mental Rolodex.

"Salar Tolazar, right?" Caleb asked as he got off the Hans Christian. "Camille, you're working for Mahmoud Abbas?"

"He pays the bills," she answered, nudging him forward with the barrel of the gun.

"You're going to take care of Valentina?" he asked. "Make sure she is safe."

"Yes, I swear I will."

"Thank you," he replied before focusing on Tolazar. "Salar, long time. I guess Mahmoud is still pissed about his son."

"Mr. Abbas, will enjoy seeing you die in person."

"I'll try not to disappoint," Caleb quipped.

"Just walk, Caleb," Camille ordered.

"There's still time for you to do the deed," he told her.

"I'll take pleasure in the fact that you know I am the one who brought about your demise."

"What's the plan?" he asked.

"You shut up and do what you're told."

"That could be a first," Caleb remarked before feigning a lunge at the closest European. The man lurched away, and Caleb chuckled. Tolazar gave Minuit a hard glare.

"We have an understanding," she told Tolazar. "I deliver you and protect his little protégé."

"Has the mighty Corsair softened in his old age?" Tolazar asked.

Caleb lifted his shoulders.

"Let's go!" Camille ordered.

41

Cartagena de Indias, Colombia

Caleb sat between two of the Europeans in the Suburban while Camille and Tolazar sat behind him. He assumed Camille still had the Beretta 92 aimed at his back in case he tried to escape. The third European drove in silence.

"Salar, does Mahmoud understand I was sent to kill his son?"

"Mr. Abbas doesn't care."

"Is Abbas one of those jobs you regret?" Camille asked.

"Not at all. Abbas is a fucker who either killed or sold weapons to other assholes who killed thousands of innocent people. If I had it to do over, I'd kill Mahmoud, too. Make it a father-son thing."

Tolazar grunted, and Caleb imagined that made Camille smile.

The Suburban cruised along the street, turning into the industrial port. The driver slowed at the guard gate to hand the guard some paperwork.

They planned to ship him to Abbas. He wondered how they planned to keep him contained. Obviously, Mahmoud Abbas wanted to torture him in person, and he'd want Caleb relatively healthy. How important was that, though? He'd wait and see what they had planned.

He thought about Amanda as they drove deeper into the shipping complex. Towers of Conex containers stood over the road. Khloe would take care of Amanda, but that didn't make him feel better. His heart ached, knowing he would never kiss his little girl goodnight again. He'd never read her another story.

Dying didn't bother him, though. Caleb didn't know what the afterlife was like, but he figured that either he'd cross over and see Audrey and Jackson waiting on him or there'd be nothing. Either way, Caleb thought that would be fine.

The Suburban pulled over in front of a building. Caleb stared out the window at the warehouse filled with shipping containers.

"You know those things turn into ovens on the open sea," Caleb pointed out. "I mean death is death, right? I just don't want Mahmoud to feel shorted."

"He pays me either way," Camille reported. "Which should be now, Salar."

"Of course," Tolazar replied, pulling his phone out. He tapped on the screen for several minutes before announcing, "Payment is made."

Caleb watched the rearview mirror to see Camille lower her gun long enough to check her phone. "He's all yours," she told him.

Salar Tolazar grinned a satisfied and lascivious smile. "Get him out."

The two Europeans pushed Caleb out of the driver's side. Once out of the car, the pair stepped back in order to avoid giving Corsair an open attack. Tolazar and Camille exited the back as well.

"Take him inside," Tolazar ordered.

Caleb didn't move. He stared at Camille. "I hope this helps," he told her.

"The girl will be safe," she assured him.

He smiled softly at his former lover. "I know. Thank you."

Her Beretta disappeared into a holster, and she crossed her arms across her breasts.

"See you later," Caleb told her.

"What's the saying, Corsair? Have a great life?"

Caleb grinned. "You were always funny. I missed that."

One of the Europeans stepped forward with a large zip tie that he wrapped around Corsair's wrists. Once secured, the men pushed him toward the building. Tolazar followed behind them.

Inside the warehouse, the men directed him to a red container with the door wide open. Caleb stepped inside to see a hospital bed bolted to the floor. Straps hung from the side of the hospital bed and two men stood beside an IV.

"Ah, you're putting me down for the count," Caleb noted.

"You won't even notice the trip," Tolazar explained.

The inside of the container had been rehabbed to include a power supply that ran a small air conditioner and a chest freezer where Caleb assumed the extra IV bags were stored.

"I get a nice nap and wake up to see Mahmoud slobbering in anticipation of my torture. This should be fun."

"Put him on the bed," Tolazar ordered. The two Europeans pointed him toward the bed still staying a few feet from him.

Caleb wondered if Camille had already left. It had been long enough that he assumed she had. He took a second to scan the room. Five people and Tolazar. Plus, he was bound. Caleb stepped toward the gurney and hopped up on it so that he faced the four men who escorted him inside.

The other two men, medics Caleb guessed, rolled the IV stand closer.

"You'll feel a pinch," one man told him as he pressed the needle into his cubital fossa vein.

"Oh, Mr. Abbas wanted me to tell you something before you drift off," Tolazar said. "While you're sleeping, he plans to bring your daughter over to see you."

There was a burn in his arm. Caleb scowled, raising his arms swiftly. The needle pulled out of his arm just before he drove his hands down.

Corsair came off the gurney as the ties snapped around his wrist. He yanked the rest of the needle free of his arm with his left hand. The two closest Europeans moved toward him. His left hand fired out, driving the IV needle into the nearest man's eye as he ducked below the other's grasp.

The drugs hit his system, and he felt like he was underwater. Still, he drove his right fist into the second man's groin. When the man doubled over, Corsair rolled across the gurney on his back, colliding with one of the medics. The pair tumbled to the ground, dragging the cot with them.

"Stop him!" Tolazar shouted.

Caleb's lips thickened as whatever they shot into him slowed his reflexes. Despite the effects, he fought through them and grabbed the medic by the throat. The man's body went limp when he snapped his neck.

Corsair took cover under the corpse as someone fired into it. He felt an odd sensation in his arm, but he pushed it away as he used the man as a shield. When he dragged the body back, he felt the cold metal of a gun. His right arm moved like molasses as he wrapped his fingers around it and came up with the barrel.

His arm screamed, and Caleb realized he'd been shot.

Shoot back, asshole.

He obeyed the voice in his head, firing into the two remaining European goons. The driver fell over. Behind him, the other medic lunged at him. Caleb went down, no longer able to hold his stance under the influence of whatever they pumped into him.

He threw his left elbow into the medic's face. The man's head jerked back, and Corsair twisted his right arm around, shoving the barrel of the Glock 19 into the medic's throat.

The muzzle flashed, spewing the man's throat out the back of his neck. Corsair rolled to the side as the remaining European, who apparently recovered from the groin strike, now fired wildly at him. Corsair couldn't raise his arm up. He leveled the barrel across the floor and fired at the man's feet. Through the drugged haze, he saw the man's right shin explode as a nine-millimeter slug tore through the bone. The man crashed to the ground, and Corsair fired another round that obliterated his face.

Crawling to his feet, Corsair saw Tolazar running for the open door. The Glock came up in his hand, and he closed one eye, trying to focus through the drugs. He squeezed the trigger, and the security chief stumbled forward, falling flat on the metal floor. Corsair shuffled his feet toward the injured man.

"No!" Tolazar moaned as he belly-crawled away from the assassin. Blood spread across his back.

"See?" Corsair mumbled with a thick tongue. "You should have left my daughter out of it."

"It wasn't me," Tolazar croaked as Corsair pushed him over on to his back and aimed the barrel of the Glock unsteadily at the man's face. "Your phone?"

Tolazar stared at Corsair without moving, and the assassin swung the Glock over and pulled the trigger. A nine-millimeter round shattered his left clavicle.

"Agh!" Tolazar screamed.

Corsair dropped down onto his haunches and let his left knee touch the container floor as he tried to steady himself.

"You're lucky I didn't hit anything vital," Corsair slurred. "Whatever that asshole pumped into me has me seeing triple. Now, pull out your fucking phone."

Tolazar's right hand moved sporadically down his torso to his pocket. He pulled an iPhone out.

"Call Abbas," Corsair ordered.

"It's him. I can help you get him."

Corsair shook his head slowly, noticing that everything seemed to blur when he moved too fast. "I don't need your help. Just call him."

"He'll kill me," Tolazar said.

"Idiot," Corsair groaned as he pulled the trigger.

The bullet hit Tolazar in the heart. For an instant, the security man's eyes registered surprise before the life faded out of him. Caleb picked up the phone and activated the facial recognition before scanning Tolazar's lifeless face. When the phone opened, Caleb scrolled through until he found Abbas's contact information.

Abbas answered, "Do you have him?"

Corsair cocked his head, staring at the dead man on the floor of the steel box. "Oh, I have him, Mahmoud. Want me to ship him to you? I think the freight is already paid."

"Who is this?"

"You crossed a line, Mahmoud. Now I have to come across the fucking ocean and kill you."

"Where is Salar?"

"He's lying at my feet. I'll forgive you for coming after me, I understand that. But if you want to live, you better vanish. If I so much as smell you around me or my friends or family, I'll send you to hell."

"Corsair, this isn't over," Mahmoud Abbas announced brazenly.

"No, I guess it's not," Corsair replied. He hung up the phone and dropped it onto Tolazar's chest. Stumbling back into the sunlight, Corsair closed the container. On the ground was a padlock, waiting to secure Corsair, and he assumed the medics for the long trip. He clicked the lock through the hasp and locked it.

Tolazar's Suburban still sat outside the building. Caleb's feet dragged along as he walked toward it. Already, he was feeling the effects of the drugs start to wear off. When he reached the SUV, he stopped.

Beside the hood, Camille Dubois stood with her Beretta hanging in her hand at her side.

"I thought you might be back," she remarked.

"Fuck," Caleb muttered. He shook his head cowered and released the magazine from the Glock. It dropped to the asphalt, and he racked back the slide to eject the round in the chamber. Caleb tossed the unloaded weapon at her feet.

"You aren't going to even try?" she asked.

Caleb's head turned from side to side. "Can I call my daughter?" he asked.

Her face registered confusion. Then she tossed her phone to him. He caught it with his right hand.

"It's long distance, do you mind?"

She replied, "I just got paid a million dollars to deliver you to Abbas. You can run the bill up."

"He might want a refund," Caleb told her.

"No deal. I left you with his people."

Caleb gave a hands up gesture. He dialed a number and waited.

"Hello."

"Khloe, it's Caleb."

"Oh, Caleb. I'm so happy to hear from you. The woman from the OOC showed up at the house. She wants to talk to you, but she warned us to leave."

"Khloe, slow down," Caleb said. "She found the house?"

"Yes."

"You have to run, Khloe. Can you take Amanda?"

"Where do we meet you, Caleb?"

He took a deep breath. "I don't think you can. I'm not going to make it."

"Oh, when will you be back?"

"Khloe, I won't. I'm sorry but listen to me. There are people who might come after Amanda because of me. You have to protect her. Remember what I told you."

"Caleb, no. We need you."

He chuckled a little, still feeling the wooziness from the drugs. "You can do it. I'm sorry I can't be there."

"But..."

"Khloe," he interrupted. "Can I speak with Amanda?"

"Oh, uh, sure."

"Daddy?" Amanda came on the line.

"Hi, sweetie. How are you doing?"

"Khloe said we had to leave the house."

"I know. Are you obeying her?"

"Yes. Mostly."

"Baby, do it all the time, okay?"

"I'll try, Daddy. When are you coming home?"

He smiled a little. It wasn't really home, but she was there, making it the closest thing he had.

"Not for a long time," he lied. "You have to stay with Khloe. It's important you do what she says, so the bad men won't find you."

"Are the bad men coming?" Her voice wavered with fear.

"I hope not. But you have to be brave."

"I will, Daddy. I love you."

"I love you, sweetie. Let me talk to Khloe."

"Caleb?"

"Khloe, you may have to use your real passport. Get back to the States. Once you get there, find a way to change your name. Use Amanda's other papers, okay?"

"I will."

"Thank you, Khloe," he muttered. "Take care of my girl."

"Are you sure you won't make it? I'll keep an eye on the drop-box." She referred to an email account they set up for communication. Each of them was to type a draft of a message and leave it for the other without sending it, keeping the record from crossing the internet. Each new message overwrote the other. It wasn't foolproof, but with the massive number of anonymous email providers out there, it would make it extremely difficult to track.

"Sure, keep an eye out, but don't hold your breath."

"Caleb?"

"Goodbye, Khloe. Kiss Amanda for me every night."

"Caleb."

He hung up and looked back at Camille.

"How old is your daughter?"

"Three."

"Fuck me, Caleb," she moaned. "You're kidding me."

He watched her.

"Fuck!"

"It's okay, Camille," he assured her.

She marched around the front of the Suburban and climbed into the driver's seat. Caleb stood in front of the SUV, watching her as she started the car.

When she rolled the window down, she shouted, "Get in the fucking car!"

Caleb's eyes darted from her face to the passenger door. He walked over and opened it. "What are you doing?"

"We have to go get Valentina," she said.

His face contorted with confusion,

"Get your fucking Glock unless you plan to kill Torres with your bare hands."

Caleb smiled at her.

"Don't fucking smile at me," she swore at him. "Hurry up."

42

Cartagena de Indias, Colombia

The Suburban sat against the curb. Minuit and Corsair stared at the white and yellow building a block away. Three officers leaned against a railing on the second-floor balcony.

"Captain Torres took my warning seriously," Camille remarked.

"What did you tell him?" Caleb asked.

"That you were going to kill him and anyone threatening the girl."

Caleb's head bobbed.

"I might have stressed that if anything happened to Valentina, I'd pay them back too."

"It's possible he's thinking if you come back for the girl, he won't have to give her to you."

"That would be a mistake," she commented.

Caleb turned to stare at the woman. "Is this why I'm still alive?"

Minuit shook her head. "No, but it can't hurt. I heard you talking to your daughter. Amanda, right?"

"Yeah."

"You aren't the same," she said.

He shook his head.

"I don't think I can forgive you, though," Camille told him. "However, I can't in good conscience take Amanda's only family."

Caleb bowed his head in gratitude. He didn't say the words, just acknowledged it. There wasn't anything that it would add to her actions.

"The captain has a lot of girls," she remarked.

"From what Valentina suggested, yes."

"Scum," she stated.

"What are you thinking?" he asked, letting her take the lead.

"I told him I was going to come take Valentina away, so that's what I'm going to do."

"If he decides that he doesn't like that?" Caleb asked.

"I'll kill them all," she told him. "If I have any trouble, you can come in after me."

Caleb tilted his head. "Okay, but don't wait too long if you see trouble."

"Don't worry," she told him as she got out of the car.

Caleb watched Minuit cross the street. He waited until she reached the front door and knocked. When it opened, she walked inside, but not before dropping her hand to her side with four fingers showing.

Four more men that she saw. With the three on the balcony, that made a minimum of seven. However, it was a two-story house, and Caleb assumed there was no way for her to see the second level. He arbitrarily added two to the list, figuring nine men total.

Might as well round up to ten.

Caleb got out of the SUV and waited as a motorcycle sped past the Suburban. He watched two girls in their late teens strolling down the sidewalk. They giggled as they ambled past Caleb.

Glass shattered overhead, and a man fell from the second-story window. The two teenagers screamed as the figure struck the concrete in front of Caleb. Both girls ran the way they'd just come. As they hurried down the sidewalk, Corsair pulled the Glock from his waistband and hit the front door with his shoulder. The front door was wooden, but not a solid core one. The metal security door provided protection for the house, but it was still swung open.

When Corsair hit the door, splintering the wooden frame, he heard a shout from the other room. "She's upstairs."

Feet pounded on the steps above him, and Corsair raised the barrel as he moved around the corner. A cop waited at the bottom of the steps, pointing a Jericho 941 up the stairwell. He didn't see Corsair behind him, and the American wrapped an arm around his neck, jerking him back. His Jericho fired as the officer fought back. Corsair tightened his grip on his carotid artery, pinching off the blood flow. The cop thrashed in Corsair's grip for several seconds until he lost consciousness and went limp in the American's arm.

Corsair dropped the man on the ground, kicking the Jericho across the room. Another uniformed man charged down the stairs. "Ramírez! What's going on?"

Corsair recognized the one Torres called Carlos the other night. The Glock came up and fired before Carlos aimed his gun. Tumbling down the stairs, Carlos stopped with his face pressed against the tile floor and his legs stretched up the steps.

"Someone's downstairs!"

"The bitch barricaded herself in there."

Corsair stepped carefully over the corpse and onto the stairs. He kept the Glock aimed up at the landing.

"Ricardo, check on Carlos," someone ordered.

Corsair sucked in a breath as two figures appeared above him. The Glock bucked twice in rapid succession. Ricardo and his comrade hit the floor before they had time to see the American. Corsair continued to the top, sweeping around the corner.

"Captain Torres!" Corsair called. "I think you have a problem."

Corsair stared down a hallway at Torres and two of the men Caleb saw on the balcony.

"Fuck!" the younger of the two shouted, grabbing the door to escape. The knob jiggled but didn't open—locked.

Two gunshots rang from inside the room. The rounds penetrated the cheap hollow door, knocking the young officer to the ground. Torres and the last cop both raised their Jerichos toward Corsair.

The Glock fired as Corsair spun around the corner. He didn't see the other cop fall, but he knew his aim was true.

"You two are working together?" Torres shouted. "I don't understand."

From behind the door, Caleb heard Minuit answer, "You're a bigger bastard than he is." More rounds tore through the door as Camille unloaded her Beretta. Corsair came around the corner, firing twice. The first shot hit Torres in the left shoulder, and the impact twirled him around. The second struck him in the lower back, shattering his spine and severing his spinal cord.

The captain fell into a heap on the floor. Unable to move, he could only moan as Caleb approached him.

"Camille, it's clear out here," Caleb announced to Minuit.

The knob turned now, but the door, riddled with bullet holes, remained jammed shut. Caleb grabbed the handle and jerked. Splinters of wood sprayed on the floor as the door gave way from the jamb.

Camille stared out the opening with the empty Beretta in her hand. Valentina lay on a bed, curled in a ball. She looked defeated, and Caleb noted the fresh bruises and cuts on her face.

"He hurt her," Camille told Caleb.

He turned to look at the now-paralyzed cop. Caleb reached down and grabbed Torres by the hair. Dragging the cop through the room to the smashed window where Camille tossed out the first cop, he lifted the man up. Torres was dead weight, but Caleb didn't struggle to get him up.

"You can't get away with this," Torres groaned.

"Maybe not, but you'll be in hell," Caleb told him as he shoved the man face-first through the broken windowpane. The thud of Torres's body on the pavement was followed by more screaming outside.

Sirens echoed through the city as the police responded to calls.

"We better go," Caleb said. Handing the Glock to Camille, he scooped Valentina up in his arms and followed Minuit out of the house.

43

Cartagena de Indias, Colombia

"What are you going to do?" he asked Minuit.

The Frenchwoman looked at Valentina, who was putting an ample amount of cream in her coffee. The girl stood at the coffee station in the little coffee shop where she began adding an excessive amount of sugar.

"I'm going to get her out of the city," Camille responded.

Caleb smiled. Camille however, scowled in return. "I'm not forgiving you," she told him.

The grin faded from his lips. "Of course not," he replied.

"I'm just not killing you. Now."

Caleb nodded. "I'll take what I can get."

"You take care of your daughter," she told him. "That's the reason you survived this."

"Camille, I will never be able to make it up to you," he said. "It's the biggest regret of my life."

She sipped the espresso and didn't acknowledge the remark.

"We might not see each other again," Camille commented.

He pulled a slip of paper from his pocket. "I wasn't sure how you'd react, but here."

"An email address?"

"Drop box," he explained. "If you ever need anything, I'm there for you."

"I won't," she said. Nonetheless, she folded the paper before it vanished into her shorts.

Caleb contained the satisfaction he had from her acceptance of the contact information. It was in her court.

"Where are you going?" she asked, glancing out the coffee shop window at the naked statue of Gertrude. Valentina appeared at the bistro table and moved the duffel bag she'd gotten from her flat. She told Izzie that Torres was gone, and the older girl said she'd get the rest of the girls out of the apartment. While Torres might be dead, there were officers under him who knew about the girls. That power vacuum would be filled soon, and the window for them to escape this prison was small. Now or never.

Caleb considered staying in the area long enough to prevent someone from interjecting themselves as the new warden to the small prison. But his face had been all over the news, and he currently made the list of the top ten fugitives in Colombia.

Answering Camille, he said, "I doubt I can fly out of Colombia at all. I'll head south and catch a flight out."

"Where are you going?" Valentina asked.

Caleb shook his head. "I just have to get back to Amanda."

"Where is she?" Valentina pushed a little harder.

Camille raised a hand. "Let him have his secrets. They'll protect him and us."

"I don't understand," the girl remarked.

"There are people besides the Colombian police that are after me. Those guys would pull your toenails out one by one to get my location. If you don't know, they can't hurt you."

Valentina's brow furrowed. "Wouldn't that just ensure that I'd be tortured forever? I couldn't give them the answers they want."

Camille shook her head. "If they find you, it won't matter." The words were ominous.

Valentina only nodded. Caleb wondered if the nonchalant demeanor of the girl was simply a lack of fear because she'd been subjected to so much. It was unlikely Valentina came out of this unscathed despite the inner strength the girl possessed. It took an iron resolve to survive the way she had, and Caleb hoped that she'd hold on to that earnestness.

"Did you talk to your daughter?" Camille asked.

"I left Khloe a message. Hopefully, she'll see it and get back to me."

"We need to go," Camille told Valentina.

The girl faced Caleb. "Thank you for everything."

Caleb dipped his chin toward her. "You stay strong, girl."

The girl's eyes twinkled.

Camille locked eyes with Caleb. The two of them didn't speak, but they held that gaze for several seconds. Then the

Frenchwoman grabbed Valentina's hand and led her out of the Juan Valdez coffee shop.

Caleb watched the pair cross the street and blend into the crowd, taking turns touching Gertrude's breasts.

He waited for half an hour, hoping that Camille might return, but knowing it wasn't going to happen. While he pondered over the last few days, he also plotted his own escape from Colombia. He needed to get out of the city and head south. Caleb estimated a two-to-three-day drive to Ecuador, where he could charter a private plane in Quito. However, it could be a few more days just trying to cross the border unnoticed. He needed to stay under the radar for a week.

By now, the news sources in Cartagena were reporting the massacre of a police unit and its captain. Caleb needed to avoid contact with anyone watching the news reports as speculation already grew that the unknown American might be responsible. So far, no one had mentioned the Frenchwoman, and Caleb thought that would help Camille and Valentina slip away unnoticed.

Caleb had a plan; he'd steal another motorcycle and take off. He could sleep in the jungle and stay off the highways.

He looked down at the empty coffee cup and considered that he hadn't eaten since yesterday. He'd grab an *arepa* from a street vendor. Or two *arepas*. He could save one for later.

His head came up to watch the crowd still groping the sculpture. He froze when he saw a white Volkswagen Phaeton with a taxi logo on the door stop at the curb. A woman exited the car and stared up the side of Valentina's building.

Caleb recognized the woman. He'd encountered her twice now—once in Florida and a few months back in Mexico. The OOC agent. Was this the one that spoke with Khloe?

He groaned. No doubt the OOC saw the description being aired on the Colombian television.

Shit!

Caleb stood up and walked to the counter, keeping his eyes on the woman's reflection. He ordered another coffee, and when the agent entered Valentina's building, Caleb exited the coffee shop, heading south, away from Gertrude.

He flagged a taxi at the next intersection. Keeping his face down, he slid into the back seat.

"Marina district," he informed the driver in his North English accent. The cabbie nodded, shifted into gear, and drove away from the curb, carrying Caleb away from the walled city.

Check out the bonus teaser scene:
https://dl.bookfunnel.com/9tepq0hyxm